*I dedicate this book to God,
to all my family, and my friends.*

Fairy Rock © 2024 Jeffrey Roy Ford. All Rights reserved.
No part of this publication may be reproduced or transmitted in any form or by any means, electronic, mechanical, including photocopy, recording, or any information storage and retrieval system, without permission in writing from the author.

This is a work of fiction. Unless otherwise indicated, all the names, characters, businesses, places, events and incidents in this book are either the product of the author's imagination or used in a fictitious manner. Any resemblance to actual persons, living or dead, or actual events is purely coincidental.

Table of Contents

Part 1:
Chapter 1: Tevin Jenkins	11
Chapter 2: Tevin Jenkins	16
Chapter 3: Tevin Jenkins	23
Chapter 4: Tevin Jenkins	27
Chapter 5: Rock	30
Chapter 6: Tevin Jenkins	32
Chapter 7: Rock	37
Chapter 8: Gilbert III	41
Chapter 9: Richard Johnson	45
Chapter 10: Tevin Jenkins	47
Chapter 11: Rock	49
Chapter 12: Richard Johnson	53
Chapter 13: Tevin Jenkins	55
Chapter 14: Richard Johnson	57

Chapter 15: Serenity Cooper   60
Chapter 16: Richard Johnson   62
Chapter 17: Tevin Jenkins   65
Chapter 18: Tevin Jenkins   68
Chapter 19: Gilbert III   71
Chapter 20: Rock   73
Chapter 21: Gilbert III   79
Chapter 22: Rock   84
Chapter 23: Richard Johnson   86
Chapter 24: Gilbert III   90
Chapter 25: Rock   92
Chapter 26: Rock   96
Chapter 27: Rock   99
Chapter 28: Rock   103
Chapter 29: Serenity Cooper   107
Chapter 30: Tevin Jenkins   110
Chapter 31: Tevin Jenkins   114

Part 2:
Chapter 32: Tevin Jenkins   120
Chapter 33: Richard Johnson   124
Chapter 34: Tevin Jenkins   126
Chapter 35: Tevin Jenkins   129
Chapter 36: Richard Johnson   132
Chapter 37: Richard Johnson   136

Chapter 38: Serenity Cooper	138
Chapter 39: Richard Johnson	141
Chapter 40: Richard Johnson	144
Chapter 41: Serenity Cooper	146
Chapter 42: Serenity Cooper	148
Chapter 43: Tevin Jenkins	151
Chapter 44: Tevin Jenkins	154
Chapter 45: Tevin Jenkins	158
Chapter 46: Tevin Jenkins	161
Chapter 47: Tevin Jenkins	164
Chapter 48: Tevin Jenkins	168
Chapter 49: Tevin Jenkins	172
Chapter 50: Tevin Jenkins	173
Chapter 51: Tevin Jenkins	176
Chapter 52: Tevin Jenkins	179
Chapter 53: Tevin Jenkins	182
Chapter 54: Tevin Jenkins	184
Chapter 55: Serenity Cooper	189
Chapter 56: Serenity Cooper	192
Chapter 57: Serenity Cooper	194
Chapter 58: Tevin Jenkins	198
Chapter 59: Tevin Jenkins	201
Chapter 60: Tevin Jenkins	204
Chapter 61: Tevin Jenkins	208
Chapter 62: Tevin Jenkins	211

Fairy Rock

Part 1

1

Tevin Jenkins

"We graduated!" someone shouts as they race up the stairs.

It's high school graduation night in the small town of Fairyville, Washington. Most of the one hundred senior class members from Fairyville High School are at Richard Johnson's party. Many are drinking and smoking pot while listening to heavy metal music blast throughout the vast, two-story, sandy brown house.

A lanky Tevin Jenkins sits upstairs with his arms folded and his knees bouncing up and down. *Serenity Cooper is going to be here. I've been in love with her since middle school. I want to ask her out, but I'm scared she'll say no.*

He rocks back and forth in his wobbly chair while his best friend, Richard, chugs down a beer, spilling half of it on his jeans. A few other people fill the room.

Richard stops drinking and yells at the top of his lungs above the music, "Tevin, drink a beer. It'll relax you!"

Tevin looks away from his drunken pal, and reaches into his bag, digging past the bottle of anti-anxiety medicine, until he finds his phone and pulls it out so he can start playing his favorite video game, *Destruction Warrior*, to calm his nerves. He tunes out the noisy sounds of the electric guitar music from the radio, moves the buttons on his phone, and destroys hundreds of zombies in the game.

"Hey! I beat my highest score again!" Tevin exclaims proudly.

Richard—and a few of their other friends who are nearby—crowd around him.

"Tevin, as shy as you are," Richard says, "I've never seen you talk so loud. Good job, buddy."

Tevin grabs a cup of beer like a first-place trophy and gulps it.

"Tevin! Tevin! Tevin!" his friends cheer.

He slams it on the kitchen table and coughs up some beer on his blue jean outfit.

"Slow down. There's plenty left," Richard says, grinning.

Tevin's buzz kicks in as he marvels at how Richard can roll a joint between his chubby fingers, light it up, and blow a kiss at Susan Davis, his girlfriend of three years, all at the same time.

Susan gestures at Richard and goes into his bedroom.

Richard pats Tevin on the shoulder and follows her with his eyes. "I may not be good at video games, but I will score tonight."

Tevin high-fives his lucky pal and takes a puff of the joint. He gags from the smoke, and his friends laugh at him.

"Don't inhale so hard."

"It's my first time."

Richard pats him on the back. "I know, amateur."

Tevin's friends circle him and pass the bong. He sucks on the pipe, convulses the smoke from his lungs, falls to one knee, and gasps for air. He closes his eyes to embrace the dizziness and smiles at all the attention.

His friends help him to a chair and take pictures of him, caught up in the moment. Tevin sticks his tongue out, making the photo funnier.

**

Richard shakes Tevin awake. "Dude, I got a text message from Steve. Serenity's here."

Tevin's eyes burst wide open, and his high almost instantly vanishes.

He races to the bathroom and frantically brushes the waves in his short black hair. Turning on the faucet, he splashes his cheeks with water, trying to clean the crust from the side of his freckled-filled face. He stops for a moment and stares at his reflection in the mirror, despising his acne. He uses his fingernails to pick the small chunks of chicken tenders out of his teeth. Richard passes him a toothbrush freshly out of the package and a half-empty bottle of minty-fresh toothpaste, and he rinses his mouth and wipes it off with a bath towel.

"I'm too drunk," Tevin says.

"You'll be okay." Richard holds him up as they make their way downstairs.

Tevin staggers while trying to keep his shaky knees straight. As he reaches the landing, he sees Serenity. She's tall, in a tight red silk dress with round hips, perky breasts, and a flat stomach. Her beauty makes his mouth water. He gawks at her as she plays with her circular-shaped afro, and he fantasizes about French kissing her as he looks into her pretty brown eyes.

She's making her way around the room, hugging her friends. "I'm going to miss you all. I leave for college in the fall."

Richard waves his hands in front of Tevin's face to break his trance and says, "Stop staring, dude." He passes him a flask with Hennessy. "Here. Take a swig of this and man up!"

Tevin swigs it down, wishing it would stop his heart from beating so fast.

His stomach drops at the sight of Serenity's boyfriend, Daniel Turner, and his two biker friends walking by. They reek of whiskey and cigarettes.

"Richard, why did you invite him?" Tevin asks quietly.

Richard pulls hard on the braids in his long brown hair. "I didn't invite the jerk. I invited Serenity, and she must have brought him. I got to get them out of here before they start trouble."

Tevin stares at Daniel and stumbles, knocking over the nightstand by the staircases. Daniel looks up at him, swallows what's left of his whiskey, and drops the bottle. It smashes on the ground, and the glass shatters.

"Serenity," Daniel barks. "I told you to stand by me. Get over here!"

Serenity immediately rushes to his side. "I was just catching up with some old friends, baby."

Daniel sticks his finger in her face. "I don't care. Don't leave my side again!"

He removes his black leather coat with a symbol of a tarantula from his tall body and drapes it over her shoulders. He has a gray tarantula shirt that matches the tattoos on his well-built arms. Serenity holds his coat, and she appears to be scared to death. She's not making eye contact with him as he scolds her for leaving his side.

Tevin sweats through his blue jean outfit. *I don't want to see her hurt like this. She looks like she wants to cry. What do I do? I'm so afraid. I love her—I must help her.*

As Daniel grabs Serenity by the arm and pulls her toward him, Tevin's body pumps with adrenaline, and he takes a deep breath and stutters the words, "S-stop it."

Fairy Rock

No one hears him because he speaks so low.

"Stop it!" he says again. This time, it's loud enough for Daniel to hear.

Daniel turns toward him quickly and glares at Tevin, causing him to flinch, fearing that the tattooed, muscular, bald man will pound his face into the newly renovated ceramic floor.

Daniel rolls his eyes and turns back to Serenity. Black mascara tears run down her face. She grabs Daniel by his biceps. "Daniel, listen. I did walk away from you, but it is not like I'm here to be with another man. Relax, baby." She kisses him on the lips.

He lights a cigarette, then grabs her by the hand, dragging her out the door.

Tevin drops his head in shame. He wipes the beer off the sleeves of his jacket and walks out into the night.

***

"Tevin, wait," Richard says.

Richard catches up to him. "Are you okay?"

Tevin stands there sullenly, brushing wet dirt off his shoes.

"Let's go for a hike," Richard says after waiting for a reply.

"Now? Are you crazy, man? It's the middle of the party."

"Trust me. It's important."

They walk in silence for about thirty minutes, until they reach the trail's end and enter the Fairyville Woods. The cool nighttime breeze blows lightly, and the crickets chirp loudly. It is dark, and the only light is from the stars and a half-moon.

They take a shortcut through a grassland full of chickweeds and dandelions until they reach Fairyville Mountain, and Richard motions for him to follow him up the path to the mountain's top.

There is a spot on Fairyville Mountain with a gigantic, muddy, gray boulder called Fairy Rock and it's a tradition there for people to carve their names into it. Children of the past painted stick figures and drawings of hearts on the side of the enormous boulder. A long rope nailed in the center allows people to climb to the top.

From Fairy Rock, Tevin and Richard look down at the hundreds of oak trees crowding the Fairyville Woods and the lights in the enormous skyscrapers of Fairyville, towering high in the sky. They listen to cars and semi-trucks honking their horns, driving through the downtown.

"She kissed him right in front of me. I don't want to imagine what they're doing in the bedroom now," Tevin says finally.

Richard places his hand on Tevin's shoulder. "You can't think about that. Focus on yourself."

Tevin tries to fight back his frustration. "I'm not tall enough. I'm too skinny. I have freckles on my face, acne, and crooked teeth. She'll never leave him for someone like me."

Richard shoos a group of gnats away. "I'm not the best-looking or the tallest guy either. You must have more confidence, like when playing that video game."

Tevin weeps. "I want her so badly. It's all I can think about."

The stars shine brightly in the dark sky as the two sit near the famous, mammoth-sized boulder.

Tevin points down below them. "Legend has it that if you jump off Fairy Rock, magical fairies will come and rescue you. Not only will they rescue you, but they'll help you achieve your dreams."

Richard shakes his head. "That's just a myth."

Tevin gazes at the dirt, crying harder. He closes his eyes. "I have to do whatever it takes to win her heart."

Richard removes his hand from Tevin's shoulder. "Wait a minute. You're not thinking about jumping off Fairy Rock, are you?"

"I can't live without her."

"Dude! There are so many amazing girls out there."

"Not like Serenity. "

Richard tugs on his braids. "How about you don't harm yourself, and I'll help you win Serenity's heart."

Tevin cheeses, showing all his crooked teeth. "Can you do that?"

"Anything is possible."

Good, then there's no reason to jump off Fairy Rock. Tevin hugs him tightly. "I love you, best friend."

"Love you too, buddy. We'll start tomorrow."

2

Tevin Jenkins

The next morning, Tevin wakes up and jumps out of bed to the smell of bacon. He steps over the wrinkled shirt, grass-stained pants, muddy socks, and tattered shoes he wore last night. He stretches, then puts on a fresh T-shirt and stone-washed jeans and races downstairs to the kitchen. His parents sit eating their usual scrambled eggs and turkey bacon breakfast and sip their coffee before work. Both of them look crisp in their police uniforms.

"How is my science whiz doing?" his mom asks.

"Okay," Tevin replies.

"Ouch!" His dad touches his mouth. "I burned my tongue on this bleeping coffee."

"Take your time, sweetheart," Tevin's mom says gently as she takes a wrinkled napkin and cleans the hot coffee off her husband's face.

Tevin hugs both of his parents and runs toward the door without eating.

As he bursts outside, the fresh air of the summer day sends a jollying smile across his face so big that his cheeks stick out. It's shaping up to be a great day! The roses in his mother's garden are gorgeous, and he imagines handing a bundle of them to Serenity and getting a kiss from her.

He daydreams about dancing to jazz music with her on his parents' long brown porch. The rhythm of the drumbeat and saxophone fills his imagination, making him leap and spin around the patio. He gets down on one knee and practices proposing to the woman of his dreams. "Will you marry me, Serenity?" *No, that's not good enough. She needs a better proposal.*

He stands up and gets right back down on one knee again. "Serenity, you are the love of my life. You are the most astonishing and elegant woman in the world. You are more beautiful than a sunset on a tropical island. Will you marry me?" *Yeah, that'll work.*

He jumps for joy. As he spins around, he spots his parents watching him through the black bars on the living room window.

He can feel his cheeks burn with embarrassment, and he pulls his t-shirt over his head, hiding his face as his parents laugh at him. He dashes off towards Richard's house. *Richard can do anything. I believe in him because he was our high school valedictorian.*

When Tevin arrives at Richard's house, Richard opens the door, holding a black leather jacket in his hands.

"What's that for?"

"This, my man, is your new coat."

"Thank you! I'm glad the weather is still cool enough for me to wear it."

"Stop blushing. This jacket is supposed to make you look like a bad boy."

"Why?"

Richard takes his durag from his black khaki shorts and ties it on his head. "All of Serenity's boyfriends have been bad boys."

Tevin puts the smooth black coat on while hunching his back and folding his arms with his head down.

"Stop staring at the floor and make eye contact with people. Bad boys aren't supposed to have low self-esteem."

"I'm sorry."

"And stop apologizing. Bad boys don't apologize."

***

As Tevin walks into East Tech Mall later that afternoon, his hands shake slightly. He can't help but glance around. His eyes dart nervously from side to side at the mall's scenery. Richard jumps up and down, whistling at a group of drop-dead gorgeous women texting and taking pictures of each other holding their shopping bags near the second-floor elevators.

"Why are we here again?"

"If you're going to win Serenity's heart, you'll have to practice talking to women."

"But talking to girls freaks me out."

"Do you want to win Serenity's love or what?"

Tevin wags his head like a bobblehead doll. "Yes, I do."

"Then you've got to learn to show the same confidence you have in playing Destruction Warrior to the girls."

A young woman with long brown hair, wearing a blue mini skirt, stands at the wishing well, gazing at her iPhone and laughing at what appears to be a text message.

"Okay, Tevin! See that girl over there? Go talk to her."

"I don't know what to say."

"I'm right here with you, my man. Just introduce yourself and ask how her day is going. That's it."

Tevin takes a deep breath as he listens to the splashing water from the wishing well, hoping that the soothing sounds will dull the thoughts of rejection from his head. He hesitantly moves a few steps toward her. *She's going to be mean to me. She's going to blow me off.* He reaches the woman and blurts out, "Hi, my name is Tevin."

The woman blankly stares at him. "What?"

"I said my name is Tevin," he mumbles.

"Speak louder. I can't hear you."

His mind goes blank as she gets up and leaves.

Richard pats him on the back. "It's okay, buddy. We're going to get this right."

No security guards are nearby, and Richard hands Tevin a metal flask filled with vodka. "Drink this for courage. When you see a girl, introduce yourself to her and compliment her. That's it! You don't have to get her number."

***

By the late afternoon, there's a bit of improvement.

"Tevin, you're getting better."

"Thanks. I've approached four women so far. Three got up and walked away, but one chatted with me until her phone rang, and she left. I feel bad the ladies keep giving me weird looks like I'm ugly."

"Don't worry! We will get it right."

They go to the food court for hamburgers with fries from Tim's Burger Joint. As they eat, Richard swigs a shot of vodka and slides it to Tevin under the round, silver table. Suddenly, he looks up. "No way. Look who's here," he whispers to Tevin, nodding slightly.

Around the corner, Serenity is eating by herself. She is ravishing in her red leggings and red shirt with a heart shape in the center. Tevin rocks back and forth. "What do I do?"

"Now is the time to make your move."

Tevin's stomach churns, and he feels like vomiting. "Not now! Should I wait until I have more practice?"

"Better now then never! You might not get another chance while she's alone."

Richard pushes him toward Serenity.

Tevin squares his shoulders and does his best to look cool as he makes his way towards her. He clutches his heart; there's a stabbing pain in his chest. *What if this doesn't work? She's going to turn me down; I know she is. I don't want her to hate me.*

He approaches her table, and she glances up as he interrupts her strawberry milkshake.

"Hello, Serenity. How are you?" he mutters meekly.

"What did you say, Tevin? I can't hear you."

He sees an empty chair next to her and bravely claims it. Her perfume has his hormones racing. From the corner of his eye, he sees Richard encouraging him.

"Congratulations on your music scholarships," Tevin stammers.

"Thanks, Tevin. You're so sweet."

He blushes. *Oh my gosh, she said I was sweet.* He moves his right arm and accidentally knocks her milkshake into her lap.

"Oh—" She jumps out of her seat and screams as the milkshake drips down her knees.

Out of nowhere, Daniel appears next to her. Tevin looks around quickly, trying to figure out where he came from. Daniel pounds his fist on the table. "Serenity! What's this boy doing here?" He slams Tevin onto the floor, creating a colossal-sized knot on the back of his head.

"Ouch!" Tevin screams, whining like a baby.

Daniel is standing over him, and Tevin cowers. "Why are you around, my girl? Did you throw that milkshake on her?"

It's getting bad. People start to crowd around and take out their phones.

Richard races over and starts to pull Daniel off him. "Hey, man! chill out."

Daniel chokes Tevin. "What are you doing here with Serenity?"

Tevin cannot breathe and feels the veins popping out of his eyeballs.

Serenity tugs on Daniel's arm. "Stop! He didn't want anything. He was saying hi. We went to middle school and high school together."

Daniel pushes her away with one arm. "What did I tell you about talking to other men?"

She grabs his waist and yanks him off Tevin. "He was just saying hi."

Tevin rolls over, gasping for air, and milkshake stains stick to his clothes and face. He moans, rubbing his sore head. Richard quickly rushes him from the mall.

***

Richard walks into his room and tosses a gray jogging suit at Tevin. "I threw your clothes in the laundry. Here's your leather coat on my dresser. I cleaned it off."

Tevin flops down on Richard's king-sized bed, sniffling his running nose. "Was today that bad?"

Richard's phone vibrates. He takes it out of his pocket and checks it. "Oh, no. Your incident with Daniel? It's gone viral. "

Tevin puts his hands on his face and falls on the carpet. "The whole world saw me get beat up. My life is over, and Serenity will never date me now. I'm going home."

Hair from Richard's braids sticks out from his head, and he tries to hug his boy, but Tevin pushes him back and sprints out of the house, hurrying through the neighborhood. People point their fingers at him. One of the kids in the neighborhood laughs. "That's the guy that got beat up at the mall." He covers his face and trips into a puddle of water, soaking the outfit that Richard gave him.

When he finally gets home, he races past his parents, up the stairs, and slams his bedroom door.

"What in the heck is wrong with you, son?" his dad asks, prying the door open gently and peeking in.

"My life is over now. Serenity will never want to be with me," Tevin cries.

His mom and dad sit on his bed.

"Why would you say that? Have you been taking the new meds that your psychiatrist prescribed?" his mom asks.

"No, those meds have side effects." Tevin sniffles.

"You shouldn't take yourself off the meds until your psychiatrist tells you," his dad says.

They sit with Tevin for several hours to comfort him. As the sun sets, they quietly leave to give him time to rest.

He lies in his bed, sulking gloomily. *There's no way Serenity will ever be with me after today. I completely messed up. I'll never forgive myself for not being that guy that she wants.*

He tosses, turns in his bed, and buries his face in his pillow, hoping it will stop his heart from hurting. *I have no choice. I must jump off Fairy Rock. It's the only way to win a chance to be with Serenity.*

***

It's midnight. Tevin tiptoes out of his parents' house and down the block, staying low and trying to avoid detection by his neighbors. As he makes his way toward the dark and creepy Fairyville Woods, he pushes through the damp bushes, ignoring his wet and muddy shoes.

A skunk digs for berries in the bindweeds near the oak trees before it flees into the darkness. The sounds of the owls hooting force him to scamper through the tall grass, fearing what they will do to him.

***

As he reaches Fairyville Mountain, he sprints up to the top of the trail. Panting in a cold sweat, he puts his hands on the legendary Fairy Rock. He feels around in the dark until he finds the muddy rope attached. Straining with all his might, he climbs to the top of the boulder.

The bright lights of the skyscrapers and the honking cars stretch out below him, and he sits sullenly, looking down on it all. *I was never good enough for her. I'm worthless. I can't stand that someone other than me will be with Serenity. Daniel's lucky to be with her. How could he treat her that way? I wasn't strong enough to stop him. I hope the legend is true. Serenity, I'm doing this for you, my love.*

Tevin stands up at the edge of the boulder.

One…

Two…

Three…

He jumps off Fairy Rock and falls fast, but his eyes can still see the jagged stones at the bottom of the surface getting closer to him. *No—No—I'm going to die!*

Fairy Rock

In an instant, magical yellow pixie dust surrounds Tevin's body. Some goes up his nose as he coughs it out. Before his body reaches the ground, he disappears into thin air.

3
Tevin Jenkins

Tevin opens his eyes to an atmosphere of heavy fog. He gets up and finds himself surrounded by a field full of grass above his waist. He scratches his head. *Am I dead? Am I in hell?*

He shuffles through the thick, cool, gray mist. The trees, grass, and bushes are black as night. Glancing up, he looks at the dark sky—nothing but a single burning orange star, providing a faint light. *Why did I jump? I may never see my family, Richard, or Serenity again.*

Crouching down, he can barely make out an array of bright purple lights heading in his direction, illuminating a group of tiny people the size of butterflies. The magical white wings on their backs carry them through the air. They wear purple body armor with purple helmets on their heads.

"Are those fairies? Aargh!" Tevin runs in the other direction and yells at the top of his lungs. "Help!" He swings his arms and feels his way through the haze, only stopping and stumbling as he nearly falls off the edge of a waterfall full of purple water. The ice-cold water splashes on his body, causing him to quiver.

"Somebody, help me!" The tiny fairies fly around him, blowing purple pixie dust in his face. He inhales the magical powder, and instantly, his brain becomes woozy and his tense muscles relax as he falls into a trance.

The powerful, pint-sized creatures grab and lift Tevin in the air, capturing him as they fly him to a dark cave full of spikey, purple rocks, where bats rest on the ceiling's stalactites.

They drop him in a shallow pond full of purple water. In the center of it stands the queen of the fairies. Her face appears mature as if she's in her fifties, and her expression is cold. The slender queen has a purple evening gown that matches the crown on her dark purple hair.

"Welcome to the World of The Fairies. You are in the West Forrest of this world. I am Queen Vanessa," she says.

He raises himself out of the water, still feeling the effects of the calm buzz. "My name's Tevin."

"Why did you jump off Fairy Rock?" she demands.

Queen Vanessa spreads green pixie dust into the air and sniffs some of it, and the substance causes her eyes to dilate. "The magical pixie dust tells me you're here because you desire a woman's heart."

"Her name is Serenity. Can you help me?"

She grins an impish grin and turns to look Tevin in the face. "Before I answer your question, let me give you a brief history of this cruel world so you can understand more about us."

As he watches her, Queen Vanessa flings green pixie dust in Tevin's face. His mind goes blank, and a crunching noise throbs deep in his head as he dozes off…. Then a strange vision forms in his head of a time when knights, horses, and peasants lived in the village of Fairyville.

He can make out an evil wizard dressed in a black cloak as he raises his spell-binding cane in the air. A supernatural aura of dark magic energy seeps out of his body, infecting his rod. A booming sound erupts, and a black laser shoots out of it, darting into the sky. The sorcery of power spins in circles, forming a hurricane that sucks the townspeople inside it. The villagers scream, wailing for mercy as their skin burns. They shrink and become fairies. The witchcraft cyclone blows its mighty wind. It smashes houses and huts into millions of pieces and sends the poor citizens to The World of The Fairies, where they remain imprisoned.

Tevin snaps out of his nightmare with a heavy heart. "Those poor people."

"Indeed," The queen says angrily. "That wizard, Gilbert III, put this heinous curse on us because of a gambling debt that King Thomas of Fairyville owed him. To protect his identity, the wicked wizard used his dark magic to trap us and remove all traces of us. We need your help, young man."

Tevin sways back and forth, trying to remain conscious. "Me? What can I do?"

"Fairies can't leave this world without a human. It's the rules set by this awful curse."

"I'm sorry," Tevin stammers.

"I have a daughter named Sparkle. She's never left this place and seen Earth's beauty and wonders. If you could show her Fairyville, she will grant you any wish you want."

The queen turns to a timid fairy standing just next to her. The small fairy is a puny teenager wearing a red evening gown with a matching top hat that partially covers her face. "Come, Sparkle. Don't be afraid to go near him, my daughter. He is just as shy as you," Queen Vanessa says.

Sparkle floats onto his shoulder after realizing that he is still under sedation. "Um, um, it's nice to meet you, Tevin."

"I never had a girl this close to me," Tevin says with a weak grin.

"Oh my gosh. I-I've never been this close to a boy."

"Girls don't usually like me."

"I'm here to change that. What's your wish?" Sparkle blasts green pixie dust into Tevin's face.

"That's too much, my daughter," Queen Vanessa says.

"Sorry, I want to understand his desires."

"Make me into someone Serenity would want to date," Tevin says.

Sparkle closes her eyes. "I must remember my training. Please, give me time to study your mind and your heart."

"Sparkle, concentrate on your magic," Queen Vanessa commands.

Sparkle sprays blue pixie dust all over Tevin. Her eyes open wide with excitement as his body begins to transform. He promptly grows four inches taller and his arms widen, growing huge muscles. Black dreadlocks spring from his scalp and grow all the way down to his newly broad shoulders. A blue aura glows around him as blue smoke covers the entire cave.

Tevin is in awe of how much his hands have grown. He observes his robust legs and wonders how he's now wearing black Escada custom-made jeans with brown leather Louis Vuitton shoes. He touches his muscle-bound, beefy chest as it sticks out through his brown silk shirt. "Is this my new body?"

"It's a temporary body, Tevin," Queen Vanessa says quickly.

"Um, um, as long as I'm near you, you can stay in this body," Sparkle offers, as she flutters around him.

Tevin has a newfound confidence he has never experienced, and a rush of adrenaline pumps through his freshly built body as he flexes his muscles in multiple poses. *Never in my wildest dreams have I ever felt so alive!*

"Are you ready, Tevin?" Queen Vanessa asks.

Fairy Rock

"Don't call me Tevin. Call me Rock," he replies, smugly.

Queen Vanessa claps her hands. "Sparkle, you did a fantastic job!"

Sparkle blows a puff of yellow pixie dust into the air, and there is a static sound as it forms into an immense, beaming square yellow portal big enough for her and Rock. The two enter the portal and return to Fairyville.

4

Tevin Jenkins

The fog vanishes and as they emerge from the portal, the sun is shining brightly and there's a brisk wind. The moment they set foot in Fairyville Woods, the portal evaporates. Rock takes a minute to smell the fresh air as the sun shines below Fairyville Mountain and by the valley where he and Sparkle stand. The young fairy sits on his shoulder, delighted as she gapes at the clear blue sky.

"Um, I have never seen anything so magnificent. Is this how Fairyville always looks?"

"Yes." Rock carries her as she marvels in wonder, smiling at the lovely squirrels and chipmunks nibbling on the acorns by the Oak Trees. She claps her hands at the mockingbirds fluttering out of the leafy, green apple trees with pieces of sweet fruit in their beaks. Rock strolls with his head held high and a massive pep in his step as he moves through the high, clover weeds.

Sparkle sniffs some of the pollen in the air and sneezes. Rock laughs as she takes a deep breath and exhales, blowing all the dead grass and dirt off Rock's pricey outfit and shoes as the two leave the forest.

It doesn't take long for them to reach the city, and Sparkle flies into Rock's jean pocket, remaining undetected as they cruise down Main Street. Rock grooves through the hordes of people crowding the red brick sidewalk. He points his finger, showing Sparkle the young children running around the water fountain, splashing each other as they laugh joyfully.

"Wow," Sparkle says.

Some people text on their tablets, and others talk on their cell phones as they enter the newly constructed department stores.

Fairy Rock

Sparkle's nose twitches after inhaling cigarette smoke from the citizens walking past them and she coughs violently.

***

When Rock and Sparkle reach East Tech Mall, Rock goes through the automatic doors. *This time, I'm going to get it right.* He walks with a swagger like he owns the place. As they pass each department store, women stare at the perfectly aligned goatee on his handsome face, and they catcall at him.

"Mmm, who's that guy? I've never seen him before," one of the shoppers says.

"He is so cute," adds another.

Rock winks at a group of women staring at him outside Brenda's Nail Shop. "What's up, ladies."

The women blush.

He rolls up the sleeves of his silk shirt and flexes his muscles, showcasing his fantastic biceps.

A third shopper cools herself with a plastic fan. "He's incredible."

Halfway through the mall, he visits Pam's Bar and sits at the main counter on an orange leather barstool. A husky bartender notices Rock's chiseled chest and tries not to peek. "What can I get you to drink?"

Rock rubs his dreadlocks, pushing them back, and snaps his fingers. "Hey, I want a club soda. No, make that an ice-cold club soda."

The bartender gives him a doubletake. "You can have the club soda for free."

A middle-aged woman wearing a pencil skirt suit sits at a barstool near him. She removes her wedding ring as she feasts her attention on him. "Excuse me, sir. Buy me a drink?"

He shrugs his shoulder at her. "No, but you can buy me one."

The woman sighs orders two shots of whiskey. Rock downs the liquor like water, slamming the glass on the wooden counter, leaving a scratch. He gets up and starts to exit.

She blows a kiss at him. "I didn't catch your name."

"Don't worry about it," Rock replies.

With a sigh of dejection, she sips her drink, smearing her lipstick on the crystal glass, and eyes him down from head to toe as he leaves the bar. "What a gorgeous man!" she says.

Further down the mall, Rock and Sparkle stop by the food court. Rock stares at a reflection of himself in the eatery's big windows, and he smiles at the tightness of his unique long dreadlocks, thin eyebrows, and Nubian nose. Man, I look good.

Sparkle interrupts him and brings him back to reality. "Um, Rock. Look over there. I can sense Serenity."

Rock looks in the direction of Sparkle's glance and notices Daniel and Serenity are arguing with each other a few tables away. "I see her, fairy."

He listens closely. "Daniel, you're too controlling, and you're insecure. For the last time, I'm not seeing anyone else!" Serenity shouts.

Daniel bangs his hand on the table. "Give me your phone. I'm checking your messages."

He snatches the cell phone out of her hand, and Serenity shoves him as she attempts to get her phone back.

In a flash, Rock gets out of his seat and yells, "Hey, everyone! Get your cameras out. Let's make this go viral."

Sparkle springs into action, feeding red pixie dust into Rock's body. Red electricity spreads inside of him, strengthening his muscle fibers as his ability to fight increases. He charges at Daniel and seizes the phone from his hand. Daniel throws a punch, but Rock dodges it and uppercuts him in his stomach. With a whimper, Daniel falls to his knees.

People are filming the incident with their cell phones. Rock grips Daniel's arm and twists it. "How does it feel, punk?" Rock pins him face-first into a puddle of spilled cola. "If you ever bother this young lady again, next time will be worse."

Daniel's face grimaces as he clutches his sore arm.

Serenity holds her hands over her mouth, speechless. Her eyes are glued to Rock as if he's her knight in shining armor. Rock gives her the phone back.

"Thank you," she says.

Without a word, Rock turns and leaves the chaos behind as he and Sparkle walk straight out of the mall.

5
Rock

Rock and Sparkle spend the afternoon sightseeing. On David Avenue they walk on the green brick sidewalks as teenagers pick fruit from the cherry trees by the benches and throw them at each other.

Further down, they stop by the great bronze statue of King Thomas, and Sparkle peeks her head out of Rock's pocket. "Fairyville is beautiful."

Rock smiles, showing his straight white teeth. "I know."

"You were unbelievable today."

"Tell me about it. It feels so good to put that jerk in his place. And the way Serenity looked at me, I could tell she wanted me. Let's give her some time to think about me, and then she'll want me more. Meanwhile, I want to show you another cool place."

***

He takes her to Fairyville Coast, the only amusement park in the city. Her jaw drops hearing the people screaming as they go up and down the monstrous roller coasters. The tallest roller coaster is seven hundred feet and the line for the ride is so long that it starts from the souvenir shop and goes on for a quarter mile.

Rock stops by a concession stand to buy some Elephant ears, Tevin's favorite food.

After stuffing his mouth full of the sweet bread, he swaggers to the front of the line and cuts in front of everyone.

"Um, um, some of the people look mad," Sparkle says.

Rock shrugs his burly shoulders, popping the bones in his neck. "They'll get over it."

He places himself in the first black leather seat and fastens his seatbelt. A chunky man with a fuzzy black beard sits beside him. He covers his mouth, trying to control his wheezing cough. "Why hello, good sir. My name is Mitch Davis. I saw your fight with that boy at the mall. You've got unbelievable skills."

"Are you a cop or something?"

"Ha, ha, ha, no. I'm a fight promoter. How would you like to train at my MMA gym?"

"Why?"

Mitch coughs and sneezes again. "With your skills, you can become a multimillionaire."

"A millionaire? Really?"

"Take my card and come to this address tomorrow morning, and we'll have you ready to fight in a month."

All passengers are seated, and the Mega Death Roller Coaster rolls up seven hundred feet in the air, racing down at 150 miles per hour. Everyone on the roller coaster shouts except for Rock and Sparkle. Rock laughs the whole way down. Sparkle waves her hands from Rock's pocket. "Fun!"

"This is only the beginning of the fun we're going to have, fairy."

As Rock and Sparkle leave the amusement park, Rock stretches and yawns. "I'm ready to go home and see my parents."

Sparkle shakes her head. "Um, no, you can never see your parents in this form. They will never believe you."

Rock nods as he listens to her. *She's right. Plus, I don't want anyone to know I'm Tevin yet. Let me get Serenity first, and then I'll return to them as Tevin.*

Sparkle conjures up a portal, and, once they make sure no one's looking, they return to the World of The Fairies for the night.

6

Tevin Jenkins

Rock knows they are back in the World of The Fairies by the thick fog, but he's surprised they come to rest in the crown of a gigantic, black willow tree. Sparkle's purple house sits high up, nestled among the tree's eight enormous branches, covered in black leaves. As the portal closes, Sparkle flutters to her miniature bed, while Rock begins to shrink back into Tevin. Hanging on for dear life, he clings to one of the branches, hoping he does not fall to the ground. "Sparkle, please help me. I don't want to die."

The young fairy blows purple pixie dust out of her window into his face, sedating him as he breathes the magical substance into his lungs.

Tevin draws in deeply as the purple magic relaxes his tension. He slides down to the base of one of the branches and finds his footing to lie down. *Man, this purple stuff puts me in a jolly mood. It's way better than the weed Richard gave me. Being Rock feels so good, and I have already accomplished so much. I'll never forget how beautiful Serenity looked when I smashed Daniel. Serenity, I promise I'll never let Daniel hurt you again, and I'll protect you with my life, my love.*

He briefly takes a picture out of his front pocket of Richard and his parents in Fairyville High School's parking lot at their graduation and prays. *God, please look after my family and Richard and let them know I'll return soon. In Jesus' name I pray, Amen.*

As he puts the picture away, Queen Vanessa flies towards him. "How are you feeling, young man?"

"I'm scared." Tevin snivels, and his nose starts to run as he sobs. "I want to stay as Rock and win Serenity's heart, but—but I miss Richard and my family."

Queen Vanessa splashes a more potent purple pixie dust on his face. It enters his brain and puts his mind at ease. The queen gently touches his forehead until his stress disappears. "I can see that many people care about you," she says, "but Rock is who you need to be. Have faith in the fairies. We know what's best for you."

Tevin shuts his eyes, exhaling the misty air. "I will do anything to be with Serenity, but…." His words start to slur as he fades into a deep sleep.

***

Tevin is groggy when he awakes in the morning. He tries to turn over to get more sleep, but Sparkle nudges him. "It's time for training at the MMA gym," she says.

She returns to his shoulder and gives him another batch of blue pixie dust. The transformation into Rock is instantaneous this time, and she applauds herself as she forms the portal. "I'm getting so much better at this."

When they appear in Fairyville, this time, Rock feels an immediate sense of dread. Something's wrong. The forest is full of people searching the woods.

"Fairy, what's going on?"

"I don't know."

A search party wearing red t-shirts with a picture of Tevin on each of them are putting up posters with photos of him on all the trees in the woods. "Tevin was such a good kid," one of the people says softly. "He mowed my lawn for free when I had no money to pay him."

"He helped me with my science project, and I got an A," another replies.

"Tevin used to babysit my son when I had to work," a third member says.

Rock's knees buckle with sadness. He can see his parents and Richard nailing pictures of him on an old oak tree with the bark peeling off it. His father hugs his mother, and she buries her face into his hefty chest. Then she pulls back and hollers at the top of her lungs. "Tevin!"

Nearby, Richard holds a tissue and wipes his grieving face. Rock turns his head. "Sparkle, this is a bad idea. I can't see my mom like this, and I want to return to being Tevin."

"Remember: your goal is to get with Serenity."

"My parents are devastated. I can't do this."

"But—"

Rock screams at the top of his voice, "Momma, I'm over here!"

The rescue dogs bark and the whole search party turns toward him. "Who is that man?" his mom asks.

Rock runs towards his parents.

"Stop! You can't do this. It won't work," Sparkle begs. She frantically reinjects purple pixie dust into him, slowing him down.

Rock stops to catch his breath and she flutters near his head. "I know your desires, and I want to ensure you get them. We must leave for the gym now," Sparkle says.

In a trance-like state, unable to control his legs, Rock leaves the search party.

***

They make their way to Mitch's MMA Gym and enter the 3,000-square-foot facility where the most brutal men in Fairyville train. Rock gets a gauge of the fighters punching and kicking the heavy bag. He sizes up the wrestlers, imagining pinning them on the red mats. A giant, sweaty fighter with skeleton tattoos all over his body finishes wrapping his hands. He locks onto Rock like a hawk hungering for its prey. "What are you looking at, new fish?" he asks.

Rock laughs. "I dare you to attack me."

Sparkle peeks out of Rock's pocket to take in the scene, and retreats, pinching her nose from the smell of funk in the gym.

Serenity is working at the juice counter, putting chocolate protein mix into a blender and mixing it with whole milk.

"Say something to her," Sparkle whispers.

He walks over with all the swagger he can and puts his arms on the counter, showing off his well-built biceps and chest muscles sticking out through his new black shirt.

Serenity glances at him. "You're the guy who fought Daniel."

"He's a jerk," Rock says. "I hope he doesn't bother you anymore."

She shakes her apron, removing some of the protein powder. "Why did you stick up for me?"

"I didn't want that jerk hurting you anymore."

"You're so brave. Daniel is one of the toughest men in town."

Rock flexes his biceps. "Not tougher than me." He leans forward. "So, when are you asking me out?"

"Excuse me!"

"You heard me."

"First, thank you for helping me, but you're too cocky for me."

Sparkle whispers, "Rock, I sense you're getting more arrogant the more you mature in your body. I sense Serenity's heart and what she wants from a guy."

While Serenity is fixing another protein shake, the young fairy slowly pumps orange pixie dust into Rock's body. Tiny, heart-shaped, orange magic flows through all his cells, making him sensitive to Serenity's feelings as it teaches him game.

He shakes his head and focuses, feeling something new. He grins at Serenity and chuckles. She turns toward him. "You know I was joking, right?" he says.

"It wasn't funny!"

He runs his hands through his hair. "You're an amazing artist, and very creative. You should let me take you to The Fairyville Museum of Jazz and Arts."

Serenity pushes the button to stop the blender's clattering. "How did you know that I like Art History? Daniel would never take me there."

"I can see an intelligent and articulate woman from a mile away."

Serenity's cheeks blush. "You know I'm still in a relationship, right?"

"You're still with that jerk? Daniel's a loser."

"We've been together for a long time. It's hard to let go."

Rock uses a rubber band from his side pocket to tie his dreadlocks into a ponytail. "You mean to tell me he's been with you that long and doesn't know to take you there? He's an idiot."

"Daniel's stubborn." She hesitates, then continues. "For some reason, I feel an instant connection with you like I've known you for years. Plus, your brown eyes are cute. You know what? I'll take you up on your offer."

After they type each other's cell phone numbers into their phones, Rock leaves the juice stand and says, "I'll call you when I get a chance."

Sparkle pats Rock on his sturdy back. "You were fantastic back there."

"I know. I'm so great." He says, grinning, as he heads toward the back of the gym.

He finds Mitch in his office creating a poster for next month's fight card. As he walks in, Mitch looks up at him and stands up, crossing his arms and grinning. "My big-time celebrity!"

Rock's eyes wander around the room, admiring all the posters of great MMA fighters who came out of Fairyville.

"Look," Mitch says, waving his hands to get his attention, "That fight you had with that kid went viral. It has over fifty million views!"

Rock nearly jumps out of his pants and chuckles from hearing the good news. "I finally got my revenge."

Mitch opens one of his desk drawers, grabs a contract, and holds it up so Rock can see it. "How'd you like to fight Benny 'The Destroyer' Reid in our main event?"

"For my first fight?"

"With all the media attention you received from saving Serenity, the fight could make well over six figures. Maybe even more."

"I'll beat anybody you put in front of me."

"Let's lock it down." Mitch holds out his hand for Rock to shake, and three heavily tattooed, hefty men enter the office. They're wearing black T-shirts that say Team Rock. "Meet your training team," Mitch says.

Rock shakes his head. *I cannot believe this stupid man, Mitch, picked the ugliest, muscular freaks to be on my training team. I don't need them. I'm Rock, and I'm the most amazing man ever.*

"My name is Denver, and I am your striking coach," the first man says.

"Yo, my name's Ron, and I am your grappling coach."

The third man starts beatboxing like an amateur rapper. "My name is Rhyme, and I'm yo' cutman who gon' make sure you don't bleed all the time."

Rock ignores them and turns to face Mitch. "When is the fight?" he asks.

"July 24th at Fairyville Arena."

"I'll see you then," Rock says.

He ignores his team as they try to talk him into staying and leaves the office, searching for Serenity.

7
Rock

When Rock returns to the juice stand where Serenity works, the line is full of sweaty, thirsty fighters waiting for the vital foods they need for their workout. He skips the line and goes straight to the counter, where she's cutting pineapples to make a smoothie for one of her customers. "Hey, sweet lady, why not take off early, and we can go now?"

"I don't get off until 11."

"Don't worry about it! I'm making Mitch so much money, there's no way he'll fire you!"

A broad-shouldered fighter with a blonde goatee seizes hold of him. "There is a line, you disrespectful rookie punk."

Rock pounds his fists on the counter, leaving a dent in it. "Boy, if you don't take your hands off me…" he says with a clear threat in his voice.

Many of the gym's MMA fighters surround Rock, and they get in their martial arts stances, ready to inflict pain on him.

In a rush, Mitch runs over to the crowd. "Hey, hey, hey!" he shouts. "Don't hurt my cash cow!"

"Ain't nobody gon' hurt me," Rock snickers.

Sparkle flutters nearby as she prepares a healthy dose of red pixie dust for him in case an intense battle occurs.

Serenity interrupts and her voice calms the crowd down a bit. "Mitch, is it okay if I take off early?" Serenity asks. "I can get Rock out of here."

"Perfect," Mitch replies.

She takes off her apron and leads Rock out of the gym.

***

Rock puts his hand on Serenity's shoulder. "You didn't need to save me. I had it under control."

Serenity rolls her eyes. "Sure, you did."

They make their way down Main Street, moving towards the museum. The warm summer breeze blows through his dreadlocks as Serenity takes pictures of the green leaves from the pine tree on the clean red brick sidewalk.

"Are you okay, Serenity?"

"I'm just admiring how beautiful this world is."

"You are really into art."

"Art and music. I want to be a jazz musician."

It takes just a few minutes before they arrive at the Fairyville Museum and walk through the metal doors. Serenity hits "record" on her iPhone, so she can film the gigantic fossils of the Tyrannosaurus Rex. She races across the ceramic floor, aiming her phone at the Sauropod display. "This is so amazing."

Rock feasts his eyes on her thin waist and red apple-bottom jeans that perfectly fit her curvy physique. He smells the aroma of afro sheen in her soft hair as he strolls with her to the museum's marvelous jazz exhibit.

Serenity continues to get footage of the wax statues of the many great jazz artists from Fairyville wearing zoot suits and elegant gowns.

"Hey, Rock, I never told anyone this, but my father always took me to the museum. They were some of my best memories of him before he passed away."

"I'm sorry for your loss."

Sparkle hides behind Rock's belt, whispering, "Please remain compassionate to her."

"I appreciate this," Serenity says. "I always wanted someone to go to museums with me. Daniel's so controlling and wants us to do what he wants."

Rock's eyes light up, and he inches closer to her. His voice fills with warmth and excitement. "We can go all the time if you want."

Serenity's lips widen into a gentle curve as she peers up at him and reaches out to sweep his dreads aside, revealing his eyes. "So, where did you grow up?"

Rock pauses momentarily, and his eyes roam around the room, glancing at each statue, trying to figure out what lies he will tell her. "Rockwood Mountains."

She frowns slightly. "That's pretty far from here."

***

After a few hours of bliss, Rock and Serenity leave the spacious building and head to the Fairyville Arcade. Just inside, Rock spots Richard standing by the *Destruction Warrior* game. He's handing out flyers to everyone waiting to play. He has bags under his eyes, appearing not to have slept in days.

Rock begins to approach him. "Don't do this, Rock," Sparkle whispers shrilly in his ear.

He gets close to Richard as the other customers root for the game's two players. Richard hands him a flyer with a picture of Tevin playing the game. "This is my friend," Richard says glumly. "He's been missing for three days now. Have you seen him?"

Rock tries to clear his throat, but he chokes up. "I haven't seen him, man."

Sorrow fills Richard's face, and he shakes his head sadly, turning towards the game console. "This was Tevin's favorite video game."

Serenity takes a flyer. "I always liked Tevin. He was a sweet kid and very shy." She hugs Richard. "It's going to be okay. I'm sure Tevin is safe."

Rock can feel the guilt nearly exploding out of his muscular body. He puts his hand on Richard's shoulder and starts to pull him close so he can whisper in his ear. "I have something to tell you."

"No, Rock! You can't go back to being Tevin yet," Sparkle says quickly. She flies up Rock's shirt and starts tickling him. His body twists and turns, and he starts laughing hysterically.

Richard pushes him away in disgust. "Yo! What's so funny about my best friend being missing?" Richard demands. He smacks Rock's hand off his shoulder and storms out of the arcade, leaving Rock feeling guiltier than before.

Serenity crosses her arms and grows unexpectedly cold. "Why were you laughing?" she asks angrily.

"Something was tickling my stomach."

"Weird," she says, frowning. She stuffs the flyer in her back pocket and glares at him. "I want to go home."

Fairy Rock

***

They walk in cold silence for several blocks until they reach the corner of Main Street, two blocks away from where she lives. "I have to walk alone from here because I'm unsure if Daniel is at my house."

"I'll get rid of him for you for good," Rock offers.

Serenity thaws a bit. "I don't want to see anyone else get hurt." She hugs him tightly and kisses him on the cheek. "Thank you for today. It meant so much to me."

Turning quickly, she runs down the street toward her home.

Rock stands there with his hands on his head, pacing back and forth. *Serenity just kissed me. Wait a minute. I'm Rock, the hottest man alive; of course, she kissed me. She must feel so lucky that she met me. Dang, I didn't mean to hurt Richard like that. When I win Serenity over, I'll make it up to him.*

8
Gilbert III

Neither Serenity nor Daniel sees him, but hiding in the bushes, peering out, a thin older man with a hunchback and a gold eye patch over his left eye ties a rope around his black robe and adjusts his black cone-shaped hat. He waits anxiously as he watches Serenity walk up to her front door, where Daniel sits waiting for her on the porch of the old, beaten-up house.

The older man crinkles his cheeks with disgust at the crickets chirping near him. His eye patch spins, and an array of dark magic gas seeps out of it and covers the annoying insects, causing them to evaporate into dust. He shifts the leaves for a better look, just in time to see Daniel get up, walk off the porch's squeaky wooden steps, and snatch Serenity by the hand.

"You're hurting me, Daniel," she says, struggling to pull away.

He shouts at her as he pulls her closer to him. "What were you doing with that man? I got people watching you."

Serenity yanks her hand back. "He's just a friend."

Daniel shoves her into the dry grass of the front yard. "I'm going to hurt that punk, and we'll settle this later. You're my woman. No other man will ever have you." He pulls a switchblade out of his pocket and stands over her. "Where does he live?"

She rolls over, feeling along the ground until she finds a rock, and flings it at him as she gets up. "I don't know."

He moves quickly towards her and gets in her face. "So, you're going to protect this punk after what he did to me? He'll never have you. You're mine!"

Fairy Rock

She wipes the tears from her eyes. "Daniel, it's not like that."

They're interrupted as Serenity's mom bursts from the front door, holding a shotgun. She pumps it and points at Daniel. "How dare you hurt my daughter?!"

Daniel drops the knife and steps away from Serenity, putting his hands in the air, and talking quickly as he moves towards the street. "I'm sorry I lost my temper, Mrs. Cooper. I love your daughter, and this will never happen again."

"You have to the count of three to run before I blow your brains out!" Mrs. Cooper shouts.

Daniel runs into the street. Mrs. Cooper follows him until he's out of sight, and she lowers the weapon. Serenity runs to her mother's arms, and Mrs. Cooper holds her in a close embrace. "Honey, are you okay?"

"No, I'm not."

"I don't want you talking to Daniel again. Has he ever done this before?"

Serenity glances at the ground. "He's been aggressive, but not like this."

"If I had known, I'd have never let you date him."

"He used to be a sweet guy, Mom. He just started to get more and more controlling over time."

"Why did you stay with him for so long? I taught you better."

"I thought I could change him back into the sweet guy I used to know."

Mrs. Cooper groans. "I'm calling the police."

He's seen enough. The older man spins his eye patch disappears. A moment later, he reappears in front of Daniel, who is blocks away, bent over, catching his breath after a two-block run.

Daniel gasps in surprise.

The older man furrows his brow and steps forward, placing a comforting hand on Daniel's shoulder. "Relax," he says, his voice steady and reassuring. "I'd can see the fire in your'd eyes. You'd want payback on Rock, don't you'd?"

Daniel jumps back. "Who the heck are you?"

The older man spins his eye patch and shines a bright gold light. "Let's just say I'd be another man who wants to kill Rock."

Daniel turns his face away from the irritating ray. "Why's your eye patch glowing?"

"I'd be powerful, boy."

The mysterious man points his eye patch at an old, abandoned house in the neighborhood. He fires a large, yellow-hot, magical laser beam out of it at the dilapidated home, blowing it into thousands of pieces.

42

Daniel puts his hands over his head, protecting himself from the debris showering down on him. He stands there, dumbfounded. "What did you just do?!"

Neighbors spill out of their homes, drawn by the sudden commotion. Their outcries resound through the neighborhood as they witness the engulfed house. Soon, a crowd forms on the street. Their expressions reflect a mix of awe and confusion.

"What happened?" one of the neighbors asks.

"I don't know. The house just exploded," another replies.

The older man turns his focus back to Daniel. He puts his hood over his hat and head, masking his eye patch and wrinkled face.

"Who are you?" Daniel asks.

"My name be Gilbert III."

The clouds turn dark as sprinkling rain falls from the sky, and the wind strengthens.

"How do you know about Rock?" Daniel asks.

"Do you'd want your revenge or not, boy?" Gilbert III asks.

"I do."

Gilbert III's eye patch glows again while his other eye rolls in the back of his head. He extends his arms out in the air, using his black magic to darken the clouds.

The thunder and lightning force the neighbors back into their houses.

Daniel's face goes blank. He backpedals and falls on his butt. "Did you just make it rain like that?"

"I'd once be the most powerful wizard in the world."

"What?"

"That boy you'd fought be no normal boy. The fairies are helping him. We have a mutual enemy. Come with me if you'd want to kill him."

"So, the Myth of Fairy Rock is true?" Daniel says quietly, unable to hide his disbelief.

Gilbert III's eye patch turns a light as bright as the sun. Daniel squints and turns his head. The magical light surrounds them, and they disappear in no time, appearing moments later in an abandoned warehouse in the south part of town. It is hot and empty inside, with nothing but a table with potion glasses and a gold bracelet on top of it. Daniel confusedly looks around. "How did you take me here? What are you?"

"I'd be a former wizard and now fairy hunter."

"Fairies are real?"

"Yes, I'd see one has escaped the World of The Fairies with the help of Tevin."

Daniel scratches his head as ashes and wood particles fall from it onto the cold cement floor. "How did Tevin end up with the fairies? What does he have to do with Rock? That kid is a wimp, and I embarrassed him at the mall."

"With the help of a fairy named Sparkle, he'd be turning into Rock to win the heart of Serenity."

Daniel grits his teeth and slowly shakes his head. "He's creepy, and he always stares at her. I'm going to beat on him again."

Gilbert III grabs the gold bracelet on the table. "You'd not defeat him as Rock—he'd be too strong. Put this bracelet on and become my protégé. Then victory will be yours."

Daniel slowly puts the bracelet on his wrist. The bracelet tightens and shakes, bringing out a blue light around him. The veins in his body pop up as he screams and falls to his knees. Blood gushes out his nose, and his eyes and skin turn blue. He grows five feet taller, and his muscles bulge out of his arms. His teeth and nails enlarge, becoming sharp as blades. He roars like the monster he has become.

Gilbert III smiles as he sees what he's created. As Thrasher Goblin roars, raises his hand in the air to quiet him. "Your'd new name be Thrasher Goblin."

The wizard steps forward and, in a quick motion, takes the bracelet off his arm, and in a flash, the Goblin disappears and Daniel reappears, nude and drenched in sweat.

Gilbert III stands over him. "Do you'd know what happened, boy?"

Daniel kneels, and saliva drools from his mouth. "No, I don't. I feel weak and hungry."

Gilbert III twirls his index finger, magically forming a black robe. He gives it to him.

Daniel puts it on as he finally musters up enough strength to stand.

"Keep this bracelet in your'd pocket until you'd find Rock. When you see him again, I'd be wanting you'd to destroy him and capture the fairy."

"You got it." He grinned darkly.

9
Richard Johnson

Richard slams his door and punches the wall in the living room, cutting his hands. His knuckles are bloody with bits of drywall on them.

Susan comes out of the kitchen. "What's wrong, babe?"

"I was passing out flyers at the arcade trying to find Tevin. This jerk named Rock has the nerve to laugh at me for looking for him."

"Why would he laugh? That's so twisted."

"I know." Richard storms up the stairs into his room and jumps on his bed. He throws a pillow at the poster of the hip-hop group *The Blams* and knocks it off the wall onto his comforter. *Where in the world can Tevin be? I hope and pray he's not dead.*

His ringtone blares, and music from the heavy metal band *The Slayers* plays on his Android phone. Mrs. Jenkins is on the other end.

"Richard, a detective called and said that someone has been using Tevin's debit card at the mall and the museum."

"Did they catch the jerk who used it?"

"No! But I wanted you to know that there was news. I have to go. I'm so worried about my baby. I'll talk to you later."

Richard hangs up, gets out of bed, and pulls his braids.

Susan enters the room. "What's wrong now?"

"It's weird because as soon as Tevin disappeared, that Rock guy showed up, and he was with Serenity. I wonder if he has something to do with Tevin's disappearance?"

"Do you think he hurt Tevin?"

"He could've because he was laughing when I mentioned Tevin." He glares and crosses his arms. "Who does that?"

"We need to find him."

"If he's done anything to Tevin, I will kill that jerk."

Susan lights her cigarette. "Babe, calm down. No one needs to get hurt."

"Nobody but Rock."

10

Tevin Jenkins

A bolt of thunders startles Tevin awake. He yawns and stretches, trying to remember where he is. He's outside Sparkle's treehouse. He covers his shivering body from the cold, rainy weather with a specially made purple blanket by Queen Vanessa. *Richard was so mad at me. I feel so bad.*

Moments later, Queen Vanessa flies to him with three fairy generals – Butch, Baker, and Benard – in their full purple armor. Bernard is clean-shaven and has a white mohawk. Butch and Baker are identical twins with matching bald heads and brown beards.

"Do ya want something to eat, Tevin?" Butch asks.

"What do you have?"

Baker pulls down on his beard. "Do you like dragons, Tevin?"

"Dragons aren't real, are they?"

"In the World of the Fairies, they're quite real, and it is what we eat, lad," Butch replies.

Tevin's lips quiver. "Aren't they big and scary?"

"Do not be afraid. We fairies are highly skilled and can easily bring down a dragon," Baker says.

Fire covers the air in a flash, giving off a blaze of heat.

"The dragons are coming!" Queen Vanessa shouts.

Tevin glances up, and an enormous blue creature whose long body fills the sky soars toward the treehouse with its gigantic wings. Its vast teeth are more orange than the fire it breathes. The dragon's blue scales glow, releasing a black aura around it. It roars and makes a choking sound as it

Fairy Rock

spits out a wave of fire that nearly touches Sparkle's Tree.

Tevin screams and runs into the black leaves to hide. Butch and Baker bend their knees into a lunging position. The fairy generals rapidly flap their wings and take off.

As they fly near the beast, the dragon roars and breathes fire at them, filling the hot atmosphere with smoke. They maneuver around the flames as they bolt toward its dark red eyes.

Baker blows black, poisonous pixie dust into the monster's face. The toxic powder forces the dragon to gag and vomit, causing its blue scales to fall off. The three-hundred-foot-tall dragon falls from the sky, causing a thunderous thud as it crashes into the ground.

The treehouse rumbles as dirt flies in the air.

"Baker! You always get in my way of killing a dragon. Let me do it for bloody once," Butch says.

"Shut your trap," Baker replies coldly.

Tevin sticks his face outside the wet, black leaves. *What just happened? The World of the Fairies is like nothing I ever imagined.* He turns his head toward Queen Vanessa as she blows silver pixie dust into the air, creating a shiny, sharp silver sword.

"Dragon meat is a great source of our strength and power," Queen Vanessa explains. As she flutters to the ground, Sparkle and a host of other fairies fly out of their treehouse to feast on the meal.

"Would you like to try some dragon meat, Tevin?" Sparkle asks.

Tevin dry heaves at the burnt, blue meat and the grease dripping off it. *That stuff looks disgusting and poisonous.*

"Do you still not trust the Queen of the Fairies?" Queen Vanessa asks slyly, holding out a piece for Tevin. She takes another piece of dry dragon meat. As she swallows it, magical blue energy glows over her. "This sensation of power is making me stronger. Tevin, how do you feel when you're Rock?" As she speaks, she blows purple pixie dust in his face, and he becomes discombobulated.

Tevin's body relaxes, and he is no longer crying. He pauses, then answers slowly. "I feel better."

Queen Vanessa nods. "Of course you do. I am like a mother to you, Tevin." She speaks softer and more soothing, and he begins to relax even more. She smiles. "Serenity will be in your arms soon. Your parents will be so proud of you," she continues.

Tevin smiles as he falls asleep.

11
Rock

The next day, Rock arrives at Mitch's gym, and his trainer, Denver, yells, "You finally feel like training? You have a fight coming up!"

Rock ignores him, strolling straight to the juice stand where he cuts the line and leans on the counter. "Serenity, let's get out of here," he says smugly.

She is in the middle of making a vanilla protein shake and stops the blender. "I can't keep taking off work like that."

"Yes, you can, and Mitch will pay you. Ain't that right, Mitch?" he shouts.

Mitch sighs deeply and shrugs his shoulders. "Serenity, go with him, and I'll pay you for the day." He turns to Rock. "Just as long as my cash cow shows up for the fight."

Rock shrugs and stretches while Serenity finishes making the protein shake, gives it to her customer, takes off her apron, and walks out the door with Rock.

The other fighters curse and shout at him as they leave the gym.

***

Once they're alone, Serenity starts to open up. "Rock, you wouldn't believe what happened the other day. Daniel attacked me."

Rock bites his bottom lip. *What? He came near her and attacked after what I did to him? Is he stupid?* He leans in close to her and gently strokes her hair. "For real? Are you okay?"

"No. I don't want to be with him anymore."

"Then don't."

Serenity puts her hand on Rock's arm. "You're so cocky, yet you seem so sweet."

"Keep the compliments coming."

Serenity laughs and holds his arm tightly. "So, where are you taking me?"

***

At Fairyville Park, Serenity smiles, showing her perfectly aligned white teeth as they head down the nature trail. She touches the beautiful green grass and freshly grown pink tulips near the flower garden, and Rock picks one for her. She smells it and blushes.

They both relax on a damp park bench and giggle at their soggy bottoms. Rock wraps his arms around her and whispers in her ear. "Do you love me?"

She puts her hand on his lap. "I just met you but can't stop thinking about you."

As they kiss, the soft touch of her tongue, the smell of strawberry ChapStick on her lips, and the peppermints on her breath makes him fall deeper in love. *Finally, this is happening. I have the most incredible girl. She is intelligent, articulate, and a sweetheart. She's almost better than me. How can anyone ever want to harm her?*

Serenity rests her face on his shoulder. "I love you, Rock."

"I love me, too."

"You're so arrogant." Serenity laughs, but then she stops. Her body stiffens.

Daniel appears in front of them. He's stone-faced and breathes heavily, pointing his finger at her. "Serenity, get away from him."

Serenity freezes in terror, her voice trembling. "Daniel! What are you doing here?"

Rock jumps to his feet and stands between Serenity and Daniel. "Relax, babe. This woman-beating-fool can't hurt you around me."

"What happened to you, Daniel?" Serenity asks, sneaking around Rock to try to see what's going on.

She gasps. Veins pop out the side of Daniel's face and down his arms. The pores on his face begin to bleed green slime down his black muscle shirt.

"Serenity, I'm only going to say this one more time. Get away from him," Daniel says as he takes a switchblade out of his pocket. Rock smiles and puts his fist up to fight. Daniel swings his knife, and Rock maneuvers out of the way and uppercuts him, knocking out his front tooth.

"Let's get out of here, Serenity," Rock says. He takes her firmly by the hand, and they start to leave, but before they can flee, Daniel takes a bracelet from his pocket and puts it on his wrist. The bracelet tightens as yellow light surrounds his body. Slime splats out of his pores, drenching his muscle shirt and jeans with ooze. His nails turn into claws, and his teeth become sharper. He grows, turns blue, and transforms into Thrasher Goblin.

"Not a smart move," Thrasher Goblin says.

Serenity clings to Rock. "Daniel! Daniel! What happened to you?"

He tries to calm her. "Relax, baby. I won't let him touch you."

Sparkle peeks out of Rock's pocket. "Um, um, *he* must have gotten to him."

"Who?" Rock asks.

"The wizard who imprisoned us, Gilbert III."

With green slime oozing out of him, Thrasher Goblin charges at Rock, bulldozing him to the ground. The creature swings its slime-covered claws at his face, but Rock blocks them with his arms.

Sparkle flaps her wings. "This is my first fight with a Goblin. What do I do?"

She skittishly blows a large amount of red pixie dust into Rock's body. His muscles grow tremendously as his strength and ability to fight massively increase.

Rock kicks the monster off and gets back up. As Serenity hollers like a baby, he hits the beast with a left hook and a right hook, hammering the Goblin backward. Rock ducks as it claws at him, but it still clips a chunk of hair out of his freshly interlocked dreadlocks.

"I'm mad now," Rock roars. He dropkicks the Goblin, and it falls, landing on its back. He gets on top of the creature and repeatedly punches it.

The Goblin spits green slime into his face. "Ahhh! This stuff is burning my eyes!" Rock screams.

Immediately, Thrasher Goblin rolls him over and then gets on top. Sparkle sticks her head out of Rock's pocket and blows black pixie dust into the monster's face, poisoning him. Thrasher Goblin coughs up black fluid and runs away.

Rock finally gets the glop off and staggers over to where Serenity's crouching behind the park bench, crying. "You, okay?" he says, gently.

"No, I'm not. I just saw my ex-boyfriend turn into a monster."

Rock sits on the bench, catching his breath.

"What's that thing in your pocket?" she asks.

He puts his hands over his head.

"Tell her," Sparkle whispers. "She caught us."

"It's a fairy, Serenity."

Serenity's head jerks back, her mouth opens, and she appears dazed as her fingers touch her parted lips. "A fairy?"

"Her name is Sparkle, and she helps me out."

"Why do you need a fairy, and who are you?"

Rock pauses.

Serenity takes a Kleenex out of her grass-stained purse and dots his wounds. "You look like you're in a lot of pain."

"I'll be okay. I'm still handsome."

Serenity grins for a moment, then gets serious again. "Thank you for saving me," she says quietly. "Can I meet the fairy?"

Sparkle slowly creeps out of his pocket, tensing as she excessively blinks at Serenity. The two make eye contact until Sparkle ducks her head back down.

"It's okay, don't be afraid of me," Serenity says. She inches near his pocket and peeks inside it.

For several minutes they sit, quietly studying each other, before Rock stretches and breaks the silence. "It's getting late. I should take you home so your mom doesn't get mad at me."

Serenity looks over her shoulder. "What if Daniel comes back?"

"I poisoned him pretty well," Sparkle says. "It'll be a while before he comes back."

12
Richard Johnson

Richard hides behind the apple trees in Fairyville Park. He fidgets with a chocolate brownie edible between his fingers. The chilly air of the night gives him chills. *What the heck was that? Am I high? I only took one bite out of the brownie. I just saw Daniel turn into a blue creature. I've followed that fool Rock since I saw him and Serenity walk by the arcade. Tevin would have a fit if he saw that idiot kissing Serenity. I saw a small woman inside his pocket. Was that a fairy? Nobody else was around to see that monster. Will anyone believe me?*

As Rock and Serenity leave the park, he quickly moves to go home. Once there, he stands on his front porch, sorts through the array of keys on his Slayer keychain, and sticks his house key inside the doorknob.

Susan opens the door for him with a cup of brandy in her hand. "Hey, what happened?"

Richard takes off his filthy blue t-shirt and rubs a mosquito bite on his forearm. "I've been hiding behind the trees spying on Rock."

"What did you find, babe?"

"I saw him fight a monster with a fairy in his pocket."

Susan sips some of her liquor. "Have you been drinking?"

"No. I saw what I saw."

She smirks at him good-naturedly. "So, the myth is true. There are fairies in this town."

"I'm trying to piece things together," Rickard says, leaning in and whispering quickly. "Tevin disappeared. Rock shows up with what looks like a fairy in his pocket, and he's with Serenity."

Susan nods uneasily, and they sit quietly in bed, staring at the ceiling fan.

After a few minutes, Richard groans. "No, he didn't. Wait, he might have." He rises out of his bed. "He didn't. Wait. He did. Tevin must have jumped off Fairy Rock!"

Susan stumbles out of bed. "What?"

He swallows a shot of Susan's brandy. "Think about it. Tevin wanted Serenity badly. He disappears, and Rock shows up with a fairy in his pocket, dating Serenity."

Susan finishes off the bottle. "My grandpa has been telling me about the myth of Fairy Rock since I was in kindergarten."

"I thought that our town's forefathers made up the Fairy Rock legend as a tourist attraction, but I guess they weren't lying about the myth."

"What are you going to do, babe?"

"I'm going to go to Fairy Rock and try to find my best friend."

"Whatever you do, hon, don't jump off the Fairy Rock to find him. We still don't completely know everything."

"I won't."

13
Tevin Jenkins

Tevin awakens in an enchanted garden, and he knows that he's back in the World of the Fairies. The soothing sounds of the purple waterfalls near the river put all who enter at ease. He lays in a bed of purple calla lilies and the scent of the lovely flowers briefly takes his mind off the sharp pain as he sleeps in a trance. His body has bruises and sores from the fight with Thrasher Goblin.

A diminutive elder fairy named Selena nurses the wounds by applying gold pixie dust on the cuts, instantly making them evaporate across his skinny physique as he starts to heal. She scolds him gently. "Tevin, you are lucky to be alive. The Goblin could have killed you."

Sparkle rests next to him. She seems unable to stay awake as she goes in and out of consciousness. "I wasn't ready for a battle with a Goblin. He was big, blue, and scary," she mumbles.

Queen Vanessa massages her daughter's thick hair. "You are very inexperienced, but you fought well." The fairy queen puts her powerful yet petite fingers on Tevin's head. "You protected Serenity and impressed me with your fight."

"Thank you, ma'am."

"You two must be better prepared next time because the Goblin will grow stronger as he matures into his body," Queen Vanessa warns.

Tevin turns to look at her. "Did Gilbert III help Daniel? Isn't he the one who imprisoned you in this world?"

"Yes, and they will come for Serenity again. You must kill them both if you want to save her."

Tevin sighs. "I'll do what it takes to save and protect the love of my life."

Sparkle is uneasy and waits for a moment before speaking. "Mother, you should go with Tevin. You're better than me," she says sadly.

Queen Vanessa shakes the gold particles off her daughter's evening gown. "Relax. You and Tevin have bonded. He is your human and only yours, my dear daughter."

"But I'm scared I'll fail in defeating it."

"My dear, precious Sparkle, you won't. After you two recover, I will take both of you to the Cave of Nightmares to train." The queen unleashes loads of red, blue, purple, yellow, pink, orange, turquoise, and silver pixie dust into her daughter, increasing her pixie count in all areas of her body.

Tevin and Sparkle fall asleep in the garden as their bodies heal.

14

Richard Johnson

In the darkness of the microfilm room of the Fairyville University Library, Richard and Susan read quickly as the microfilm machine spins, and an assemblage of old newspaper articles from the *Fairyville Press* whirl across the screen.

"What in the world?" Susan says. "Stop right here. Five people in our city were reported missing, and nobody ever saw them again. All of them went missing after being seen going to the Fairyville Woods."

Richard slumps back in his chair, running a hand through his braids in frustration. His voice tings with irritation. "Why hasn't this made national news?"

A short, thin, freckle-faced library assistant in a navy-blue tweed dress opens the door to check on them. She sees the headline and leans in. "Whoa, is that an article about those missing people?"

Susan acknowledges and pulls a half-smoked cigarette from her green XXXL sweater pocket that nearly covers her leggings. "Do you mind if we smoke in here?"

The library assistant adjusts her glasses. "Go ahead. We're the only three here this late besides the janitor in the corner sleeping. I'll clean up before anyone finds out."

Susan lights up. "You're a lifesaver."

The library assistant sits in the chair next to them. "Thanks! By the way, you can call me Sarah." She scans the article as she talks. "You know, my grandma was big into the Fairy Rock myth."

Susan breathes out smoke. "Do you know anything about it?"

Sarah turns the knob on the machine and stops it. "Yeah. You see that picture over to your right? That's a painting of the first pirates who came to the Village of Fairyville back in the day."

Susan interrupts. "Wait a minute. I had never heard of pirates coming to Fairyville. I heard something about a wizard or something invading the town after King Thomas lost some bet. Then he turned the villagers into fairies and trapped them in a different dimension or world."

"That's not what I heard," Sarah replies. "I heard that a band of pirates, led by their Captain, Vanessa Purple, pillaged the village, murdering people. The wizard Gilbert III turned them into fairies and trapped them in another world as a favor for King Thomas."

In shock, Richard bangs his head on the desk. "Oh no."

Susan shakes her head agitatedly as she turns the machine again.

Sarah pauses it as they come across an article about a painting of Captain Vanessa of the Purple Clan Pirates. "See! Check this out! It reads: Captain Vanessa is wanted for multiple crimes of robbery, murder, treason, and kidnapping. Her total bounty was one million dollars."

"I thought fairies were the good guys?" Richard asks.

Sarah shakes her head. "From what I heard, they were criminals sentenced to The World of the Fairies as a severe punishment for their crimes."

Susan groans. "I hope Tevin is still alive."

"If Tevin jumped off Fairy Rock, his life would be in danger. The fairies are bad apples," Sarah says.

"I thought they granted people wishes and whatnot?" Richard says.

"Yeah." Sarah frowns. "But at what price?"

Richard stands and puts his jacket on. "I'm going home to get some gear. Then I'm going back to Fairyville Woods."

"Why?" Susan gasps.

"To save Tevin. I'll be back, I promise," Richards replies.

***

Moments later, Richard hurries through the Fairyville Woods holding a flashlight. The cool breeze of the summer night does nothing to calm his nerves. He waves the bright light through the forest, scaring off a raccoon running through the bushes as he passes it.

Jeffrey Roy Ford

As he races up the muddy nature trail of Fairyville Mountain, he moves his legs faster as the frightening wind intensifies, and owls fly out of the oak trees.

Abruptly, he reaches Fairy Rock and climbs the rope nailed to the top of the gargantuan boulder.

How did Tevin know where to jump? He unzips his dusty jacket, wrestles off his heavy book bag full of mountain climbing gear from his dad's garage, and pulls out a half-pint of cognac. He gulps half the potent liquor and looks down the steep mountain at the trees and rock piles below it. *Ain't no way I'm jumping off Fairy Rock.*

The night hawks fill the sky, blocking his image of the luminescent, full moon. Before taking another drink, he stops to think about a time in the third grade when he went on his first field trip to Grateville National Park, thirty miles outside Fairyville. He was a new student and forgot his lunch. He cried under a maple tree, and a shy kid named Tevin sat next to him and shared half his peanut butter and jelly sandwich. They laughed as jelly fell on both of their t-shirts, and they have been best friends ever since.

He finishes off the bottle and tosses it in the grass. *Tevin, I'll find you and bring you home. I promise you, buddy.*

Standing on top of the distinctive boulder, he glances at the stars throughout the night sky, the mountains from far away, and the lights turning off in the skyscrapers as the businesses close for the day. *I'm scared to death. Tevin, you're like a brother, and I'll do this only for you.*

He stares down at the steep ground from the mountain. He grabs his dad's revolver from his book bag and loads it with six bullets.

I must jump off Fairy Rock now because it may be the only way to save him.

He takes a breath and leaps.

15

Serenity Cooper

Serenity sits in her plaid pajamas on the satin sheets in her unmade bed, attempting to play the saxophone, but her notes fall flat. *Darn it. I haven't slept in two days. My ex-boyfriend turned into a creepy monster right in front of me. How did this happen? Is it my fault?*

She puts the saxophone mouthpiece in her mouth and blows another tune. *Dang, flat again. I can't concentrate. Where is Rock? I haven't heard from him. I feel so bad that Tevin is missing too, and I haven't put much effort into finding him. I've been so selfish.*

She stands up and gazes in the mirror, trying to pat down her uncombed hair, which is going in every direction.

She reminisces about her first-ever talent show in front of the Fairyville Junior High School students. Her hands trembled as she tried to remember how to play the song "What an Angry World" by the Fairyville Jazz great Dennis Winestrong on her alto sax sheet.

She played terribly, and no one clapped. Some of the students stuck their fingers in their ears to plug them. When she finished, there was complete silence in the auditorium.

But then, a gift: A skinny, nerdy kid stood out from his aluminum chair and gave her a standing ovation. The kid was Tevin, and he was the only one who supported her that day.

Tevin, please be alive and come back safely. I'm so overwhelmed by all this. Daniel will kill me, and I can't let that happen. I have so much that I want to accomplish.

The sweet sounds of the song "What an Angry World" plays on her Android phone as it rings. She picks it up. "Hello."

"Serenity, this is Mitch. Where in the world is Rock? Have you seen him?"

"I haven't seen him in two days."

"He better not bail on that fight, or I'll sue. Find him."

She hangs up the phone, puts her favorite red bath towel over her face, and wails.

Her mom barges into her room, nearly tripping over the heart-shaped wool rug, trying to get to her daughter. "Serenity, what's wrong, sweetheart?"

She clutches her mother's soft, tall body with a stench of cigar smoke on her flannel jacket. "Three men are fighting over me. One is missing, and another turned into a monster. The last one is walking around town with a fairy in his pocket."

"Serenity, have you been drinking?"

"You know I don't drink."

"Well, who's missing? Who turned into a monster? Who is walking around with a fairy in his pocket?"

"Mom, Tevin is missing. Daniel's a monster now."

"That does it!" Mrs. Cooper shouts. "I'm going to get my gun and kill him."

"No! I don't want you to get hurt."

"Serenity, Daniel came around you again, so we'll go to the police. Hopefully, they'll do something about it, like issue a restraining order against him."

Serenity grabs her mom's shirt. "Daniel's not human anymore. Who will believe me, Mom?"

"Come now. We're going to the car."

16
Richard Johnson

Richard appears in the thick fog in The World of The Fairies. The moisture is abundant, and he cannot see his own hands. He digs through his open bookbag for the half-pint of cognac he packed. "Empty! " He throws the bottle back on the ground in disgust and staggers through the fog, desperately searching for his best friend. His voice slurs, "Tev! Tev! Tevin, can you hear me?!"

Bright purple lights appear, and tiny flying people in purple armor surround him. He trips and falls backward as the wee men and women fly around him. "Oh, snap. You all must be fairies."

"Yes, we are, lad," Butch responds.

"Where's Tevin?" Richard asks.

Baker smirks and covers his mouth. "This boy is drunk."

"Come with us, lad, and meet our queen," Butch orders.

"I know who you all are. I'm not going anywhere with you," Richard replies as he tries to stand up defiantly.

Baker flies closely around his face, sizing him up. "Butch, we're going to have to sedate him."

Richard pulls out his revolver. "You're not going to sedate anyone."

The fairies scatter.

Swooping in, Butch blows purple pixie dust in Richard's direction and misses as he jumps out of the way of the attack. Richard fires his pistol. The fairies scatter again, unharmed.

Baker pulls and tugs on his beard. "I'm going to capture him."

"Let me do it. You got to kill the dragon," Butch says.

They soar through the mist, charging at Richard, who turns and sprints away. His eyes are sore from trying to squint through the gloomy atmosphere. Racing through the fog, he stops abruptly when he hears a waterfall. *They're too fast for me to shoot. I'm going to have to jump in the water or hide.*

He crawls into the log of a dead tree near the creek's ledge and listens to the commotion around him.

Baker calls out mockingly to him through the fog. "You should come with us peacefully if you know what's good for you."

"Let me do some of the threatening. You always have fun," Butch says.

"Quiet," Baker warns.

Thunder and lightning saturate the sky as purple smoke appears around the fairies. Selena emerges from the vapor wearing a vintage, purple Renaissance dress. "The boy is here for Tevin. We must not let him find him. We need Rock to kill Gilbert III," she states menacingly.

"I'm going to find the lad, and Baker better not get in my way," Butch says proudly.

Selena glows fiercely. "You know that Rock is vital to our fate. Queen Vanessa and I do not have the time to find the boy as we must train Tevin and Sparkle. I'm sending the dark wolves after him. They will be enough," she orders.

Richard breathes heavily but stifles the sounds as he quietly inserts more bullets into the revolver's chamber and slowly moves his head out the log's hole to view what's happening. He watches fearfully as Selena blows blue pixie dust into the wisteria weeds. "I summon the dark wolves." The world quakes as the ground in the black field near them splits open, and a hole corrupted with black magic dirt emerges. Two bear-sized grizzly wolves creep out of it. Selena pets their thick, black fur.

"Find the intruder," she says. The vicious, dark animals' loud howls disperse the bats out of the trees, and the evil wolves take off to find him.

Richard sees the evil beast coming towards him through the mist. *I got to get out of here!*

He crawls from under the log and dashes toward the edge. *I have no choice. Tevin, I'm doing this for you.*

Richard jumps off the cliff into the waterfall. Down he goes into the watery darkness, until he begins to rise up, the pressure squeezing the air out of him. Breaking through to the surface, he flails and kicks, fighting his way out of the water, and gets to the shore of the beach. Black seaweed sticks to his wet clothes. He lies exhausted in the muddy sand, his legs badly bruised and sore.

He takes a minute to take in the fact that he survived. *I must have dived at least 200 feet.*

But the danger hasn't fully passed. The area's trees, grass, bushes, dirt, and mountains are pitch black. He can barely see. The sounds of howling make him squirm.

I must get up. He grabs his gun and limps through the fog.

In the darkness, the wolves bark. With a shaky hand, he points his pistol toward the sound. *What the heck is coming?*

He hides in the bushes' leaves and camouflages himself with dirt. Two glowing, dark red eyes emerge from the water onto the beach.

What is that? Richard bites down on his fist to keep himself from hollering as dark wolves sniff the sand-filled surface. The foul odor of drool comes out of the beastly creatures' tongues. His hands tremble, trying to hold his gun with his sweaty palms. The wolves show their long, sharp fangs.

Richard tries not to groan as the throbbing pain in his legs gets worse, and his mind races with thoughts of death. He puts his finger on the trigger. *I'm not going out like this.*

As they sprint toward him, he screams and fires.

The bullets do not affect them. They jump on Richard and begin to maul him. The pain is excruciating, and his blood covers the ground.

"Help!" he screams.

A little man about three feet tall with pointy ears and a long white beard dressed in a green robe appears from behind one of the trees. He points his bow with two glowing brown arrows at the dark wolves and fires them, hitting the wicked animals in their necks. The mystical arrows explode, setting the dark wolves on fire, and they run away.

The pointy-eared man rushes to his aide. "I'm here to save you." He strips Richard's jacket and t-shirt off and rubs glowing white cream all over his wounds. The blood dries up on his arms, and the soreness disappears.

He puts his hand on Richard's shoulder and rubs yellow cream on his face. Then he uses the cream on himself, and the gel causes them to glow as they beam away.

17
Tevin Jenkins

The Cave of Nightmares lies in the black mountains just outside the enchanted garden.

Queen Vanessa's muscles bulge as she heaves against the massive boulder guarding the entrance to the cave. With a grunt, she shoves the rock aside, revealing a dark, foreboding tunnel. As they enter, the air grows thick and stale. Sounds of scuttling fill the cave. Hundreds of tarantulas and scorpions pour out of the cave's depths. They crawl and skitter off the walls.

Tevin's heart pounds in his chest as he leaps out of the way.

Queen Vanessa orders him to stand strong. "Do not run away. This training will help you save Serenity," she says calmly.

Sparkle rubs his hair. "We'll be fine. My mother knows best."

Queen Vanessa gusts peach pixie dust out of her fingers, creating a peach-colored light throughout the cave, and the three go inside.

Tevin backs away as the tarantulas and spiders crawl out of the human skeletons across the cave. Rats screech as they run by him. He folds his hands. "Lord, please be my eyes and ears," he prays quietly. "Please protect me. In Jesus' name, Amen."

As they reach the cave's center, Queen Vanessa commands them to lie on the rocky surface by the stalagmites. She sprays them with purple pixie dust, and they fall asleep.

Tevin dreams of eating supper at home in his parents' living room. His mom is wearing the same purple evening gown that Queen Vanessa is wearing. She's cooking a wonderful turkey dinner with dressing and cornbread. Richard, Susan, and his dad wear black tuxedos while waiting for supper at the dinner table. "Would you like some turkey, everyone?" his mom asks.

"Ouch, I burned my tongue on this bleeping hot chocolate," his dad complains.

His mom gives her husband some ice water to cool his tongue. "It'll be okay, dear."

Richard puts his arms around Tevin. "Congratulations on being accepted into ten major universities on academic scholarships. I'm glad you picked Fairyville University, and we will be roommates. What are you going to major in?"

"Chemistry."

Susan pats Tevin on his back. "Thank you for teaching my little cousin how to play Destruction Warrior and buying him those cool comic books. He loves you."

Tevin raises his hands as he celebrates with everyone in the room. He smiles at his beautiful mother.

He abruptly becomes serious as Serenity appears in the room with Thrasher Goblin. She's in an extremely tight, red gown with slits that expose the skin of her round hips, while the Goblin is dressed in a red suit.

The mighty Goblin roars at his family, and everyone jumps out of their seats. Without warning, Gilbert III enters the room.

The wizard fires a magical laser beam out of his eye patch, hitting Richard, Susan, and Tevin's parents with it, making them quickly disappear.

"No!" Tevin screams.

Serenity laughs hysterically and kisses Thrasher Goblin on his cheek. "You will never have me, Tevin," she cackles.

Gilbert III aims his eye patch at Tevin. "You'd and Rock be doomed."

He fires the laser beam at him.

Tevin wakes up from his dream, sweating profusely. He looks around, and seeing Queen Vanessa, he struggles to speak. "Was that a nightmare? Are my family, Richard, and Susan okay? Is Serenity back with Daniel?" he stammers.

"It was a dream," Queen Vanessa states flatly. "Welcome to the Cave of Nightmares. Here, you will learn to fight while facing your fear."

Sparkle comes out of her own trance. She looks like she's about to cry and her voice is a soft whimper. "Mother, I had a dream. I saw my father in his tree house, and he was alive. He was lying in bed. He didn't look too good. He said he loved me and would find a way for us to be free. Then Gilbert III came into his room and killed him. I miss my father," Sparkle cries.

Queen Vanessa hugs her. "My sweet, beautiful daughter, it was just a dream."

"Where's my father?" Sparkle asks.

"I don't know, Sparkle," Queen Vanessa replies. She flies into the air. "There's no time for fear. The two of you made several mistakes in your fight with Goblin because you were afraid. Your enemies will kill you if you do not fight better."

"I'm sorry, Mother," Sparkle whimpers.

"Sorry won't cut it next time," Queen Vanessa snaps. Her eyes turn dark purple, and her aura glows. "Ogres! My ogres come out of hiding." Loud footsteps vibrate the cave, forcing black rocks to fall from the black stalactite-filled ceiling as swarms of bats screech and fly out of it.

Three ten-foot-tall monstrous, naked, gray-skinned giants with large, yellow teeth emerge out of the shadows, roaring and beating on their chests. They tower over Tevin and appear at least six hundred pounds, with oval-shaped heads, flabby arms, chunky legs, and plumped bellies over their waist.

The purple pixie dust wears off Tevin and he screams.

Sparkle is by his side, sizing up the five-hundred-pound creatures. "Calm down, Tevin. We'll be fine," Sparkle says bravely.

Queen Vanessa smiles. "I'm impressed by your courage, my daughter." She gestures to the monsters. "These ogres will be your opponents. Work together and face your fears to defeat them."

Tevin thinks of Serenity. *I love her so much, and I must save her.*

Sparkle goes into his pocket and injects blue pixie dust into him. Blue smoke covers Tevin, transforming him into Rock.

"Ogres, attack them," Queen Vanessa demands.

Rock, sporting his new blue suede jogging suit, laughs hysterically. "This is going to be easy."

18
Tevin Jenkins

As Queen Vanessa calls the first naked ogre to the center of the cave, Rock stretches and loosens his muscles, preparing for battle.

He hops back and forth, taunting the ogre. "I'm gonna crush you!" The bald, gruesome ogre swings his massive fists. "No!" Rock blocks the punch and stumbles back, nearly falling from the impact.

Queen Vanessa blows a whistle and they both stop fighting and look at her. "Rock, you are scared. I smell your fear," she says calmly.

Rock shrugs his shoulder and scoffs. "What? I'm not scared of anything." He flexes his muscles and kisses his biceps.

Queen Vanessa shakes her head. "You're wrong! I can sense your fear, and you need to control it if you want to save Serenity."

She nods her head, commanding the ogre to attack again, and the gray-skinned behemoth tackles Rock, pinning him down on the snaggy stones. The floor cracks open and spews purple water, soaking Rock's fancy jogging suit. Debris falls from the top of the cave and onto everyone in it. Rock strains with all his might to move, but he can't.

When she sees that he's in peril, Sparkle rushes in and sticks red pixie dust into him, growing his muscles and strengthening his bones as his fighting ability increases, but he still cannot move.

"Sparkle, you are just as afraid as Rock," Queen Vanessa scolds her.

Sparkle rushes back in and blows toxic black pixie dust into the ogre's hideous, scarred face, causing it to cough. It yells, barbarically beats on its chest, and fiercely glares at the young fairy. "But my pixie dust isn't working.

I don't know what to do," Sparkle cries in frustration.

"You did not use enough. Dig deep and concentrate. You two have the power to defeat your opponent."

The ogre begins pounding Rock to a pulp, splattering his blood across the rocks.

Sparkle shrieks and flies closer. Her warm hands touch Rock's back as she climbs up his shirt, and she releases a ton of red pixie dust into him. His muscles expand, and his suede sweater tears to shreds. In seconds, he's back in action. With his rejuvenated strength, he swiftly kicks the ogre off him, and it lands on its back.

"Control your fear, and you will defeat it," Queen Vanessa says.

"I ain't scared, queen fairy lady," Rock says.

"Concentrate and focus on its movements then."

Rock wipes the blood from his mouth and observes the beast's shoulders and hips. The ogre swings, and he ducks. It kicks at him, and he dodges it. He jumps and viciously throws an overhand right to the ogre's head, knocking it out cold.

Queen Vanessa claps her hands. "Wonderful! Wonderful job."

Sparkle uses gold pixie dust to bring the swelling down on Rock's face. "Good job. We did it."

"It's not over yet. This time, you will fight two more of my pets simultaneously," Queen Vanessa says.

She snaps her tiny fingers, and two monstrous ogres enter the cave's center. They roar and stomp on the ground, causing the place to vibrate as the stalactites up top break and fall to the cave's floor.

"Oh, snap!" Rock shrieks, and he dives out of the way as the pointy stones break into pieces around him.

"I thought you weren't afraid," Queen Vanessa snickers.

Rock arrogantly sticks his nose up. "Nah. Nah, I ain't scared. Put some clothes on those things."

"Mother, I'm too tired to keep going! I'm exhausted from fighting the first one," Sparkle complains.

The queen's eyes change to dark purple as she commands thunder from the sky. Rock flinches as Sparkle hides behind him. "Mother is upset," she wails.

"You two are acting like cowards!" Queen Vanessa yells.

Rocks rubs his dreadlocks. "Who are you calling a coward?"

"Show them no mercy," Queen Vanessa demands.

The ogres charge them, and Rock steps back.

"Don't back up. Fight like a man," Queen Vanessa orders angrily.

"Sparkle, your mother's tripping out," Rock says.

The ogres punch him simultaneously, and Rock covers up. He grabs one of them. He body slams the beast, putting it to sleep.

Sparkle takes her head out of Rock's pocket. "Rock, hold your breath."

A black aura comes around the young fairy, and she inhales the air.

Her belly bloats. She exhales and spreads black pixie dust throughout the cave, poisoning all the ogres. The beasts' skin turns pitch black, and they stumble around the cave, vomiting black fluid until they faint.

"Great job," Queen Vanessa says, flying near them. "You two have learned to control your fear." The queen claps her hands and blows kisses at them both.

After the poisonous pixie dust clears, Rock sits on a boulder and tries to put his hair back in place. "Queen, I'm going to need some new threads. I want to go back to Fairyville in style."

Queen Vanessa gives an exasperated stare and at that exact moment, Selena teleports into the cave.

"You came just in time. Heal Rock and Sparkle and prepare them to return to Fairyville," Queen Vanessa orders.

"I shall obey, my queen," Selena says.

19
Gilbert III

Gilbert III paces the floor of his lair—an old, abandoned warehouse. The wizard leans against the sink of the men's restroom and wipes the paint chips off. They land on the floor, and ants crawl on the cracked tile scattered across the room. He takes his pocketknife and shaves the white stubble off his puny, prune-shaped face.

When he's finished, he turns and enters a small laboratory, full of fluorescent lights blinking on and off. The floor is full of sticky tar, piles of lumber, and boxes of chemistry flasks. He checks on his protégé, Daniel, who lays across the room, resting on an old, bent metal cot with an IV bag connected to his arm as the rest of Sparkle's poison drains out of him.

The heavyweight-sized Daniel squeezes on the torn, dirty mattress, pulling the yellow foam out as he mutters cluelessly to himself. "Serenity left me for that stupid jerk. I want my revenge."

After several more minutes of mindless muttering, he tries to get up, but Gilbert III pushes him back into bed. The wizard injects a unique serum into his protégé. "You'd better be calm." The elixir flows through Daniel as it cleans the poison out of him. "You'd must get healthy, boy," Gilbert III tells him softly.

Daniel pushes Gilbert III out of the way, grabs his distinctive bracelet off the rusty metal laboratory table, and storms out of the lair. "Serenity is my woman. Mine!"

As the door slams shut, Gilbert III spins his eye patch until a yellow light glows. He disappears and reappears directly in front of Daniel, who is running down the street bare-footed. Instantly, he grabs Daniel and pushes him to safety as a Mercedes Benz swerves and nearly hits them.

Daniel struggles, but Gilbert III holds him down and leans over him, muttering, "Calm down. I'd be trying to help!"

The effect of the medicine appears on Daniel's weary face, and he lays back quietly.

Gilbert III crouches down to try to blend in better with the wet street. He notices people getting out of their cars. Thinking quickly, he uses his glowing eye patch to create a magical yellow portal and transmits Daniel to his hideout. Once there, he rests his protégé back on the metal cot in the laboratory.

Daniel opens his eyes briefly, and he whispers to himself, "I dreamt of the first time I met Serenity. I had just earned my stripes from the Tarantulas. My big brother, Mookie, was so proud that he gave me a Harley Davidson as a gift. I turned the engine on and inhaled the exhaust fumes like a fragrance. It was a sunny day, and I rode through Fairyville Park. I saw her playing the saxophone by the pond. Her notes were off rhythm, but it didn't bother me. She was the prettiest woman I had ever seen in my life. And as she played, a man dressed in black with a ski mask snatched her saxophone and took off running. I rode over to the mugger and beat the breaks off him. We've been together ever since… until Rock showed up."

He closes his eyes and tears up, the tiny drops slipping down his cheeks. "My parents are dead. My brother is dead. I can't let Rock have her. She's all I have left."

Gilbert III shakes him roughly, and Daniel's eyes come in to focus. The wizard stands over him sternly. "I'd do not want to hear your pity, boy. If you'd want her back, then destroy him."

Daniel sniffles then sits up a bit. He turns to Gilbert III. "I'm ready to face Rock again."

Gilbert III's eye patch glows a brown light, flashes a ray, and transforms into a long, heavy brown ax. He hands it to Daniel and laughs haughtily. "By now, Queen Vanessa has trained Rock and the young fairy. This unbreakable ax can cut through anything. When you'd turn back into the Goblin, use it to kill Rock, and I'd take care of the fairy."

Daniel grins darkly. "I can't wait to shed his blood."

Gilbert III touches his wrinkled face. "If I'd were younger, I'd destroy him myself."

Daniel grabs the magical bracelet and the ax. "Don't worry. I'll finish him."

20
Rock

Rock unzips his new blue Fendi Denim outfit's pants pocket, and Sparkle flies into it. As she gets comfortable, she casts a handful of yellow pixie dust from her itty-bitty palms to form a magical portal that fills the cave with a bright yellow light.

As Rock and Sparkle enter the portal, Queen Vanessa cheers them on. "I have faith in both of you to destroy Gilbert III and the Goblin," she shouts to them as they vanish.

They arrive in the Fairyville woods, and the two of them travel through the ragweeds and bushes, past the pollen-filled tall grass only to see another search party posting pictures of Tevin and Richard to the bark of the oak trees.

Rock kicks one of the trees, rattling it as green leaves and acorns fall. "How can this be? How is Richard missing?!"

The search party members stop and glare at him.

"Calm down," Sparkle whispers.

"Calm down? My best friend is missing!"

"I know, but we still have a mission to save Serenity."

Rock storms by the crowd of searchers, lost in his thoughts. What happened to Richard?

Sparkle shakes purple pixie dust out of her little red puffy hair, and she inhales, expanding her lungs to blow it onto Rock.

But Rock sees what she's doing and blocks her. "Hey, Fairy, don't you dare put that stuff in me."

Sparkle steps back and shrugs. "Okay, I won't. I promise we will find him, but we must get to Serenity."

The searchers don't notice the fairy, but they're distracted by the young man making a scene, and many of them stop the search and watch him warily as he moves angrily through the muddy field of shrubs and dead leaves. On the outskirts of the woods, he spots Mr. and Mrs. Johnson, Richard's parents, weeping by a dying oak tree.

"I have to help," Rock says.

Sparkle flies out of his pocket and goes up his brown Versace silk shirt to get close to his ear. "Please focus! We must save Serenity, or the Goblin will kill her."

"I know," Rock says coldly, pushing her back into his pocket. He leaves the crowded forest for Mitch's MMA gym. "Serenity should be at work right now."

***

As Rock bursts through the door, Mitch turns away from the array of fighters wrestling on the mats in the main gym and gets in his face. "Where've you been?!"

Rock pushes him out of the way and goes straight to the juice stand. No one is in line as he goes to the counter where Serenity is busy fiddling with her saxophone.

"Hi, honey," Rock says nonchalantly.

She pulls him across the counter in a burst of frantic hugs and kisses. "Where've you been? I have been so worried about you."

"I was training in the fairy world. Did you hear Richard's missing?"

"Yes! I don't know what's happening in this town, but it's scary. I know Daniel is coming for me."

"I'll make sure he never hurts you again."

Mitch has recovered from his shock, and as he approaches, he sneezes into his handkerchief and then taps Rock on his shoulder. "We need you in the auditorium. The press conference for the big fight is about to start."

Rock looks at Serenity, and she waves him towards the door. He takes her by the hand, and together, they walk into the large, rectangular-shaped room full of reporters. Cameras flash as they go to the podium, where his trainers Ron, Denver, and Rhyme, await him.

The first reporter asks Rock a question. "You are an internet sensation for saving Serenity from that terrible man. How does it feel?"

"I feel good, I smell good, my girl's good, I'm good-looking, and everything's good," Rock responds.

"I see you're sitting next to her. Are you two an item?" reporter number two asks.

Serenity blushes at the camera. "Yes."

The reporters applaud, celebrating the couple's newfound love.

"How do you two feel about being Fairyville's new number one couple?" another reporter asks.

Rock says, "Any woman with me is the luckiest woman in the world."

"How is your fight preparation?" the first reporter asks.

Rock pauses as he looks at his trainers, all wearing black t-shirts with gold letters that read Team Rock. He sighs at the balding Ron and his ugly chain tattoo around his shoulder.

He grits his teeth at the clean-shaven Denver as he sprays minty cologne around his barreled chest and gives Serenity the side eye. He snubs at Rhyme in a black beanie, mumbling a freestyle. His hip-hop trainer appears to have added another microphone tattoo that goes along with the hundred other microphone tattoos on his abnormally large but well-toned body.

Ron attempts to speak, but Rock interrupts him. "Hey, this is my press conference. Mitch pays these trainers to watch me knock out Benny the Destroyer, not to talk."

The sound of trumpets fills the room. Everyone in the auditorium looks around to see what's going to happen. Two tall, round, overweight bodyguards kick the room's double doors open. Benny the Destroyer's entourage enters, smearing their muddy feet on the carpet. They are wearing pink lavender suits. Some play the trumpet, while others throw rose petals on the ground.

Thirty-five-year-old Benny the Destroyer walks in wearing a pink robe that matches his shiny pink hi-top fade.

"No way! The champ is much shorter in person. He must be about 5'8," one reporter says.

"He has the build of a human tank," another adds.

Benny gets to the podium and removes his robe, showing off his hairy chest and stomach.

He pulls out a raw steak and chews on it.

Serenity puts her hands over her mouth and gags as he swallows the uncooked meat.

"I'm Benny the Destroyer, the world champion, and I come to Fairyville to face my challenger, who calls himself Rock," he says.

Rock purses his lips from the stench of Benny's musty armpits. "I can't believe that I have to fight this loser."

The champion faces Rock and Serenity. He continues to eat the uncooked, bloody meat.

Serenity puts her red shirt over her nose from the smell. "Yuck."

Rock pounds on the table, rattling it. "Listen, man. You're creeping my girl out. I'm going to knock you out for that."

Benny throws the steak at him. "You disrespectful punk! I am a six-time world champion fighter, and I will not let an internet sensation disrespect me!"

He attempts to charge at Rock, but his entourage holds him back.

Rock takes Serenity by the hand. "Let's go. We have bigger things to worry about."

The reporters snap pictures of them as they leave Mitch's MMA Gym.

"You better be there on fight night," Mitch hollers after them.

"I'll be there," Rock says.

The couple hurries off the premises and heads toward Serenity's house.

"That man was so disgusting," Serenity says.

"He was a very stinky human," Sparkle says.

"When I fight him, I'll finish him quickly and make him shower," Rock responds.

***

Trouble is clearly brewing as they near Serenity's neighborhood. The smell of smoke is thick in the air, and as they get closer, it's clear that the roof of her house is burning. The street is full of neighbors and fire trucks and flames are pouring from the windows of the house.

Serenity desperately searches for her mother, and she's not there. She screams and sprints toward the flames. Her neighbors grab her and pull her back while the firefighters try to extinguish the blaze with their water hoses.

Then, over the noise of the trucks, Mrs. Cooper wails from inside the house.

Rock hears it and with a glance, he can see the panic in Serenity's face. He bulldozes through the neighbors, making his way inside the home. Once in, he realizes the danger he's in. The smoke blocks his vision.

Sparkle reaches out of his pocket and listens. "Rock, she's upstairs. Just run upstairs and grab her. Your body can take the heat."

Rock races through the fire and up the stairs. "Mrs. Cooper, where are you?!"

"The bathroom," Mrs. Cooper calls through the smoke.

He follows her voice, feels his way to the bathroom door, and kicks it down. Mrs. Cooper leans against the toilet. He pushes past the flames, picks her up, and carries her down the stairs.

As they make their way to the lawn, the ceiling rumbles and caves. Bricks and lumber hit Rock in his head and shoulders, but he bravely pushes his way through, bringing Mrs. Cooper outside.

"Mom! Oh my God—are you okay?" Serenity cries.

Mrs. Cooper coughs profusely.

Serenity tries to get the soot and wood chips off her mother's red nightgown.

In the light of the flames, Rock and Serenity notice a humongous goblin footprint on the lawn.

Rock, Sparkle, and Serenity get in the ambulance with Mrs. Cooper. "She's lost consciousness," one of the ambulance workers says. "We must perform CPR."

Serenity gets on her knees and prays. "Wonderful and merciful Lord, please let my mother survive this. In Jesus' name, Amen."

***

Sometime during the trip to the hospital, Serenity's mother revives. When Serenity sees her, she's frail, but the color's starting to come back to her face. Serenity rushes to Rock's side. "The doctors say my mom is going to be okay. Thank you for saving her life."

Sparkles pokes him and whispers in his ear. "Rock! We must take Serenity with us. It's not safe for her here."

Rock sighs deeply and runs his hands through his dreads. "Serenity, I'm going to take you to The World of The Fairies," he says.

"I heard Sparkle," she says sternly. "I have ears too, you know!"

Rock holds her hand. "Do you trust me?" he asks.

"Yes," she says calmly. "I know you won't let Daniel hurt me." She pauses, then continues. "But what about my mom?"

"When the Goblin realizes you're gone, he will not bother your mother. He wants you," Sparkle says.

Fairy Rock

Serenity appears to be thinking, and then she nods. "I trust both of you."

***

An hour later, Rock and Serenity stand on Fairy Rock. The full moon is out, and the heavy wind blows the leaves on the trees sideways below the mountain.

Rock tightly embraces Serenity, and she cries. The scent of *Oil Sheen* in her hair is smooth. He softly kisses her lips. "It's going to be okay, sweetie."

"Rock, I'm scared to death. Are you sure I'm not going to die?"

"Trust me. I won't let anything happen to you."

"When this is over, do you think the fairies can make me a better jazz musician?"

"I don't see why not."

Rock picks Serenity up. Her long, slender legs dangle off his arms.

"Um, um Rock, we need to go. *Now*," Sparkle says.

They jump off Fairy Rock.

21

Gilbert III

As dusk falls in Fairyville, Gilbert III strolls down Main Street. He's wearing a black jogging suit, a hood covering his liver-spotted bald head, and the eyepatch on his skinny, aging face. He uses a cane to help himself walk down the packed road.

Helicopters hover over the city and shine their searchlights over the street's department stores and skyscrapers.

The town is in chaos as Serenity is now missing, too. Crowds of search party members check the roads with flashlights as they look inside some of the vacant businesses and trash cans in the alley to find clues.

Gilbert III continues down First Avenue to Fairyville City Hall, where the mayor, Sally Brunson, has called an emergency town hall meeting. It's standing-room-only, and the conference hall is full of loud chatter as people try to figure out what happened to the three missing teenagers.

Police Chief Eric Bailey turns on the air conditioner, keeping the overcrowded room cool, and the mayor beats her gavel on the podium. "Order. Order." She waves her frail hand to calm the unruly audience.

"Three of our high school graduates have gone missing. Is there a kidnapper in this town?" one of the town members asks.

"How will I protect my children?" another person says.

"One question at a time," Mayor Brunson shouts, trying to keep order.

She's interrupted as a third person blurts out, "We saw a big, blue lizard-looking creature destroy Mrs. Cooper's house. What will you do about that?"

Mayor Brunson slams the gavel on the podium and the room becomes quiet. She wipes the sweat off her forehead, takes the microphone from the mic stand, and begins walking around the stage. "I know you are all scared. Chief Bailey and I have taken every precaution to keep this town safe."

Gilbert III hides in the corner of the room as a drunk man, stinking of scotch, rises out of his chair. "*Hiccup*, you haven't said anything about helping those missing kids yet."

"We have many search parties looking for them. If anyone has any information on their whereabouts, please call The Fairyville Police Department."

"The lizard creature is going to kill us all!" a senior citizen resident calls out, then faints on the floor. The people sitting next to her help her to her seat, fanning her as she regains consciousness.

The mayor waits until the room quiets down and then speaks into the microphone. "I can assure you that there is no lizard creature. It is probably just a criminal dressed in some costume trying to scare people. I promise we will apprehend the criminal." She sighs and realizes that she's not getting anywhere with the crowd, so she excuses herself and makes her way back to her office.

I'd have to do something before the town catches on to my plan. Gilbert III spins his eye patch and disappears, reappearing moments later in front of the mayor's office door and peeks through the crack. The mayor and the police chief are alone in the room, talking to each other.

"What do you want?" Chief Bailey asks.

The mayor shoves the heavyset Chief into the bookshelf, pummeling the books off it, and slaps him in his thick, gray-bearded face.

"What did you hit me for?"

She throws her red, high-heeled shoe at him. "I'm up for reelection this year, and I cannot lose because your police department can't protect this town."

Chief Bailey straightens the collar on his police uniform and adjusts his hat. He gets in her face. "Mayor, I hope you know you just assaulted an officer."

She punches him in his head, her ring causing a small cut on the hairline of his long, curly hair. "Don't forget who looked the other way when you stole money from the Police Charity Basketball game to pay your gambling debts."

"You weren't complaining when I took you on a cruise with some of that money."

She pauses and then holds the Chief's hand. "Listen, just get this town under control so I can get reelected."

He caresses her ponytail. "I got this, honey. We only have to keep this quiet so my wife doesn't find out and kill us both."

The mayor smiles, and they both relax together on the couch.

***

Later that night, Gilbert III and Daniel creep outside the Jenkins' home, hiding behind the tall, blue juniper bushes on the side of the two-story brick house. The cold water drizzles on his head from the busted gutter above him, and it splatters on Daniel's shoulder. He squeezes his fists. "I'm ready to kill those people now," he whispers angrily.

Gilbert III taps him with his cane. "Be quiet. You'd get your chance."

He looks through the kitchen window. Susan, Sarah, Richard's parents, and Tevin's parents are all talking by the kitchen counter. His eyepatch churns counterclockwise, releasing dark magic into his ears, allowing him to hear their conversation from outside.

"Martha," Mr. Jenkins says, "Why do you keep making this hot chocolate so bleeping hot?"

Mrs. Jenkins cleans the hot chocolate off his polo shirt. "Wait until it cools off, then drink it, Harold."

Susan takes a bent-up notebook out of her designer book bag and clears her throat. The others turn their attention to her. "I know this is crazy, but I believe Tevin, Richard, and Serenity are in the fairy world."

Mr. Johnson pauses, then slowly puts tobacco into his pipe. "Do you mean my son jumped off Fairy Rock? That's absurd."

Mrs. Johnson puffs her pipe. "Jumping off Fairy Rock is just a silly myth."

Sarah leans forward and talks fast, drawing the others in. "Susan and I have researched a lot about the fairies. We believe that Tevin, Richard, and Serenity are alive … for now."

"We also have proof that the internet sensation, Rock, is Tevin," Susan interrupts.

Mrs. Jenkins nearly falls out of the kitchen chair. "What!"

"Hogwash," Mr. Jenkins scoffs.

Gilbert III steps away from the window and moves toward the front porch, motioning for Daniel to follow him. As they reach the front door, he spins his eye patch until the air fills with magic yellow light. The kitchen light bulb mysteriously goes out.

Daniel puts on his bracelet, and he's enveloped in a swirl of light as he transforms into Thrasher Goblin. Defiantly, he roars a loud, thudding noise and stomps his mutant foot in the middle of the front porch, caving it in.

Gilbert III steps back and fires a yellow laser beam out of his glowing eyepatch, melting the front door, and in a rush they enter the house, wrapped in fog and swirling dust.

Mr. Jenkins grabs his nine-millimeter handgun. "Everyone, get down."

Mrs. Jenkins pulls out her Beretta. "You all stay down. Harold and I will take care of this."

Gilbert III stands in the living room next to the growling goblin as the others dive behind Mr. and Mrs. Jenkins who draw their weapons and stand facing the invaders. Mrs. Jenkins cocks her Beretta and braces herself, ready to fire. As Thrasher Goblin roars and steps forward, they both unload several rounds into him.

With an angry scream, he's hit, and though he bleeds slime, he continues forward. The Jenkinses keep firing, changing out their magazines every few bursts, and as the Goblin keeps coming, they turn their aim to Gilbert III.

But realizing his danger, his eye patch spins at an incredible speed, creating a light shield in front of him, blocking the bullets.

The Goblin rushes at them, clawing at Tevin's parents, forcing them to the kitchen floor in a pool of their own blood.

"Leave them alone, you psycho!" Susan shouts.

They seem unable to stand as they aim their weapons at the Goblin again.

It kicks their weapons away from them.

Mr. Johnson jumps forward and hits the Goblin with a kitchen chair, breaking it across its back. The Goblin headbutts him into the table, smashing it, then grabs Mrs. Johnson and squeezes her.

Susan and Sarah snatch knives from the sink.

Gilbert III walks calmly into the kitchen. "If I'd were you, I'd be putting those weapons down."

Susan and Sarah back up against the wall.

"Who are you?" Sarah asks.

The two girls lock arms with each other.

"I'd be Gilbert III, and I'd have a message for Rock. Tell him if he'd want to see his parents again, then he'd return to Fairyville and face me."

Jeffrey Roy Ford

He uses his spiraling eye patch to fabricate a brown ray throughout the room. The beam goes around the bodies of Thrasher Goblin, Tevin's parents, Richard's parents, and himself.

The wizard snaps his fingers, and everyone disappears except Susan and Sarah.

22
Rock

Rock can't help but notice that the fog is heavier than usual. As he and Serenity rest on a tree branch outside Sparkle's treehouse, she stays hidden deep in his pocket. Serenity shivers, and Rock reaches around her to hold her tightly. She leans into him and begins to play a purple saxophone that Bernard created for her.

Rock kisses her on the cheek. "Don't worry; you're with me. I won't let anything hurt you. Just keep playing, sweetheart."

She snuggles against his chest, puts her mouth on the reed, and her saxophone lets out beautiful, smooth music.

Rock relaxes as the slow, romantic melody of her tune has him rocking back and forth.

But moments later, he takes his arm off Serenity as he spots Queen Vanessa beside Susan and Sarah. They're approaching, and they look rough, with grime smudged across their faces, clothes covered in mud.

"Rock, I need to talk to you," a teary-eyed Susan cries.

Serenity stops playing and looks up in surprise. "Susan? Is that you?"

"How did you find me?" Rock asks.

"We jumped off Fairy Rock to tell you that Gilbert III and the Goblin kidnapped Tevin and Richard's parents."

Rock's chest tightens. He stumbles and nearly falls off the firm branch. "What do you mean, kidnapped?"

She touches his forearms. "If you don't face them, they'll kill them."

"This can't be happening. I must save them!" Rock groans, running his hands through his dreads.

Susan looks at Rock quizzically. "Hey, aren't you Tevin?"

Rock freezes momentarily, and Sparkle pulls on his pant leg and quietly whispers to him. "I can tell your blood pressure is high from hearing the news. But we can't let them find out your identity. I'm s-sorry, but I must give you the pixie dust." She releases hordes of purple pixie dust into Rock, ever increasing the dosages until his nerves calm and his dilated pupils return to normal.

He shakes his head and stands up straight. "No, I'm not Tevin."

Queen Vanessa casts yellow pixie dust in the air, and it flows in circles as it turns into a magical yellow portal. She flies forward and calls out to them with a fury. "Now is the time," Queen Vanessa orders. "Kill our enemies. Kill them both!"

Without a moment's hesitation, Rock jumps through the portal.

23

Richard Johnson

Richard wakes up shirtless in a room full of lit candles with sticky cream over the wounds on his arms. He bumps his head on the dirt ceiling, trying to escape the makeshift bed full of black leaves and grass. *What is this place? Am I still in the fairy world?*

A pointy-eared man who stands about three feet tall enters the room. "Hello, boy."

Richard flinches and quickly searches for his gun.

"I am not here to hurt you," the man says.

"Who are you?"

The weird-looking man combs his white beard and adjusts the green beanie on his head.

"My name is Elroy, and I am the leader of the elf army."

"Are you the one who saved me?"

"I am."

"Thank you." Richard reaches for his torn bookbag in the corner of the soil-covered room. He glances up at the ceiling, realizing that black grass is growing out of it. "Are we underground?"

"We are ten feet below the surface."

Richard digs through his bookbag. "Hey! Where is my gun, and where is my beer?"

"Your gun is in the other room with the other Elves, and… I drank your beer."

Richard turns quickly and scowls at the elf. "Listen, man, thanks for saving me and all, but I'm petrified. I need to find my friend Tevin, and I can't function without my freaking beer."

Elroy wiggles his ears and points his finger toward the dark hallway, signaling Richard to follow him. As Richard staggers to his feet, the elf leads him through his tiny home. Richard crawls to avoid banging his head on the low ceiling again. They go into another candlelit room, where he's surprised to find three other elves with white beards growing down to their knees. They have rum all over their green robes as they eat dragon meat at a small wooden Chester table in the back of the room.

A female elf stands nearby, posing in her tight green robe and showing off her thin, hairy legs to everyone in the room. "I see the human is awake. Do you like what I did to your hair, boy?" She grins.

Richard touches his hair—no more long braids; now has an afro. He bites his lip and tries not to curse. "Why did you do this?"

"My name is Melinda, and I thought you were cuter that way," she says with an airy laugh.

"Listen, stop calling me boy. My name is Richard, and I need to find my friend, Tevin. That's all I care about right now."

"And here I thought you wanted something to drink." Elroy chuckles as he offers Richard a cup of rum.

Richard grimaces from the bites he has endured from the dark wolves. He sits on the filthy floor of the underground bunker and quickly downs the cup, coughing while swallowing the strong liquor. The room starts spinning. He's dizzy and begins to lose consciousness as he reaches for Elroy. "What did you put in this cup?"

He falls back, and his eyes roll back in his head. Suddenly, he is aware that he's having a vision. He can see Elroy as a human dressed in a purple poet's shirt and pants. It's the afternoon, and heavy rain pours down as Elroy appears on a long pirate ship in the ocean. He's mopping the deck.

Captain Vanessa is next to him. She puts her purple captain's hat on, buttons her purple trench coat over her dress, and shouts angrily at him, "This is your punishment for not killing those villagers back in Pimoria. Because of this, you are now demoted from first mate to cabin boy." She turns to face her army of pirates dressed in purple trench coats with rifles on their backs behind her.

He can see Melinda run to Elroy. "If we don't kill anyone, Captain Vanessa may kill us for being insubordinate again," she says.

Elroy pushes her away. "I joined the crew to travel the seas, not to be a murderer. Don't lose faith. When we get to Fairyville, we will make our escape."

As Richard watches, the ship lands on the shore of the beach, and he observes Captain Vanessa and the other pirates run off the boat and raid the village. As the smoke rises, Elroy, Melinda, and three other cabin boys escape. They run through the burning town into the woods when Gilbert III stops them without notice. The wizard shouts at them and points to the distant fires of the city.

They bow quickly to the angry wizard. "We are nothing like our captain. We want to live a life of peace," Elroy begs.

But the begging does no good. Gilbert III's enchanted eye patch blinks a green light, and it flashes on them. "I'd be believing your story, but the king gave me a job, and that's to punish the pirates. Perhaps you're not like them, so I'd not turn you into fairies, but I'd be turning you into elves to separate you from your twisted captain as I'd send you away."

The forest echoes with the agony of their sobs and whimpers. Their bodies shrink, and their beards grow longer as they vanish into the mysterious World of the Fairies.

There's a flash of light, and Richard opens his eyes from the vision. "You, elves, are nothing like the fairies. I'm sorry for what's happened to you."

Elroy's undersized hands massage healing cream on his shoulder as he speaks to Richard. "We have information about your friend, but it will be challenging to get to him as we are at war with the fairies. Our intelligence tells us that he is in a treehouse. He has transformed into a very muscular man with a rather attractive female companion."

Richard pauses and takes a seat on the dirty floor. *I can't believe what I'm hearing. This is wild. So, Tevin is Rock, and the female companion must be Serenity.*

Elroy continues. "You may want to rescue him, but Queen Vanessa will kill you before that happens."

"Can you help me?"

Elroy pulls out his bow. "We both have our reasons for killing the queen. Your gun will not be enough to bring down the fairies. We elves are afraid to face Queen Vanessa, but Richard, you are brave. If I train you to be an archer, you can use special arrows to fight her. I know you'll fight her to save your friend and be the key to getting us out of this evil world."

The other elves, Reginald, Jason, and Bartholomew, crowd around Elroy.

"Here is the outstanding bow we created for Richard," Reginald says proudly,

Jason chimes in meekly, "I'm hoping the boy can do this because I'm scared to stick my head outside the hole we live in."

"I don't know how you saved the boy from the dark wolves. I haven't left this hole in years. These creatures out there are just too terrifying," Bartholomew whimpers.

Elroy puts his hand on Richard's chubby body. "Richard, you showed so much courage by coming here to save your friend. Little do you know that you may be the one to save us all."

The healing cream is taking effect and Richard stands firmly, ready to fight for his friends. He picks up the bow, and draws it, aiming at the shadows. "Train me, and I will stop the fairies!"

24
Gilbert III

Gilbert III stands in the laboratory's doorway as Daniel violently kicks a wall in the lab, leaving a muddy footprint on it. "I want to kill Rock *now*!" Daniel yells.

Tevin's parents and Richard's parents lean against a dingy brick wall, knocked out by magic, and tied with magical chains.

Gilbert III briefly stares at the busted-up wall. He lets his mind drift back to a time, centuries ago, when he was a young man studying his craft. He was sitting in his bedroom inside the ten-story castle of King Thomas, looking out the window; the falcons flew through the beautiful blue sky with the fluffiest clouds as the sun shone brightly. He can't enjoy the moment, however because of his pounding headache. He tugs on the bloody bandage covering his eye and the mark he received when the wicked Captain Vanessa shot him with her musket.

The King enters his room and stands near his bed, gently leaning over to check his bandages. "How are you doing, my boy?"

Gilbert remembers turning away. "I'd be feeling sad as my father and grandfather are dead because of those evil pirates."

The king sits down on the bed next to him. "Your father and I were great friends, and your grandfather practically watched me grow up." King Thomas rubbed the young wizard's bushy black afro. "I'm so sorry about what happened to you and your family. We can't let those monsters keep wreaking havoc. I need you to kill those pirates before they return to destroy my kingdom."

The young wizard stood and shook the tall, handsome king's hand. He admired his majesty's clean-shaven face and perfectly groomed black hair. "King Thomas, killing those pirates won't be enough. I'd will torture them by sending them to the dark world to suffer."

King Thomas put his hands on the wizard's shoulder. "Torture and punish them as you wish, young Gilbert. Just make sure they never hurt anyone else in my kingdom again."

"I'd be making sure I'd stop them, sir."

"Thank you, my young friend!"

Gilbert III recalls how he used all his newly acquired magic skills to create a sacred eye patch that he couldn't wait to put on his face. The first time he saw it reflected back in the mirror, he'd felt a swirl of pride. Lost eye or not, he would use his new eyepatch to seek revenge forever on Captain Vanessa and her crew.

He emerges from his daydream and focuses on Mrs. Jenkins as she awakes. He leans over her and taunts her mercilessly. "Why you'd not be afraid, woman? Don't you'd know that I'd be killing your son when he'd gets here? Then I'd be killing you'd all as well."

"That's not happening, I promise you that," Mrs. Jenkins shouts back defiantly. She leans against her unconscious husband and strains her thin, muscular physique to hold him up. "I refuse to cry and give you the power to see me afraid. Father and wonderful, merciful God, I pray that you send your angels to look over my husband, Timothy, and Lisa as they sit beside me. Please protect them along with Tevin and Richard wherever they are. Please show me the way to stop these evil men. I'm prepared to sacrifice my life to save everyone and for your glory. In Jesus' name, I pray, Amen."

Mrs. Jenkins collapses on the nasty floor.

Gilbert III scoffs at them and leaves them alone in the darkness. As Daniel follows him into his office, he turns and whispers to him slyly. "Daniel, you'd need to get your rest because Rock will be here soon."

Daniel flops down on his cot next to the wizard's desk. "I'm way ahead of you."

25
Rock

As Rock and Sparkle exit the portal, they land in the woods of Fairyville. It's late at night, and the full moon's rays twinkle through the atmosphere. The crickets chirping fill the forest around them.

Rock moves deliberately through the forest, fueled by anger and focused solely on finding clues to find Gilbert III and the Thrasher Goblin. But as they scurry through the forest, they quickly run into another search party with flashlights, nailing pictures of the missing people on the bark of the oak trees.

Rock stops and looks over a few of the photos of his parents. He leans against the tree, puts his head down, and chokes up. *Is all this my fault? Had I not jumped off Fairy Rock, would everyone be missing? Wait a minute. I'm Rock, the freshest, most handsome, and most incredible guy. I'll fix this because I'm the man.*

Sparkle shakes him out of his thoughts. "Get your head in the game! There's no time stop. We must hurry."

***

They race down Main Street, passing homeless people covered in blankets napping against the buildings. Rock startles them awake, shouting every few moments, "Gilbert III, Gilbert III, come out, you little punk!"

They turn right and go down Gerber Avenue, the city's party district. Bar-goers loiter outside the neighboring clubs, drinking beers and dropping cans on the concrete. A long line awaits outside the brightly lit, two-story Club Fashion.

"Gilbert III, Gilbert III, come out now!" he chants at the top of his lungs.

"Shut up, man. You're killing my buzz," a man says, slurring his words. He is holding hands with his girlfriend. They are both tall and heavyset, dressed in black goth outfits.

"Hey, that's Rock. He's going to fight Benny the Destroyer." The man's girlfriend points at Rock. She jogs over and wraps her flabby arms around him. She takes out her iPhone to get a selfie with him. "You're so handsome, and I know you will win against Benny."

Rock is busy talking between each click of the camera shutter, "Have you seen a wizard and Goblin around here?"

She snaps another picture. "No, I'm sorry. I haven't."

Her boyfriend gets angry. "Why are you getting pictures with this guy? You're with me."

"He's like a celebrity. I will get so many followers when I post this on social media," she replies.

The man shoves Rock. "Stay away from my girl."

Rock winks at his girlfriend. "Don't get mad at her for trying to upgrade."

As they finally make their getaway, Sparkle sprays pink pixie dust in the air, forming a long, straight line.

"What are you doing?" Rock asks.

"I have an idea. This is tracking pixie dust. I never used this magic before. Mother says I am the only fairy with this power. If I did it right, it should lead us right to him."

Rock nods his head. "Okay, let's do this."

They follow the pixie dust and go down the empty street of Turner Avenue, shouting for Gilbert III to show his face!

As they pass by the cars on the quiet street, the vacant warehouses and factories, a bald, hefty man emerges from one of the warehouses, holding an ax.

Rock points at him. "It's Daniel."

Daniel's bloodshot eyes stare back at Rock. He removes his leather biker jacket and throws it in the tall, gangly weeds near the door.

They face each other, circling under the streetlights, each looking for the moment to strike.

Rock puts his dreadlocks behind his ear. "Where are my parents?"

"Where is Serenity?"

"She's safe from you."

"You stole my girl."

"You're abusive. She left you for the best choice, me."

Daniel grips the heavy ax and swings it at him. Rock jumps back as the blade barely misses his neck. Daniel prepares to swing again. "I saw you kiss her."

"I kiss her every day, and she loves it."

Daniel twirls his ax at him again. "No!"

Rock ducks as the blade cuts a few hairs out of his dreadlocks, barely missing his scalp. He snatches the shaft from Daniel and throws it in the dirt. "Before I whip you, I'll teach you how to fight like a man."

Daniel steps back a few feet and puts the mysterious bracelet on. "No, I'm going to fight like a Goblin."

His body grows and mutates as his skin turns into blue scales. A black aura beams out of him. He no longer bleeds, and his slimy body is immune to his dark magic transformation.

Sparkle reinjects red pixie dust into Rock, building his muscles and getting him ready for the fight of his life.

Thrasher Goblin roars as he sizes Rock and slashes his chest with its sharp-edged claws.

Rock groans in pain as he puts his hands over his bloody cut. The Goblin picks up the ax and attempts to hit him again. Rock dodges the attack and gets his hands on the weapon. They both fight to gain control of the axe.

Sparkle flies near him and blows more red pixie dust into her friend, increasing his strength as his biceps get bigger.

Rock gets the mighty ax from him again and throws it fifty feet in the other direction.

Thrasher Goblin slams him to the concrete and bites his shoulder, making blood gush out of it.

Rock's face and clothes are covered in blood.

Rock repeatedly punches the dangerous, blue creature in the jaw, forcing it to release its teeth out of him

Sparkle injects Rock with another round of red pixie dust, giving him the strength to wrap his arms around the Goblin's thick neck. He squeezes as hard as he can.

The Goblin madly pulls on Rock's wrists to escape the choke hold. Rock keeps his grip on the Goblin's throat until it falls unconscious.

"Um, um, Rock, you're bleeding badly." Sparkle casts gold pixie dust on the gash on his chest. The unique gold particles stick to his skin and sew up his wounds, giving him energy.

Swiftly, Rock gets back up, dirt and grass stains on his torn clothes. "Thank you, fairy. I feel better."

"Help!" a woman nearby screams.

Rock pauses. *Wait a minute. That sounds like Richard's mother.*

He looks up at the old, rusty metal warehouse to the third-floor window and spots Gilbert III with his glowing, yellow eye patch. "It's him, and he must have both our parents in there."

"Um, um, it's time to take Gilbert III down," Sparkle says.

Rock pounds his fists together. "Let's do this."

26

Rock

As they enter the muggy warehouse, Sparkle sticks her tiny head outside Rock's pocket. "Be careful. We don't want to walk into a trap."

The moonlight shines through the busted windows of the factory as it reflects off the eroded walls. They cough from the mildew and sewage spilling out of the drains, and Rock moves carefully through the room, looking for signs of life. "I'm not worried about a trap. Mom, Dad, tell me where you are!"

Rock steps into a puddle of oil and slips into a pile of sawdust and broken glass. Water from the rusty pipes above him drips on his forehead as he tries to get back up.

Squeak. Squeak.

"Rock, what was that sound?" Sparkle says nervously.

Rock brushes some of the grease and debris off his Escada jeans. "Mice or rats, probably."

The room starts to erupt as plywood and dirt fall from the ceiling. A bright yellow light appears, and Gilbert III walks out of it. He wears a yellow robe and a yellow cone-shaped hat. He holds a thick cane, flashing a bright yellow light that forces Rock to squint and turn his face. His eye patch blinks a gray light, and a large metal shield appears before him.

Soot, glass particles, and wood chips are all over Rock's hair and body. He tightens his forearms and clenches his fist while getting into a southpaw stance. As he squares off, he calls out, "Gilbert III, where are my parents?"

"You'd better not be worried about them because your'd life ends now," Gilbert III responds.

"My life is just getting started," Rock scoffs. He calls over his shoulder to Sparkle, "Fairy, let's spank this clown!"

But Sparkle hides in his pocket, curled up in a ball, shivering. "I don't know why mother sent me to help. She should have sent a more experienced fairy. The wizard is much stronger than the Goblin," she whimpers.

Rock moves forward and begins to pummel Gilbert III, but the wizard blocks the ferocious assault with his shield. He smacks Rock with his cane, breaking his jaw and sending him twenty feet across the room.

Rock tries to rise to his feet again but falls back down. "The room is spinning."

Sparkle mumbles about the dark power of Gilbert III. "I'm not ready to face a wizard, but he's going to kill us both if I don't do something."

Rock slowly stands back up. "Come on, fairy, spray me with that red dust."

Before she can respond, Gilbert III teleports in front of him again and cracks his cane across Rock's ribs, bruising them. Rock falls to the floor, and the wizard beats him with his stick.

Sparkle takes her head out of his pocket again and blasts black pixie dust at the wizard. He quickly disappears out of the way. Seizing the momentary respite, she injects gold pixie dust into Rock, fusing his broken bones back together, and he springs back up, fresh for the fight.

He swings wildly at the wizard with punches and kicks, missing with each move. "I'm going to save my parents from you, you freak."

"I'd be sensing the fear of Tevin inside of you'd. After I'd kill you'd, I'd be torturing your'd parents to death," Gilbert III snarls.

The wizard twirls his fingers and releases a mysterious black power into the room. The moldy ceiling crumbles and the pipes burst, letting out steam. The wizard's sorcery eye patch beams a black light, creating a flock of black hawks.

The black-feathered birds make a hoarse, screeching noise and latch onto Rock's body, pecking at his flesh, severing his skin. He grabs one of the birds and throws it off him.

Sparkle is in a frenzy now. Flying around him, dodging the birds, she sprays all the red pixie dust she has left into him.

His muscles swiftly rise, ripping the shirt off his body. His chest is full of veins, and his muscle fibers tighten to the max. He punches and kicks the hawks, splattering them as they explode into chunks of bloody meat, their feathers flying everywhere. The defeated birds' corpses evaporate into thin air.

Rock takes a moment to breathe. He's defeated the hawks, but at a cost. He has gruesome cuts across his body, and his jeans are in shreds. He staggers as he massages his ribs. "I'm going to win this fight somehow."

"I'd be going to finish you'd," Gilbert III says. The wizard strikes Rock with his shield, and Sparkle falls out of his pocket. Blue smoke comes out of Rock, and he changes back into Tevin.

"No, Tevin," Sparkle whimpers.

Gilbert III's eye patch spins in circles as he laughs and points his cane at the shy fairy. "Is that the best Queen Vanessa can do? You'd be a pathetic fairy."

Tevin's fingers and toes tingle. The rest of his body is numb, like he's in shock.

Sparkle rises in the air as Gilbert III taunts her. "Young fairy, you'd and this boy' will die together."

Sparkle's face turns stone cold. "The last words my father told me were even though I am the youngest fairy, I have the most natural talent and potential. I can't die here because Mother is depending on me. The fairies are depending on me, and Tevin needs me."

A purple aura glows around her body, turning her hair purple. A wave of purple light comes out of her as her wings grow two inches. A sudden gust of wind pushes Gilbert III backward as purple smoke fills the room.

Tevin coughs the fumes out of his lungs as the air starts to clear. Sparkle looks stronger.

Did she reach the next level of a fairy or something?

She stares at the wizard with her new purple eyes. "Tevin and I will not die here, but you will."

27

Rock

Tevin moves his numb legs, but he is still unable to walk and remains on the ground. He cringes as Gilbert III rises, seemingly studying Sparkle's new transformation. "I'd be seeing that you'd are not so pathetic after all." The wizard smirks.

Sparkle's aura lights up the warehouse.

The floor erupts, and magical sand arises out of the Earth, surrounding Tevin. "Rest, my friend," Sparkle tells Tevin, flying close to him, then darting away again. "This will be over soon. My sand shield will protect you."

Tevin looks through a small hole in the dune, watching as Gilbert III and the young fairy square off against each other.

The wizard screams and raises his cane, creating a yellow energy beam around him. His body grows twelve feet, and his robe stretches to match his towering physique.

The wizard snatches the eye patch off his face, revealing the pink scar tissue and scabs left from the bullets of Queen Vanessa's musket. He has a crystal glass marble for an eye full of dark magic particles. "Fairy, I'd be taking revenge on you'd for what your'd mother and the other pirates did. They'd kill my father and grandfather. I'd created this eye specifically to torture you'd pixies."

Gilbert III's marble eye flashes raging yellow and expands to the size of a beach ball as it lets out an astronomical energy of brightness. The wizard launches lasers at Sparkle.

The young fairy swiftly flies out of the way, and the marble hits another wall, blowing it up. Thousands of spiders and roaches crawl out of the debris.

The marble eye shines, gravitating out of the rubble, and attaches itself to Gilbert III's eye socket. It shimmers yellow beams, and the wizard discharges them at her again.

Sparkle continues to dodge and gets in front of the wizard, blowing a massive amount of black pixie dust in his direction. It engulfs him, and he tries to spit some of it out. He falls and gags.

Sparkle seizes the moment and fills the room with poison, killing all the mice and vermin hiding on the factory's first floor. "I must use more pixie dust. He has to die so my mother and everyone can be free."

The room quickly fills with deadly toxins as the pixie dust breaks through the windows and walls, leaking outside the factory. Gilbert III groans, desperately attempting to breathe, and he passes out with one arm outstretched in defiance, now motionless.

Sparkle stops her assault.

As the black pixie dust clears the room, she removes the protective sand covering Tevin. She applies gold pixie dust to his wounds and slowly dries up his cuts and bruises until they heal and fade away. "My newfound strength has given more power to my magic."

"Thank you, Sparkle. You look so different."

"I have evolved, Tevin. Let's get your parents. I can now sense that they are upstairs."

Tevin gets up slowly and follows the young fairy. "Sparkle, please keep close. I don't want to be left by myself."

"I won't leave you, my friend."

They go up the rusty steel stairs, and Tevin squirms when he sees a pair of rats run by him.

"Tevin, don't be afraid. I'm here with you."

He puts his t-shirt over his nose, covering the rat manure stench, and brushes through the cobwebs in the dark hallway.

There is noise from people struggling inside the laboratory.

Tevin opens the cracked door. "Mom? Dad? Is that you?"

His parents and Richard's parents are in the back of the room by the lab tables, tied up in radiating, cryptic chains. Mrs. Jenkins squints to see him but recognizes his voice instantly. "Tevin, my baby. You're alive."

"Mom, I'm coming!" Tevin shouts back. Then, quietly, he turns to Sparkle. "Please free them."

Without looking back, she glides to Mrs. Jenkins and grabs the chains around her, pulling each shackle she snaps them in half, freeing her.

Mrs. Jenkins stares at the fairy with a blank expression on her face. "Thank you."

Sparkle barely acknowledges her, but instead continues as she breaks the chains for Mr. Jenkins, Mr. Johnson, and Mrs. Johnson. While she works, Tevin weeps while holding his father who lies asleep in a comatose state. "What happened to Dad?"

Mrs. Jenkins kisses her husband's forehead. "He's still asleep from the potion Gilbert III gave us."

Mr. Johnson and Mrs. Johnson embrace each other.

"I love you," Mrs. Johnson says.

"I love you too," Mr. Johnson whispers.

Mrs. Jenkins hugs her son. "Tevin, where have you been?"

Tevin sighs. "I jumped off Fairy Rock, and I was in the World of The Fairies."

Mrs. Jenkins sits back and crosses her arms. "So, the myth is true. What in the world made you do something so dangerous?"

"I wanted the fairies to help me win Serenity's heart."

Mrs. Jenkins rubs her son's face and kisses him on the cheek. "This is something that you have to learn. If someone doesn't like you for who you are, you don't need them."

Tevin wipes the tears off his face. "I need Serenity's love to be happy, and I can't live without her."

"No, son, the only one you need is God," Mrs. Jenkins says.

Tevin clings to his mother. "I'm so sorry for what I've done. I brought all this evil into the world, and I can't find Richard, and I've gotten so many people hurt."

As Tevin and his mother talk, Mr. and Mrs. Johnson approach Sparkle. They seem mesmerized by her size and her wings. As they draw near, Sparkle turns to face them, and waves them over. Mr. Johnson is the first to speak. "Can the fairy find Richard? Susan said he went to Fairy Rock to find you, Tevin."

Sparkle frowns. "My mother did not say anything about Richard, but if he's in my world, I'll find him."

They're interrupted by a loud thud, and the room starts to shake. Everyone shudders and huddles together to try to find a quick moment of safety. Sparkle takes to the air, angrily flitting back and forth.

Tevin jumps up, "Sparkle, they're not dead. Change me back to Rock, and we can stop them right here," he demands.

The fairy quickly flies into his pocket and blows blue pixie dust around Tevin, enlarging his body and lengthening his hair as he converts into Rock.

Mrs. Jenkins screams when she sees the transformation. "What happened to my baby?"

Mr. and Mrs. Johnson hold Mr. Jenkins as he wakes up.

"I don't understand anything we are seeing," Mr. Johnson cries. "I need a cigar."

"Richard gets his habits from you, dear. We have to find him," Mrs. Johnson whimpers.

Rock winks at them as he stretches his muscles, preparing for battle.

Sparkle ponders for a minute. "Rock, I'm going to give you some new power with my new strength," she says finally. She inserts silver pixie dust into him, causing him to groan and hunch over. Long, white wings grow out of his back and tear through his shirt, allowing him to fly. She blows more silver pixie dust in the air, and it changes into a double-edged sword. "I made this for you."

Rock grips the magnificent weapon, and everyone else backs into the corner of the room as a bright yellow portal burns their vision.

Gilbert III and Thrasher Goblin walk through the portal and into the room.

Mrs. Jenkins folds her hands and prays. "Almighty and merciful God, please look over my son and protect him from the evil in front of him. In Jesus' name, Amen."

28
Rock

Rock bears his fierce blade. Feathers fall out of his new wings as he moves them too fast. He flies off the floor and bangs his head on the ceiling. "Fairy, what did you do to me?"

"I made you stronger," Sparkle responds.

His enemy, Gilbert III, has his arms around Thrasher Goblin, who holds him against one of the few sturdy tables in the lab. The wizard has black fluids emanating out of his mouth and down his robe.

He points his cane at Rock. "I'd be not dead yet. Thrasher, destroy them'd."

In one fluid movement, the Goblin rips the table off its hinges and flips it at Rock.

But Rock is getting the hang of his new body. He moves back without thinking, swings his sword, and cuts the table in half, sending it back to the ground. He races down from the air and slices the Goblin's arm, and it bleeds ooze.

Defiantly, the Goblin uses his other arm and swings its ax at him, missing as Rock blocks it with his weapon.

Mrs. Jenkins runs toward the Goblin. "Don't hurt my baby."

"Momma, stay out of this," Rock says.

Sparkle blows purple pixie dust at Mrs. Jenkins, stopping her momentum.

Rock flies forward, sticks the Goblin in his abdomen and yanks the blade downwards, ripping the monster's insides open. He chokeslams the Goblin on the slippery vinyl floor, breaking the tile under him.

Gilbert III shouts in frustration. He seems to be at the end of his strength and weak from the poison. He rallies as the tide is turning. He appears to summon a fiery inner strength as he fires a yellow laser beam from his marble eye, hitting Rock on the shoulder and burning it.

Then, the wizard faints.

The Goblin has his hands over the deep slit in his stomach, trying to keep his organs from falling out of his stomach. He spews up slime and desperately jaws at Rock. "You stole my girlfriend from me."

"You treated her like garbage. I'm making her life better because she is with me," Rock scoffs. As the Goblin staggers and begins to mutter incoherently, Rock halts his attack, realizing the Goblin may be at the end of his life as the monster spews up slime.

As he flies near Mrs. Johnson, he overhears her scolding him. "All this madness over a woman. Men will do anything to get laid."

But Sparkle isn't ready to give up the fight. She flies next to Rock, pushing him forward. "We've got to finish this! Don't let up now!" She spreads extra red pixie dust into Rock, maximizing his strength as much as she can.

Rock flies directly at the Goblin and swings his sword at the Goblin's ax, rending it in half, and he punches its humongous body, crushing its chest cavity. Triumphantly, Rock rips the bracelet off Thrasher Goblin's wrist. The Goblin's lungs collapse, and its blue scales start to shed. He shrinks down in height and weight, reverting to Daniel.

Daniel lies in slime, and he looks up at Rock. "Tevin, I may have been abusive to Serenity, and I was wrong. But I don't think that you are such a good person either."

Daniel falls back with a groan, closes his eyes, and dies.

Rock swallows the lump in his throat. "Daniel wasn't totally wrong. I know I'm the man and everything, but I feel guilty right now."

He stands there for a moment, brooding, but then hears movement from the other side of the room. He turns and sees Gilbert III and moves towards him.

The ailing wizard's face is pale, and Sparkle's poison spreads throughout his bloodstream.

"You have to kill him," Sparkle says.

"Fairy, I can kick some butt, but I'm not cool with all this killing and murder," Rock replies.

"You have to kill him so that the fairies can escape our prison world."

Rock drops his sword. "I can't, fairy. I'm sorry. I'm handsome, but I guess I'm no killer."

"It's okay. You have done your job," the young fairy says.

Sparkle flies out of his back pocket, returning him to Tevin.

The visibly woozy wizard tries to speak to him. "Boy, you'd are a fool. You'd not understand how evil these fairies are. I'd trapped them in that dark world for the safety of Fairyville."

Before he can say anything further, Sparkle sprays black pixie dust into Gilbert III's face. He falls back, wheezing and gurgling for a few moments, until passing forever from the world. He lies sprawled out on the ground, his eyes stare forever into nothing, and his eyepatch lies discarded on the ground next to him in a puddle of black ooze.

Sparkle zips around the room in triumph. "The fairies are now free. Mother will be so proud of me," she rejoices.

The rest of the group rushes over to help Tevin's father.

Sparkle blows gold pixie dust over the big man. Steam comes out of his head as the rest of Gilbert III's sleeping serum evaporates out of him.

As he awakens, Tevin hugs him closely.

"Tevin, don't you ever bleeping run away from us again. I love you so much," Mr. Jenkins says.

The rest of the group seems bewildered as Mr. Jenkins is so alert.

"Dad, I'm so sorry for what happened to you. It's all my fault," Tevin cries.

"It's okay, son. I'm just glad you are bleeping okay."

"I'm glad you're safe too, Tevin, but now we have to find Richard," Mrs. Johnson says.

"Sparkle, can you please find my best friend?" Tevin asks.

"Yes. We must return to my world to get Serenity and the others," Sparkle replies.

Mrs. Jenkins puts his arm around his son. "Tevin, you are not going back."

"He must go back for the sake of the others who came for him," Sparkle says calmly.

Mr. Jenkins nods. "Then we are all going together."

***

Fairy Rock

After a quick meal, the group arrives at Fairy Rock. They trudge through the high grass and step over mud patches by the boulder. Mr. Jenkins and Mrs. Jenkins hold hands and take pictures of their names they engraved in it when they were younger.

"We haven't been here in years," Mrs. Jenkins says. "I never thought about jumping off this thing."

"I'm glad we could grab some guns," Mr. Jenkins says.

Mr. Johnson lights his cigar. "I just want my son back."

Mrs. Johnson puffs her cigar. "When we find Richard, I'm sending you both to rehab."

The group climbs the rope to the top of Fairy Rock. Tevin's chilly from the blustering wind, and everyone zips their jackets. They all look down at the steep surface, seeing the marsh puddles.

"Oh my gosh, Tevin," Mrs. Johnson says. "Are you sure about this? I'm not going to die with all that filth on my jeans. Do you know how much they cost?"

"I trust Sparkle," Tevin says.

"Why can't Sparkle just bleeping teleport us there?" Mr. Jenkins says.

"First-timers have to jump," Sparkle replies. "It's part of the rules of the fairy world. Besides, I love nature and Fairy Rock."

Mrs. Jenkins prays. "Heavenly God, I pray that we survive and find all those who came missing from jumping off Fairy Rock. I know the police department I work for is crooked and would never believe us. Please give us the strength to survive this ordeal. In Jesus' name, Amen."

They jump together.

29

Serenity Cooper

The fairies are celebrating! As they party, they use their pixie dust to create beautiful purple sparks in the air.

Serenity sits with Sarah and Susan in the black leaves on the tree branches at Sparkle's Treehouse as the fairies drink rum and whiskey.

Queen Vanessa grins and hovers around her fairy brethren. "The curse is over. We are free. My lovely daughter, Sparkle, has defeated Gilbert III. She has triumphed!"

Selena slowly wiggles her hips, twirls around, and flings various pixie dust in the air, creating more sparks. "My Goddaughter is so wonderful."

Serenity huddles beside Susan and Sarah in the foggy, windy weather, and the sparks blast the sticks and leaves off the tree branches. Her excitement becomes a frown due to the irritating smoke of the joint Queen Vanessa created for Susan. Susan's eyes are red, and she mumbles, "When Rock returns, we have to find Richard and get out of here."

Queen Vanessa waves her arms. "Fairies, gather around. The day we have been waiting for has finally come. We are free!"

"Hooray!" The other fairies clink their miniature cups with each other and swallow their liquor.

"Now we take revenge on the king responsible for sending us here. We are going to go to Fairyville, and we're going to send all the humans to this world to torture them as our prisoners."

"Wait, what?" Serenity asks.

Fairy Rock

The wings on Queen Vanessa's back flutter, and black magic comes out of the trees. "Ogres, dark wolves, and dragons, I summon you." Families of ogres and dark wolves climb to the top of Sparkle's tree. Packs of dragons shoot flames out of their nostrils as they fly toward the fairy queen.

Serenity stands up quickly. "Susan, are you seeing this?! This is bad!"

Queen Vanessa blows out yellow pixie dust, swiftly forming a portal larger than the giant tree she's standing on. "I have been waiting so long for this day. Centuries of being a prisoner of this world have done nothing but fuel my anger. Fairies, we will have our revenge today."

A crew of fairies gather around Queen Vanessa, bowing to her feet.

"Arise, my subjects. We will take over Fairyville, kidnap as many humans as possible, and return them to this world."

Serenity and the other girls remain on the branch, covering their mouths, trying not to scream.

"I think she created this thunderstorm to scare us. We must get out of here," Sarah whispers.

"Wait a minute. I remember seeing a river right under her house. It's directly under this branch. If we jump down, we can swim our way to shore. Maybe we can find Richard and hook up with Rock somewhere," Serenity says.

"We have to hurry while they're not paying attention to us," Sarah says.

Serenity and Sarah help Susan to her feet as they look down at the bottom, seeing nothing but fog. They back up after a colossal-sized dragon soars near the treehouse.

"We have to jump now," Sarah whispers.

They quickly jump off the branch into the river. Under the purple, trout-infested water, they desperately kick their legs and swim to the top. As they break to the surface, Serenity spits the water out of her mouth, and she exhales, discharging it from her nose.

"Keep kicking, ladies. We are almost to the shore," Sarah calls to them over the roar of the current.

"I got Susan, but I dropped my saxophone," Serenity says.

The women swim to the pampas grass and pull themselves out of the river and start checking on each other.

"Watch out," Serenity yells. A flock of deer sprints through the bamboo trees and nearly plows them over.

"Something's coming," Sarah shouts, pointing through the haze. Shiny red eyes blaze through the mist.

Serenity steps back, trips over a dead deer, and falls on top of it. She yelps as she sees the ribs sticking out of the decomposing corpse.

The mist gets thicker. Water trickles out of Serenity's afro, and she falters from what seems to be shadows of ghostly spirits floating through the trees. The dark jungle becomes utterly silent. There's ruffling in the purple Fountain Grass, nearly taller than the trees.

Three horrid, oversized dark wolves jump out of the grass. "Run!" Serenity yells. She stands her ground, swinging her stick as the ladies run through the shrubs.

A fairy with a bushy red beard wearing a red robe hears them and flies down to see what's going on. He blows a hoard of black pixie dust at the dark wolves, forcing them to run away.

Sarah calls back to Serenity, "Let's escape before this pixie kills us."

The fairy glides before them, and Serenity swings her stick at him. He swiftly gets out of the way. "I'm not here to hurt you. I'm not like the others. I am Sparkle's father, Leon. Follow me, and I'll protect you from Queen Vanessa."

Serenity's fingers slacken, and the stick slips from her grasp. "Sparkle's father is alive," she says, her voice barely above a whisper. "I can't believe it."

30

Tevin Jenkins

Empty rum glasses litter the leaves in Sparkle's tree's crown, and pixie dust covers her treehouse.

Chilled, Tevin puts his jacket back on, trying to stop the goosebumps on his arms.

"Sparkle, where did everyone go?" Tevin asks. "Where is Serenity? Should I change back into Rock so she won't be mad at me?"

Mrs. Jenkins touches her son. "You need to be yourself, Tevin."

Sparkle is on his shoulder, scanning the hordes of leaves and stems of her residence. "Tevin, I'm finding pixie dust, ogre footprints, dragon scales, and dark wolves' fur all over all eight branches of my tree. They must be in Fairyville."

"What do you mean?" Tevin asks.

The young fairy holds her head down. "Mother must have gone to Fairyville to take over the town. One thing is for sure now. She will make the humans her prisoners. I like you, Tevin. Hopefully, she will spare you."

Tevin stops and looks at her accusingly. "What are you even talking about? Prisoners? I'm confused, Sparkle."

Before he can finish, the mist of the world turns grayer, interfering with Tevin's vision. A massive cluster of yellow portals open, and hundreds of people seem to be falling out of them. Many of them crash land on the branches of Sparkle's giant tree. The branches bend from the weight of the civilians.

Some people yell for dear life as one of the tree's limbs breaks in half and they fall into the river.

Tevin recognizes many of them as residents of Fairyville.

He stands speechless, as waves of horror wash over him. *What was Sparkle talking about? What is happening? This feels wrong!*

At least thirty fairies swarm out of the portals. They grab some people and blow purple pixie dust in their faces, causing them to stumble around as if they're drunk.

"Where am I? How did I get here?" one of the residents asks.

"What is this place?" another whimpers.

"Is this the afterlife?" wonders a third.

Tevin squints at his father, who has his hand on his gun holster.

"We're all going to be fine, everyone," Mrs. Jenkins says. "God is going to protect us."

More people rain down out of portals from the sky. Some residents are dead; others have broken their legs from the fall.

"Oh no! What have I done?" Tevin cries.

Another portal opens. Queen Vanessa flies out with an army of fairies. As she descends, she releases her aura, and her skin and bones stretch as she grows seven feet tall. Her purple dress and wings match her body as she creates her trademark thunderstorm in the dark sky.

"It's my mother," Sparkle says coldly.

The fairy queen levitates over the townspeople in the tree as they try to hide in the leaves. Her voice is no longer friendly, but fierce. Somehow, as she starts to talk, even her face is different. "Men and women of Fairyville. This world is your new home. You will now be my prisoners and servants. You will work until I tell you to stop. If you disobey, I will kill you."

People scream as they try to find a way off the tree.

"Officers," a police captain says. "Use the rest of the ammunition to defend everyone against the fairies."

Mr. and Mrs. Jenkins pull out their handguns and run toward the sounds of other police officers.

"Your weapons will not work against my mother," Sparkle says grimly.

Tevin's chest is heavy. "I didn't mean for any of this to happen. I just wanted to be with Serenity."

Sparkle flies back onto his shoulder, and she seems stiff as an icicle. "What do you want me to do?" she asks. "I don't want to disobey my mother and the other fairies. Mother will soon ask me to round up some humans and take them to the caves. I care about you, Tevin. You're shy like me. You're my only friend. I don't want you to get hurt. If my father were here, he would know what to do."

"Send them to the caves of the wretched mountains," Queen Vanessa commands. The fairies circle the humans and use their yellow pixie dust on them, teleporting them away.

"No!" Tevin cries.

The police officers fire at the queen, but the bullets bounce off her.

She burns dark magic powder into her aura, commanding the sky to bring more rain down as the water floods the tree with puddles. "How dare you try to attack your new master?" She swoops down and shoves a man into a patch of thorn branches. She blinks, taking command of the lightning from the sky, and blasts another man into the leaves.

The other fairies continue puffing yellow pixie dust onto the Fairyville citizens, teleporting them to the caves.

Tevin plugs his nose from the burnt flesh. "Please stop hurting people."

Sparkle clutches hold of Tevin. She raises her aura, pulls protective magical sand from the jungle, and covers him.

Tevin is in the dark dune, placing his ear against the sandy walls. Through the commotion, he singles out his parents' voices.

"Tevin, where are you?" Mrs. Jenkins calls.

Mr. Jenkins says, "Don't worry about Tevin. He is the safest out of all of us. Sparkle will not let anything happen to him."

Tevin pounds his fist against the thick walls of the dune. "Mom, Dad, I'm in here. Sparkle, what's going on?"

"Your parents and Richard's parents jumped off my tree into the river," Sparkle replies.

Queen Vanessa interrupts them. "Sparkle, who are you hiding in the sand?"

Sparkle snaps her fingers, and the sand instantly disappears around Tevin.

"Mother, please spare Tevin. He's my best friend."

"I'm not sparing this human scum."

"But he helped save you all," Sparkle begs.

Queen Vanessa slaps Sparkle's tiny body into the front door of the treehouse, breaking the door. What appears to be a shadowy black ghost flies into Queen Vanessa's body, causing her face to moue as her purple aura becomes wider. "Don't you dare talk back to me!"

Tevin cowers. "You said I was like a son to you."

"You're a fool, Tevin. Do you think that I care about you dating Serenity? I can't tolerate either of you. I just used you to set us free," Queen Vanessa sneers.

Sparkle pops up from the smashed lumber. "Please forgive me, Mother. I can't let you hurt Tevin." She flies into the pack of fairies, plowing them out of the way.

Queen Vanessa shrieks a high-pitched noise, releasing demonic energy out of her mouth. "My daughter doubled-cross me!"

The World of The Fairies rumbles as people wail for their lives.

Selena waggles her wings, raising herself. "Sparkle must go on trial for treason."

"I agree," Queen Vanessa says.

Sparkle rushes in and uses her yellow pixie dust to create a small portal. "Tevin, save yourself. I'll do my best to protect you."

"Sparkle, wait," Tevin begs, but she pushes Tevin into the portal and closes it, sending him back to Fairyville.

31

Tevin Jenkins

Tevin wakes up on the red brick sidewalk on Main Street in Fairyville at the break of dusk to the warm summer air. Dirt from a shovel falls on his face. He coughs the soot out of his mouth.

The EMS workers, Homeland Security officers, FBI agents, firefighters, and state troopers from Hattonville are moving large amounts of soil into garbage bags. He rubs his eyes and tries to clear up his vision to see what they're doing. As they come into focus, he can see that they are digging up dead bodies from a sand barrier that crumbled and fell out of the sky.

One of the firefighters touches Tevin's filthy forehead. "Hey, guys, I think we have one still alive."

An EMT rolls out an ambulance stretcher. "Young man, are you okay?"

Tevin coughs up more dirt. "Where am I?"

"Fairyville." He waves for a stretcher. "Let's get him to Hattonville General Hospital. He could explain what happened to everyone in this town. No sign of anyone, not even the mayor," one of the firefighters says.

As he tries to make sense of what's happening all around him, they load him in the back of the ambulance, and two federal agents get in with him, both tall, in their mid-forties, with athletic builds.

An agent with a Kangol hat pulls out a pen and notebook from the pocket of corduroy pants and starts taking notes, talking to him with a distracted air. "Sir, my name is Agent Darryl Washington, and this is Gabby Reed. What is your name?"

"Tevin Jenkins," he mutters quietly.

"Can you speak louder? I can't hear you," Agent Washington says.

"He looks terrified," Agent Gabby says. She pulls a little mirror from her Bottega Veneta handbag, checks the mascara on her thin face, and rubs her long, permed hair.

Tevin's arms and legs tremble. *I was a fool. I got everyone captured or killed all because I trusted those fairies. I thought they were my friends. I hope my parents and Serenity are safe. I hope everyone will be okay. Where are you, Richard?*

He bangs his head on the stretcher and punches the air.

"He's freaking out. Give him something to calm him down," Agent Washington says.

Tevin screams and kicks his legs up and down, and the white sheets from the bed fall on the floor.

An EMT pins Tevin to the stretcher. "Steve, give him some Haloperidol so he can relax."

Another EMT rubs Tevin's head with his latex gloves and takes a pill from the medicine tray. "Tevin. Tevin, listen to me. Swallow this, okay? I don't want to have to give you a shot."

Tevin fights it for a minute, but then he ingests the Haloperidol medication and drinks it down with a pixie cup of water. "Yuck."

Agent Gabby holds his hand. "It's okay, Tevin. Can you tell me what happened in your town?"

The soft touch of her fingers and the beautiful aroma of her perfume reminds him of his mother. "I-I did a bad thing," he stammers. "I jumped off Fairy Rock to meet the fairies because I wanted them to help me get with Serenity. They transformed me into Rock, and my fairy friend Sparkle killed the wizard, Gilbert III. The curse is gone, but as soon as I'd saved them, those treasonous fairies took over Fairyville and kidnapped everyone."

Agent Gabby squeezes his sweaty hand. "Poor kid. He's delusional."

Agent Washington takes the top hat off, showing his hi-top fade. "The boy is delusional or on drugs. It's more likely that terrorists kidnapped the citizens."

"Witnesses outside of Fairyville said they saw a humongous dirt barrier over the town and could not get in. Then the barrier fell, covering the town with dirt, and everyone was missing," Agent Williams interrupts.

"As of right now, this delusional kid does not make a good witness, so we should assume that this was an act of terrorism," Agent Washington replies curtly.

"But how does a terrorist create a dirt barrier over a whole town?" Agent Gabby asks.

"I don't know. None of this makes sense."

The ambulance pulls up to the west entrance of the hospital about three miles from Fairyville. The big, overweight EMTs take him out of the ambulance, and the hospital care employees meet them at the automatic glass door. They roll Tevin on his stretcher through the clean, white hallways to a small room with a hospital bed. The detectives handcuff him to the rail.

"We just don't know if he is a terrorist," Agent Gabby says.

"I'll have a couple of uniforms guard his room, and we'll talk to him in the morning," Agent Washington replies as he turns away.

***

The next morning, Tevin awakens as the sun's rays shine through the closed window blinds. The cozy room has a painting of a child holding a tulip in the grass field. A cold turkey sandwich with pickles is on the nightstand by his bed, yet he has no appetite.

There's a nurse filling out a chart in the doorway and he motions to her to turn on the TV. She pauses for a moment, glares at him, and then flips the TV on before going back to work. Tevin begrudgingly looks away. *She must think I'm a terrorist.*

There's footage on the news of ashes covering the burnt buildings in Fairyville and stones, broken glass, and gobbled-up paper balls littering the streets. The coroners carry people in body bags.

The exhausting effects of the Haloperidol medication they gave him keep him fading in and out of sleep. His thoughts obsess over the people captured from his town. *My parents are the only family I have in Fairyville, and they are probably dead. I failed Serenity, I failed my parents, I failed Richard, I failed everyone.*

The television screen changes to the President making a speech. His blue suit, freshly braided hair, and clean-shaven face have the nurse winking at the screen as he begins to speak. "America, this is your president, Jaylon Bee. Today is one of the most tragic days in American History. The disappearance of all Fairyville, Washington, residents is a complete mystery. We believe this is an act of terror. We will heighten security in all the cities throughout the country to protect you. As for now, the city of Fairyville will be closed for further investigation. My American citizens, I reassure you that this country will be safe. We will find the Fairyville residents and bring those terrorists to justice. You can trust me because my name is President Jay to the Bee."

The nurse turns off the television and slams the remote controller on the ceramic floor, breaking it as the batteries roll on the ground. "See, this is what happens when an Independent gets elected for the first time. The country is in danger because this guy thinks he's so cool." She scowls, but then softens and mutters under her breath, "But then again, he is one handsome president."

Tevin puts a pillow over his face and weeps. "Terrorists did not kidnap the people of Fairyville. The fairies did."

Part 2:
Three years later

32

Tevin Jenkins

It's sweltering.

The heat is only made worse by the crowded, muggy one-bedroom apartment that Tevin calls home. He wipes his forehead and reaches for the AC. The knob falls off.

He tosses the knob down and looks out the window. It's Hattonville, and he's alone. He sits at his green, foldable kitchen table full of prescription medications with a bandage on his big toe from stepping on a splinter from the wooden floor. In disgust, he puts his head down on the table. *My psychiatrist wants me to take Buspirone for my anxiety, and then I must take Seroquel and Haloperidol to treat my schizophrenia. They won't believe my story about the fairies kidnapping everyone. If I had never jumped off Fairy Rock in the first place, this would have never happened.*

He slinks to the bathroom mirror and looks at the stubble on his unshaven, freckled face. He squeezes the remnants out of a lifeless, flat toothpaste tube. An empty bottle of mouthwash and a dented, blue hairspray can roll around on the floor.

I can't take it anymore. Mom, Dad, Serenity, Richard, everyone... I'm s-so, so, sorry. Please still be alive. There is no way I can save them by myself, and the stupid authorities think I'm crazy. If I return to the police station, they'll probably send me back to the psych ward.

He scratches dandruff from his thick black afro until the pain throbs his head. *I miss everyone so much. I hate myself, and I wish I were dead. I can't live with myself for what I've done.*

He turns away from the mirror and flops down on his busted couch, which has foam sticking out of its cushion. He takes a nearly empty plastic bottle of cheap whiskey from the nightstand and sips on it. He thinks of when he was ten and his parents took him on a bicycle ride through the neighborhood. His mother had a long, pink, ten-speed bike that matched the socks on her muscular, thin legs. His dad rode a big, blue, twelve-speed bicycle and allowed him to ride on the handlebars.

He recalls swinging his arms and legs freely, leaning against his daddy's burly body.

"Would you like some ice cream?" his dad had asked him.

"Butter pecan!"

He can still remember the way they rode their bicycles to Sugar Sweets off Main Street and Fogle Rd.

His mother hugged him tightly and told him she loved him as they all sat and watched the sunset on a bench outside the ice cream shop.

"So, Tevin, do you like any girls at your school?" Mr. Jenkins asked.

He blushed, and he hid his face in his mother's arms. "Yes."

Mrs. Jenkins rubbed her hands through his hair. "Who is it?"

"Her name is Serenity."

"Mrs. Cooper's daughter," Mrs. Jenkins said.

Mr. Jenkins pressed his thick black mustache against his forehead and kissed him. "I believe that you'll get her. We are Jenkinses, and the ladies love us."

Mrs. Jenkins hit her husband on his arm. "Oh, dear, stop it."

The alarm clock goes off, and Tevin snaps out of his daydream—time for work. He stumbles down the hall into his bedroom, where newspaper articles about reporters interviewing him about what happened in Fairyville are pinned to his wall. He turns off the alarm clock, grabs a double shot of bottom-shelf vodka, and exits his apartment.

It is humid outside, and the wind is calm on this peaceful night. Numerous couples hold hands as they take pictures of themselves outside the bars.

A few minutes later, he arrives at the newly built church where he works as a janitor. He pulls the gold bars on the double doors and goes straight upstairs to the administration office, sticks his timecard into the work clock, and punches it. *I hope I don't smell like liquor because Pastor Anderson will be angry. If I lose this job, I don't know what to I'd do with my miserable life.*

He continues to go through the motions of living, mindlessly putting on a pair of overalls and grabbing a mop bucket from the broom closet to clean the vinyl floors. Without thinking, he cracks open a window to let the hydrogen peroxide formula fumes in the soap out of the room.

Pastor Dan Anderson is watching him work, although Tevin doesn't look up. The short, heavyset, bald man with a white beard stands at the end of the hallway, and Tevin sees him as just another part of the room as he goes about his tasks until he breaks the silence. "Hello there, Tevin."

Distracted by his miserable thoughts, Tevin lets out an automatic reply. "Hello, sir."

"How are you feeling today?"

"Not too good."

"Are you having thoughts of harming yourself again?"

"Yes."

Pastor Anderson walks up to Tevin and puts his hand on his shoulder. Tevin flinches slightly, not used to physical contact. However, he can sense some warmth in the pastor's touch, and it stirs something in him. Pastor Anderson gestures for Tevin to follow him, leading him into the main chapel. Inside, he guides Tevin to a row of pews, and they sit down midway through the row.

They sit in silence for a few moments before Pastor Anderson breaks the ice. "I can tell you've been drinking, but I won't fire you," he says, leaning forward. "You know, Tevin, God does not put anything in your life that you cannot handle."

"Pastor, nobody believed me when I said the fairies kidnapped them," Tevin protests. He slouches against the hard-backed wooden bench and glowers.

Pastor Anderson rests his hand on Tevin's knee. "I believe you, Tevin."

Tevin crosses his arms and whines. "I can't go back to Fairy Rock to save them because the government has sealed off the town." He's worked up and he stands to pace back and forth through the church's aisles. "They were all kidnapped because I jumped off Fairy Rock. I thought the fairies would help me get with Serenity."

"You were lusting after her."

"Yes, and I am so sorry." Tevin kneels and puts his head down, and tears spill out of his eyes.

Pastor Anderson comes to his side. "If I can help you stop the fairies and possibly save the lives of the people of Fairyville, will you be able to do it?"

"Yes, Pastor. I'll do anything to save them all."

Pastor Anderson helps him to his feet and holds his hand. "I believe that fairies are demonic creatures. With holy water, we can make a potion to stop them all. Follow me to my office."

Tevin rubs his chin hair.

Is this a solution? I want to find a way to sneak back into town and jump off Fairy Rock. I can poison the fairies and save everyone who is still alive. I hope that Pastor Anderson's plan will work. And that his holy water is strong enough.

33

Richard Johnson

Richard and the elf Elroy crouch down in an elm tree, doing their best to shield themselves from the blistering cold and rain of the West Forest. Richard uses an eyeglass covered in magical green cream that Elroy invented, and as he looks through it, he views many townspeople from a far distance who've become prisoners working in the drizzly, foggy woods. The shivering townspeople have black mud smeared over their clothes as they work through the rain. They have chains tightly attached to their arms and legs, causing many of them to pass out from the lack of blood circulation.

He shudders at the misery they're experiencing. As he watches, the fairies scream at them, commanding them to use plows and rakes to clear the forest of the black bushes and leaves to create crops and farmland. Ogres hold whips with silver spikes at the end of them, ready to torture anyone who refuses to work at a fast enough pace.

His eyeglass glows, allowing him to hear a conversation a dehydrated man stumbling through the fields is having.

"I need water," the man pleads.

"You'll get your water when you clear half the bushes and trees," Baker replies.

"Get back to work before I have this ogre give you another flogging," Butch says.

Another man wipes black dirt off his face and begs them, falling to his knees. "Please let us go home."

The ogres smack a husband and wife trying to comfort their seven-year-old son. Both of their noses are bleeding as they lay in the pitch-black bushes. The boy throws a stone at the ogres. "Leave my mommy and daddy alone." But it's no use. They thump their barbaric chests and circle the boy, drooling.

Richard takes the hood off his green cloak. His body is lean and physically fit, as he's lost fifty pounds from years of archery training. He uses a specially made green glove given to him by the elves and removes a whimsical, flaming arrow from his bag. "I'm going to free them all."

Elroy wiggles his little, pointy ears. "Richard, we can only free so many. We don't want the fairies to catch us. If they do, these people will be trapped forever. We have to stay safe, for now. We are the entire resistance."

Richard ignores him and places the arrow on his bow. Elroy sighs as he shoots it, hitting one of the ogres in its back and setting it on fire. It aimlessly runs through the workers, hollering as the flames melt its skin. Richard loads more arrows as quickly as he can and fires them furiously, piercing all the ogres.

"We are under attack. It must be the lad," Butch screams in anger.

Baker tugs on his beard and points in Richard's direction. "I can see them coming from over there! Let's get him!"

Elroy squints as he looks through his unique eyeglass. "Two fairies are coming in our direction. We must distract them long enough for the people to escape. Remember your training."

Richard takes out three arrows that have smoke coming out of them.

"Fire now," Elroy says.

Richard shoots toward the fairies, striking them as they fall into the shrubs.

Massive amounts of smoke fill the area, blinding Butch and Baker.

The townspeople beat the ogres with their plows, take the keys to their shackles from them, and free themselves.

"We've done our job," Elroy says. "Let's get out of here."

"Did you see my parents and Susan in the crowd?" Richard asks.

Elroy takes a final look through his eyeglass. "No."

"They must be in the other prisoner fields," Richard says.

Elroy takes out a bottle of rum to share with Richard. "Don't worry. Just be patient. We will find them."

34

Tevin Jenkins

Back in Hattonville, Pastor Anderson holds a chalice bowl of clear water and sets it on a new wooden communion table he just bought. He talks softly and solemnly as he draws Tevin close to him. "Tevin, I will bless this water and turn it into holy water. Those demonic pixies will not like this."

"Thank you for doing this, pastor."

"No problem, Tevin."

Pastor Anderson puts his hand over the bowl then raises his arms and prays. "Father God, the one who is almighty and merciful, please bless this water. Give it strength to protect your people from the enemy and all demonic entities. In Jesus' name, Amen."

Tevin unfolds his hands, takes the water, and pours it into a thermos.

"Thank you for giving me hope. I know I am not strong anymore because I am no longer Rock." He starts to whine. "Can I be honest, pastor? I'm scared. I don't know how to get back into Fairyville. The government has it sealed off."

Pastor Anderson smiles and nods his head. "It's going to be a challenge for you, Tevin. But don't fear! God has blessed you with so many gifts. Please stop talking down on yourself. You have all the strength you need to defeat the fairies."

Tevin smiles for the first time in days, and Pastor Anderson gives him a bear hug. "We will pray about it, and whenever you are ready, I'll go to the fairy world with you."

Tevin closes his eyes and feels a bit of peace flowing over him. *Maybe I can save them after all!*

***

At the first light of dawn, Tevin walks through the line of people at Dan's Coffee Shop, waiting outside the small, brown, brick building for one of the café's famous caramel lattes, and moves down the street until he reaches the two-story green apartment building where he lives and leaps over a broken step to enter the building. As he enters the lobby, a woman about five feet tall, slim with rainbow-colored hair and a sun dress greets him.

"Tevin, it's me."

"Who?"

"Sparkle."

He fumbles with his thermos, nearly dropping it.

"Excuse me. What did you say?"

"I'm Sparkle. I escaped from the Dimension of Space, and with my new abilities, I can temporarily transform into a human."

Tevin rapidly blinks and makes a double take. "I thought you were dead. Thank you for saving me."

Sparkle immediately embraces him for several minutes.

"How did you find me?"

"We have a strong connection. I can sense you from anywhere. My mother put me on trial after I sent you back to Fairyville. She exiled me to the Dimension of Space. I floated in the dimension for years with no food or water. It was frigid, and I thought I would freeze to death."

She fumbles nervously with her dress, then looks up at Tevin shyly for a moment before continuing. "Spirits taunted me the whole time, but I didn't give in to them. The dimension became hot as I floated toward a big rainbow-colored star. My mother must have thought the star would burn me to death as the ultimate torture, but she underestimated me. The star gave me powers and changed my hair to a rainbow color. I used my new magic to create a portal and came here."

Tevin hesitates as a burning question lingers, almost too painful to ask. His emotions tear him apart from his reunion with her. He gathers his thoughts, breaks his silence, and asks her, "Are Serenity, my parents, Richard, and everyone else still alive?"

"Yes. I can feel their energy with my new power."

Tevin shuts his eyes in relief and winces. "If they're alive, then we have to save them!"

"I know," Sparkle says softly. "I know."

As he leads her back to his apartment, she doesn't say a word. Tevin can tell that they are both unsure of what to say or how to start. As he steps inside, she looks at the chaos and mess in silence. Quickly, he moves the paper plates and beer bottles off his brown, liquor-stained couch, clearing a place for her to sit down.

"With my new powers, I sense that my father is alive too," Sparkle says as she sits down gently. "But I'm not sure I can save them myself."

Tevin nods. "Turn me back into Rock, and I like our chances even more."

Sparkle looks down at the ants eating breadcrumbs on the wooden floor. "Yes. But that's not enough." She turns and looks Tevin in the face and mutters darkly. "I'm going to do something I do not want. I'm going to have to kill my mother!"

35

Tevin Jenkins

They sit in silence for several minutes, then Sparkle rises to her feet, looking at the pizza boxes and chicken bones on his soft, fluffy, blue rug. "Do you have any clean pillows?"

Tevin smells the odor of cheap whiskey on the pillow. "I'm sorry about my place, Sparkle. I know it stinks in here, and I have nothing clean. I'll stop by this little department store around the corner to buy some clean pillows."

"Please don't worry about it. I felt so strong earlier, but now I feel weak. Being in the dimension for three years with no food or water is taking its toll on me."

"Are you going to be alright?"

"Yes, but please, I need to rest."

She falls back, passing out on his sofa. Surprised, Tevin feels her forehead, and it's sweltering hot. She snores loudly, and her face is dark red. *She has a fever. What do I do? I don't know how to heal a sick fairy.*

He quickly runs to his bathroom and grabs a towel full of barbeque potato chip crumbs. He shakes the bits off and rinses the towel with cold water. *Hopefully this will cool her temp down.*

She sleeps fitfully, trembles, and falls off the couch. Her arms and legs jerk uncontrollably. Her eyes glow a rainbow light, and her hands involuntarily shoot out magical rainbow sand, knocking holes into his apartment's walls.

Fairy Rock

This is a disaster! I've got to help her, or she won't be well enough to help me save Serenity. She's given so much to get here! He runs into his bedroom and takes cover under his bed. The sturdy sand hits the door of his room, knocking it off its hinges. Pieces of wall and ceiling debris drop on his bed as grime and dirt bury his floor. *She's going to kill me. Almighty God, please help me. In Jesus' name, Amen.*

As he approaches her, Sparkle's energy decreases, and she stops moving. Her body shrinks back down to the size of a fairy. Her face is pale, her lips blue.

My friend is dying. Who can heal a fairy? Who or where can I take her? Pastor Anderson will know what to do.

There is some commotion in the hallway outside of his room. His landlord, Mr. Franklin, knocks on his door. "What in the Billy Jo heck is going on, Tevin? You better not be having a party. We have rules in this complex."

He moves quickly to the door and shouts, "No, Mr. Franklin, I was exercising, and the television was loud."

"Well, why are there cracks in your walls?"

Tevin scratches some ceiling paint chips from his filthy hair as he squints and strains his cheek muscles. *I must think of something to tell him.* "Um, I was shadowboxing, and I didn't know I was that strong, and I knocked that wall out."

"That doesn't make any sense."

Mr. Franklin isn't buying my excuse. I have to leave before my big landlord knocks the door down. Pastor Anderson is my only friend in this town, and I pray he can help her.

He quickly checks the lock on his front door, then rushes to his window and throws it open. Returning to the couch, he carefully lifts Sparkle, tiny as she now is, and makes sure she's secure. *The one good thing about this is that she shrunk again. I'm not sure I could lift her if she was still big!*

Tevin sneaks Sparkle out through the fire escape and dashes down Amber Avenue. He nearly trips over a stone on the sidewalk, stumbles, and almost drops her out of his hands.

After several minutes of running, he arrives at the church, where he throws open the door and sprints through the thin hallways to the minister's room inside the rectory. "Pastor Anderson! Pastor Anderson, please open your door. It's me, Tevin. I need your help."

The Reverend flings the door open, holding a King James Bible. "What's wrong?"

Tevin rushes inside. "Reverend, can you keep a secret?"

"Are you in trouble with the law? Tell me what's wrong."

Tevin opens his hands and shows the minister his tiny fairy friend. She has a severe cough, and her face is still dark red.

Pastor Anderson has a blank facial expression, staring at Sparkle as if he's in a trance.

"Tevin, is that a real fairy?!"

"Her name is Sparkle, and she's sick. Can you help her?"

Tevin tries to keep his emotions intact, but he's frantic. "Everyone I've ever cared about is gone. I can't lose Sparkle too. Please do something."

That pastor gently touches the fairy's forehead. "It looks like she's dehydrated. She needs some rest and water."

Tevin bites his fist.

My loving mother and father helped me get through school and manage my mental illness. My best friend would do anything for me, and I even earned Serenity's love as Rock. It's time I do something for them. I know that I'm scared, but I must save them now. I hope Sparkle will be okay.

"Please, look over her closely. I'm afraid she might be dying! I'm going to The World of The Fairies *tonight*."

Pastor Anderson rests the fairy on his unmade couch bed near his writing desk. "It looks like you can't wait any longer. I'll stay and do the best I can to help her. I believe that God chose you to save those people, and I believe that he will protect you. Earlier today, I met a man who said he was the former police chief in Fairyville. He may be able to sneak you back into the city so you can jump off Fairy Rock."

36

Richard Johnson

Richard moves carefully, his mind at full alert, listening for anything and everything. It seems impossible to him that he's somehow gotten used to being hunted. Used to being in danger. Used to always looking, and never finding, his parents.

He floats quietly on a small rowboat down the Purple River, where the currents are strong, making it difficult to pull and push on the oars. He rows the boat toward the orange star, hoping to find land soon. The purple water below him turns white. He puts the cowl over his green robe, protecting himself from the chilly temperature and in the stillness, he pulls out a compass made of green, round, hardened cream full of Elroy's magic. The needle points north. *I've reached the North Forest. My parents, Susan, and Tevin weren't in the West Forest. I hope to find them here.*

He rows through the pain of his throbbing shoulders. Luckily, the currents slow down as he drifts into a swamp. Dead bugs float in the water, and he sees a pink toad with navy blue spots on its back floating on a beige lily pad. It sticks its tongue in the water and swallows some of them. *I'll never get used to this world.*

He stops his boat and pulls onto an island of burgundy sand. He takes his bow and bag of arrows and walks through the beach into the North Forrest. It's hard going, but he does his best to calm his breathing, fighting the temptation to return to the boat. He passes turquoise maple trees and light blue bushes, quickly sprinting into the bushes as a stampede of light blue moose runs by him. *What in the world?!*

He puts a flame arrow on his bow as he clenches his jaw. *I must be brave. Only the strong will live in the World of The Fairies. I must find Susan, Tevin, and my family.*

"Help!" a voice screams.

Richard pauses as he listens to the sound. In a rush, he realizes, *That's my mother!*

He sprints through the blue scrubs and red bushes, passes by the purple trees, and goes through the tall, yellow grass as he throws caution behind him. As he makes his way down a white hill and braces himself, he witnesses three dark wolves digging through the roof of the human-made underground bunker. Blood and dirt cover their bleeding paws. The monsters' red, beady eyes get bigger as they stick their tongues out, waiting to taste some human prey. *There must be people in there!*

He shoots his fire arrows, striking all three beasts. They run away, engulfed in flames, and as they flee, they set the grass and bushes ablaze.

The smoke pollutes the bunker.

A group of people climb out of the hole. They look thin and dehydrated, their torn clothes filthy. Richard recognizes them! It's his parents and Tevin's parents. He quickly removes the cowl from his head, drops his bow and arrow, and goes toward them with his arms open wide. "Mom. Dad. It's me."

Mrs. Johnson covers her mouth. "Richard."

They immediately run over and embrace him.

Richard chokes up. "I missed you, Mom and Dad."

Mrs. Johnson rests her sobbing face against his robe. "We didn't know where you were."

"We never stopped looking for you, son," Mr. Johnson cries.

Mr. and Mrs. Jenkins come over to Richard and hug him.

Richard sees the bags under their eyes and the patchy gray beards on his dad's and Mr. Jenkins's face. *I can tell they went through a lot to survive over the years.*

"We're glad to see you," Mr. Jenkins says.

"I'm glad to see you too. Have you heard any news about Tevin?"

"We believe that he was sent back to Earth by the fairy, Sparkle," Mrs. Jenkins says quietly.

Richard agrees. "That makes sense." He turns and looks into the distance. "Come with me. I'll take you somewhere safe." Crouching and moving quickly, he leads everyone through the colorful forest to his rowboat, taking care not to leave a trail behind.

Fairy Rock

Once he's got them tucked safely aboard, he pushes off and moves quietly through the water. It's safer this way. Less chances to leave a trail. *Keep your eyes along the shoreline. Listen carefully. But there's only so many ways to be surprised when you're on the water!*

They row back to the Purple River. Pink trout jump in and out of the water, and Richard hears everyone in the group's stomachs growl as their mouths salivate for the delicious fish.

"Is there any food where we're going?" Mrs. Johnson asks.

"Yes, plenty of it," Richard says, motioning for them all to whisper.

"Are there any cigars we are going to?" Mr. Johnson says under his breath.

"Yes, cigars, beer, and liquor." Richard smiles.

"Hurry up and row, then," Mr. Johnson says.

An hour later, they arrive at Elroy's hideout, ten feet below the surface near a giant black sequoia in the South Forest.

Richard exhales deeply, feeling the weight of worry lifting off him. *My parents and the Jenkinses are safe. I still have to find Susan and the others, though.*

Elroy's new home has many fresh, delicious-smelling fried fish and shrimp cooked by Melinda, Jason, Reginald, and Bartholomew, but despite the wonderful food, what's catching their interest are the three-foot-tall pointy-eared elves. But when they smell the feast, they immediately come out of shock, run toward the dinner table, and chow down.

"Richard," Elroy says, "It looks like they haven't had any real food in a while."

"I'll eat now. I'm just happy that they are finally safe," Richard says.

Elroy beckons him closer and leans in. "Don't get too comfortable. They are safe for now, but Queen Vanessa will never stop searching for them."

Richard grimaces. *I guess I can't relax yet!* He cracks his neck and rolls his shoulders to loosen them up, then looks down the table at his parents before turning back to Elroy. "Okay, I guess we'd better get them cleaned up."

***

They spend several more hours resting and feasting, and as night falls, everyone is clean, wearing green robes. It's strange to all be together, but Richard finds it hard to believe they were apart for so long. The day has flown by, and it feels so natural to be together again. Richard and his father sit on a floor made of green tree bark, and they sip rum. Mr. and Mrs. Jenkins are not drinking or smoking because of their Christian faith, but Jason and Bartholomew roll up a pack of thick cigars for everyone to smoke.

"Make sure that cigar is great because my dad hasn't smoked in a while," Richard says.

Reginald lights up one of the cigars, and hands it to him. "You are courageous for leaving this hideout. I wish I had your courage."

Bartholomew slurs, "Blah, blah, w-we will fight with you. S-someday."

"Bart, you're much too drunk to do anything," Jason laughs.

"Blah, blah, I-I'm not a drunk, okay. Nah, nah. Now pass me some liquor," Bartholomew mumbles.

Melinda stands up and dances, most likely trying to lighten the mood. The other elves laugh and holler as they admire the beauty of her brown eyes, luscious red lips, and shiny, freshly shaven legs.

When the music finally stops, they smoke the remaining cigars and drink the last drops of their drinks. Sleepiness appears to set in as everyone prepares to rest for the night.

Richard's parents and the Jenkinses lie down on the new, makeshift beds filled with soft, scented orange leaves. As they doze off, Elroy combs his beard and finishes his fifth glass of rum while standing beside Richard.

He whispers softly, and only Richard can hear him amidst the gentle snores. "Your parents have had years of malnourishment, and these leaves will slowly regenerate them back to health. It will take time, though."

"I'm so glad that they're going to be fine," Richard says, trying his best not to cry. "But I'm not done yet. I need to find Susan now."

"I know, but stay vigilant. I know you're tired, but it's very dangerous out there. We are lucky that we avoided capture this long."

"I'll try. But either way, she is my girlfriend, and I have to save her, even if I have to put myself in danger!"

Elroy rubs his chin. "Let me think. We searched almost everywhere for her. The only other place she can be is in the East Forest."

Richard looks down at his sleeping parents and turns to Elroy. "I'm leaving tonight to find her. I can't wait any longer. Take care of my parents and the Jenkinses."

"You are our best archer, but you're no match for Vanessa. Be careful."

"I will."

37
Richard Johnson

Richard rows the small rowboat through the Red River in the East Forest, pushing through the storm as heavy, red rain showers the area. He lifts his hood to keep his braids from getting wet.

I must be here.

An enchantment of thick fog circles the river, shrouding his vision.

Richard lies in the boat, resting from the hours of rowing. He tries to find the energy to sit up and row again. His eyes are droopy, and his legs are cramping from dehydration.

I must stay awake because I don't know what—or who—is coming to attack me. I want to drink some rum, but I should save it for Susan. I know she is going to enjoy some when we finally meet again.

The rain stops, and the one orange star in the night sky is more transparent. Richard's mind begins to wander.

This is one of the few beautiful sites of this evil world. Susan, my love, I hope you are still alive. I miss you so much. You are the best thing that happened to me, and I am coming to save you. Without you, I would never have made high school valedictorian. Your beautiful black hair is probably much longer now. It's been so long since I touched your smooth, silky skin and kissed your soft lips. You always smelled like expensive perfume and weed, but in a good way. I can't stop thinking about your amazing brown eyes, and I want to rub my fingers in your wooly hair and hold your tender, soft hand. I'll give you a long, passionate kiss when I see you. I love you, Susan.

He reaches into his pocket and pulls out a small gold ring Elroy has made for him with magic.

I'm going to do right by her. I will ask her to marry me and get everyone out of this disgusting world.

The sturdy little boat drifts further through the river. Richard gains enough strength to start rowing again. The light wind makes it easier for him to navigate the water as he sees the shore.

He thinks of Tevin. *Tevin, I'm not mad at you for jumping off Fairy Rock because you did not know this would happen. Things will improve when I kill Queen Vanessa and return everyone to Earth. I will show you how to win Serenity's heart by being yourself and not that cocky Rock.*

The boat lands on the red, sandy beach of The East Forest. Richard pushes the ship into the black bushes and covers it with leaves. He carefully sneaks past the gray trees and through the gangling, red weeds.

Where should I start looking for Susan? He can barely see through the fog. *I remember what Elroy told me. Where there is fog, there are fairies.*

As he gazes through the long red grass, he runs into four humongous ogres dressed in purple armor, carrying giant axes. Two fairies, Butch and Baker – now generals in Queen Vanessa's army – fly above them.

Richard sticks his unique eyeglass on his eye, allowing him to hear the fairies' conversation.

Baker tugs on his beard. "You are the lad, Richard, who has given us so much trouble."

"You are much stronger than you were when we first met," Butch says.

"This cannot be the same drunk lad who nearly pooped in his pants when we first saw him," Baker argues.

"It's the same lad. The elves made him very strong, but he is still no match for us," Butch replies.

Richard uses his gloves and grips his bow. "You fairies make threats, but you will all die by my arrows."

38

Serenity Cooper

It is pitch dark in the hideout where Susan, Sarah, and Serenity live.

The earsplittingly loud explosions and the screams of ogres wailing in pain have everyone rattled, as the East Forest is ablaze. Serenity quickly scoops dirt on the magical fire in the fireplace, putting it out to avoid detection, while Sarah and Susan hide for cover under the enchanted black leaves that work as a shield.

Leon, Sparkle's father, peeks from the tent's black straw roof.

The elder fairy scratches his head. "Who is that fighting? Is it just one man battling Queen Vanessa's troops? I need to help him, but I don't know how much I can do at my advanced age. It's been years since I held or saw my daughter. Sparkle is my world, and I hate how her mother separated us. She brought me joy in this dark world. I enjoyed our talks and the time we spent together by the river. I taught her that there's more out there than this evil place. I know she will return to join this fight and free us all. I love you, Sparkle."

The scent of the burning trees is strong, and the other girls plug their ears from another ogre's scream.

Serenity stands up from her leaf bed and pokes her head out of the black straw tent to look for herself. Many trees burn up, and buzzards fly out. Smoke rises into the clouds, and sparkling pixie dust shines in the atmosphere. She quickly wipes any evidence of tears on the sleeves of the red robe that Leon made for her, hiding her emotions.

Who is that fighting? Could it be my boyfriend? Rock, I knew that you would come back to save us. You are the love of my life, and I pray you're okay. I know you can be cocky sometimes, but you are a sweetheart deep down inside. You're a good man who believed in my dreams of being a jazz musician and appreciated my love for art. Unlike Daniel, you listened during our conversations and told me to pursue my dreams. Since hearing that my mom is in one of these prison camps, I need your help to save her. I know that you will save her. I love you, Rock, and I miss you.

Sarah emerges from the corner of the tent and removes the healthy leaves from her wrinkled, red robe. She reeks of marijuana smoke and hemp. The former librarian's assistant staggers to Serenity and lifts the hood from her head. "Who is that fighting? Could it be my grandmother? Before she retired, she was a major in the army. She must have finally got the federal government to send reinforcements to this evil place. I miss my grandma. She sparked my fascination with books by reading me bedtime stories. Reading books is a passion of mine. I read so many books in my lifetime. I know that my grandmother will rescue me from this world. When I return to Earth, and things return to normal, I'm going to the library."

Susan rises from the floor, brushing the dirt and dry leaves off her green robe. "I explicitly asked Leon to create this green cloak because it reminds me of the pot I like to smoke."

Her dilated eyes peek through a small hole in the tent. "Who is that out there fighting? I don't know, but I miss Richard. He is my first boyfriend and my first love. Since my mom and dad passed over the years, he is the only real family I have left. I wasn't always a drunk. I was into volleyball and tennis. When Mom and Dad got sick, I got depressed. The marijuana eased my pain. The liquor and cigarettes relaxed me. I know drugs and alcohol are unhealthy. Someday, I'll stop. I don't know if we will ever leave this fairy world, but I hope to see Richard again before I die."

Susan embraces Serenity, and she hugs her back.

"Serenity, hold me tighter. I need it," Susan says.

"Everything is going to be okay. When the fighting stops, and it's safe, I will play jazz for you," Serenity says.

"It will never be safe," Susan cries.

Sarah rubs Susan's back.

Leon flies over to the ladies. "Keep her quiet! We do not want the fairies to hear us and find our location." He sprinkles magical silver pixie dust around his red robe, and it hardens, transforming into battle armor. "It has been a very long time since I was in battle. I must go out there and find out who is fighting the fairies, as we need all the allies we can get!"

Fairy Rock

The fairy blows silver pixie dust with black electricity around it in three directions. It transforms into three magic swords for the women. "Ladies, I'm going to see who is out there fighting. If I don't come back alive, use the sword skills I taught you to defend yourselves. You all have become so good that I believe you can fight without me if you have to."

"We should help you, Leon," Serenity says.

"No, stay here. Your safety is important to our cause."

"Leon, come back alive, okay? We love you," Sarah says.

"You are all like my daughters. I love you too," Leon says.

He rushes from the tent and heads into the fight.

39
Richard Johnson

Richard takes the last two flaming arrows from his backpack and aims them at the fairy generals. He tries to catch his breath while struggling to hold the bow straight. The sweat from his forehead drips onto his lips, and he spits to get the salty taste out of his mouth.

Richard straightens the eyeglass on his face to keep the tiny fairy generals in focus. He fires directly at them.

Butch and Baker maneuver out of the way of the fiery arrow as it scrapes pieces of their tiny, white wings off and leaves black marks all over their dented armor.

Fatigue consumes Richard, and he keels over into a black-grass patch near three dead ogres.

Butch and Baker lower themselves to the ground.

Baker pulls hard on his beard until the skin on his face stretches. "This archer lad is skilled. We would have been dead if he had hit us with that attack."

The fairy generals toss pebbles at Richard and laugh.

"He doesn't look like he has much strength left to fight. Before we kill him, let's torture him," Butch says.

"How does it feel to lose, human?" Butch chuckles. He throws a dirtball and hits Richard's braided hair. "After we kill you, we will kill everyone you know."

Richard tries to stand, but his legs and shoulders are too sore to move. The dusty wind blows the eyeglass off his face, making it more challenging to see as the bullies taunt him.

Fairy Rock

I can't die here. I must get back up. Everyone depends on me. Mom, Dad, Susan, Tevin, and the city of Fairyville. Who am I kidding? None of us should be here. I'm twenty-one years old. I'm supposed to be drinking beer out of a keg at a bar, getting drunk, or at a frat party. If this had never happened, I would have been smoking a blunt before class in my third year of college. Instead, I'm in this dark world, getting spit on by fairies.

The two fairy generals float around him with a purple aura around each of their bug-sized bodies. They mutate and grow seven feet tall. Their muscles bulge out of their bodies as powerful, magical purple light fills the sky.

Butch and Baker flex their pecks and pump out their brown, hairy chests. They step on Richard's back and head, digging his body further into the mud.

"Uggh!" Richard screams.

Out of nowhere, black pixie dust comes from the sky and blows into Butch's and Baker's faces, forcing them to cough and gag.

Leon swoops down and screams as a red aura surrounds him. The power of his aura knocks the fairy generals into the bushes as they choke on the poison.

Richard realizes the aging fairy is lifting him up and together they fly into the sky. Hordes of vultures are beside him, and Leon raises his aura, scattering them.

They fly him over the black trees and land by the tent's entrance.

"Ladies, where are you? I found the man fighting Queen Vanessa's troops, and he needs help," Leon says.

The girls circle Richard as the noble fairy removes the barrier around him.

Susan's eyes widen, and she puts her soft, gentle hands on Richard's face. "It's my boyfriend."

Richard is barely conscious, weak, and unable to speak. Cuts and scrapes cover the bruises on his cheeks. Susan's fingers brush against his neck as if trying to check his pulse. Her face floods with tears. "Leon, my baby is dying. Do something."

"I will do my best to heal him," Leon says.

Her wet lips kiss his cheeks as she rests his head on her lap.

Serenity and Sarah pull her up.

"Let Leon help him, okay?" Serenity suggests.

"I have a little bit of hemp left to calm you down, Susan," Sarah says.

Leon injects him with gold pixie dust and Richard's bleary vision clears as he spots the fatherly fairy in a red robe continuing to apply the soothing pixie dust.

Where am I? Who is this fairy that's helping me?

"He is awake," Leon tells them gently.

Susan wipes some black mud off his skin and kisses him again. "I missed you so much, babe," she whispers.

Richard smiles as her long brown hair, sensational smile, and the marijuana scent in her clothes instantly bring him tears of joy. "Susan, I can't believe that is it you. I love you, and we must never leave each other's sides again."

They caress each other as Leon, Serenity, and Sarah turn away, giving them privacy.

"We still have a problem," Leon says. "Butch and Baker are still alive, and they will find us."

The sound of trees falling nearby gets everyone's attention.

"Here they come," Leon says.

Sarah draws her sword. "Serenity, get ready."

Serenity seizes her blade. "My family, friends, and dreams are up to me and this blade. Now is my turn to help defeat these fairies."

40
Richard Johnson

Richard and the others peep out of the cracks in the tent's straw walls. Baker and Butch are just outside of the hideout. Their aura burns steam out of the grass. Butch and Baker increase the power of their aura.

Richard's ears pop from the rumbling noise. The ladies holler and plug their ears. The ground quakes. Branches, leaves, and coconuts fall from the trees, littering the steaming grass with debris. Squirrels and rabbits flee from the gray bushes. Rattlesnakes and rats scatter out of holes in the muddy ground, hurrying through the woods.

The strings loosen in the straw hideout as the surface cracks, and the roof caves in.

Everyone dives out of the hideout as a thick mist surrounds the gang.

Richard grimaces from the pain in his lower back as the women help him to his feet. They prop him up against a black willow tree near a line of gray bushes. "The fairies are using fog attack," he stammers. "I don't have any arrows, but I can still fight!"

Susan pulls a green sword from her robe's holster. "Babe, you're hurt. Stay behind me. These two huge freaks are right next to us. They don't make enough weed to dream this up. But Leon told me that this sword would glow and give me the power to know how to use it naturally. He said it would also allow me to move incredibly fast. He calls it the Sword of Speed."

Sarah straightens her bifocals and draws a maroon sword. "I have read stories about monsters and all types of evil. Who would have thought that I would be a warrior going into battle with some psychotic fairies in real life? Leon calls this weapon the Sword of Power. He said this blade was strong enough to slice an oak tree in half with one swing. It's weird, Susan, I feel like I've been using it forever."

Serenity unleashes a red sword and slightly turns away from the scintillating red light it's triggering. "Leon told me what this sword could do. It's called the Sword of Medicine. It's a weapon that helps heal my comrades in battle. Leon's magic gave us the knowledge to use these weapons."

Richard notices the fairies are only paying attention to Leon.

Butch and Baker blow silver pixie dust in their hands. The silver particles crackle, pop, and explode. The silver smoke clears, and two enormous silver axes appear in their hands.

"Leon, you traitor. You will die first," Baker says.

Leon flies off Serenity's shoulder in the direction of Queen Vanessa's generals, generating a red aura around his body. As he draws more power, he clutches his heart and grimaces.

"Leon, let me help you," Serenity says.

"I'm much older now and way past my prime. Your sword cannot reverse the process of aging. Get out of here. Save yourselves."

His tiny body stretches and grows seven feet tall in a flash. His thin physique chisels as his arms and legs have thickened. The good fairy shrugs his shoulders, and magical sand radiates from the ground. His eyes turn red, releasing a burst of magic, turning the sky and the clouds above them red. Electricity beams out of him, hardening the spellbinding red armor around his skin.

"There seems to be no limit to these fairies' powers," Susan says.

"There must be," Richard replies.

Serenity touches Richard with her sword, and red energy seeps inside him, healing his injuries.

"Thank you," Richard says. He leaps forward, spinning his bow and creating a green shield. *I still have no arrows, but I can't just stand here and do nothing. I must fight on.*

Leon squares up with Butch and Baker, pointing at them with a cold, expressionless look. "I'm stopping both of you right now."

41
Serenity Cooper

The battling fairies raise their auras, releasing their dark magic into the atmosphere. The high wind kicks dirt, sticks, and leaves into the air, bending the trees in the area sideways and nearly pulling them out of their roots.

Serenity, Susan, and Sarah stick their swords into the ground, bracing themselves.

The air is nearly blowing the skin off Serenity's face. She concentrates on holding onto her weapon and keeping thoughts of death out of her mind. *I don't want the wind to wipe us away. Leon is fighting, and he needs our help.*

Richard spins his bow faster, creating a magical green light to block the piercing wind and debris.

Butch and Baker swing their axes at Leon but do not come close to hitting him. He's just too fast for them. They hover high in the air and increase their purple aura. They blast black pixie dust throughout the region, and the poison burns trees and bushes, leaving a massive hole in the black-grass field.

Out of nowhere, Leon dashes at the fairy generals and knocks them into a pile of gray boulders, cracking their heads open. Blood splatters their armor as the evil generals stagger back to their feet.

As Leon goes in for the kill, he clutches his heart and grimaces. The tornado stops, and the red sky turns purple as Butch and Baker's aura takes over the sky again.

The group remains near the ruined hideout. The fog is getting thicker as it changes colors to dark purple.

"The fairies are doing this to blind us!" Richard shouts.

Serenity pulls her sword out of the dirt. She hears the buzzards yapping, the rats squeaking, and the snakes rattling, but nothing from Leon. "I'm going to find him!"

She uses the light from her weapon as a guide and creeps through the high gray weeds. Her comrades follow her, swinging their blades and bow through the field, knocking the grass and weeds down as they get taller and taller along the way.

Their robes are muddy as they enter a strange field with steam and static electricity popping out of it.

"Oh, no!" Serenity screams.

The wicked fairy generals tower over the ailing Leon, who looks beaten to a pulp as his face swells and broken bones stick out of his limbs. "Give me your power," Butch demands.

Long, skinny, shadowy figures emerge from the grounds, and the fairy generals inhale them into their lungs. Butch and Baker seem to enjoy consuming these creatures as if they were a drug.

Serenity and her friends huddle together. "Are those ghosts going inside of them?" Susan asks.

"I don't know," Sarah responds.

Richard sticks his hand in the air, and his enchanted glove generates small green particles around it. "With these gloves that Elroy made for me, I can create more arrows that might be able to take them out, but I'm going to need some time to make them."

Serenity steps forward. "I'll buy you some time, Richard. I've learned a lot from dating Rock. He made me realize that confident people can do wonders with their lives. No matter how big these fairies are, we can beat them." She marches boldly toward the fairy generals.

Butch and Baker show their oversized axes. There are chunks of Leon's flesh on the weapons.

Serenity cringes but quickly regains her composure. She charges the fairies. "It's now or never! We must strike now!"

42

Serenity Cooper

Serenity concentrates on the monstrous fairy generals directly in front of her.

The gloomy field cradles Leon as he lies on the grass with a swollen and broken jaw, his wings bent and torn.

She tightens her grip on her glowing, red blade and swings it violently at Butch and Baker, missing the target as the fairy generals soar away.

"I see we have a feisty one," Butch says.

Baker picks black mud out of his beard. "Let me be the one to kill her."

"I'm not going anywhere," Serenity says. She swings her shining blade at Baker as he gets close, cutting his jaw.

He touches the mark on his hairy face. "You caused me to bleed."

The fairy general attacks her with his ax, but she blocks every blow with her magnificent sword.

Serenity grunts and flails her weapon, desperately trying to stab the bleeding Baker.

"I'm not going to let you hurt Leon anymore."

The sparks fly from the impact of their blades. Serenity can hear her friends behind her.

"We can't just stand here and do nothing," Sarah says, and Serenity glances over her shoulder.

Sarah trudges forward through the marshy land. Her sword repeatedly flashes maroon energy, and she smacks Baker with it, knocking the armor off his torso.

The fairy general escapes to the air, saving himself.

"You are just weak!" Butch yells.

Baker aggressively jerks his beard, tearing chunks of hair off his skin. "Do not insult me again!"

Butch rips off all his armor, exposing his naked body, and screams as veins pop out of his bulky muscles. "I'm going to kill you all."

He drools as his yellow teeth become fangs. Enormous amounts of purple aura gorge out of his body, causing the ground to shake. He extends his arms and uses his magic to make purple lightning bolts fall from the sky, striking the grassy field and setting it on fire. The trees fall from their roots and thud to the surface, making dust and mud splash into the air.

Serenity and Sarah sprint through the burning weeds, coughing black smoke.

They turn as Butch emerges from the vapor, swinging his sharp ax, and cuts half of Serenity's afro off. She falls back. The fairy rams her into a pile of burning grass and pins her into the flames. He smirks and laughs at the sounds of her screams.

Sarah rushes into the fumes to her aide, swinging at Butch, but he blocks her strike with his sturdy ax.

"Get away from my friend," Sarah says.

Susan catches up with them and comes into the fight. "Leave us alone. We're too young to die."

As the gleaming, green power around Susan's blade gets more robust, she swings her weapon and, with one true swing, she chops off Butch's head, shrinking him back to the size of a tiny fairy.

The dark wind begins to blow, clearing the smoke.

Serenity lies in the grass, staring at Baker above them. Her muscles are sore, and she can no longer fight as she's pushed herself to exhaustion.

He growls at them angrily, and he tugs most of the hair off his chin, causing more blood to gush out of his face. "My brother is dead. I'm going to kill you scum who murdered him!"

The power of his purple aura fills the sky. His chest inflates as he prepares to spread the field with poisonous, black pixie dust.

A flaming arrow hits the vengeful fairy in the neck, and he bursts into flames.

He shrieks terribly as supernatural purple sand rises from the ground, extinguishing the flames on him. He shrinks back down to a bug-sized fairy, flies down, and grabs Butch's head and body. He flings yellow pixie dust into the air creating a portal, and teleports away.

Richard sprints to the girls with his bow and new arrows. "Are you all okay?"

The group gathers around Serenity.

"She's hurt badly," Susan cries.

Sarah puts on a replacement pair of bifocals from her robe's pocket. "We need to grab Leon as well. He's in pretty bad shape."

"Thank you all for saving me," Serenity whimpers.

Richard looks around quickly. "I know where we can take Serenity and Leon: To the hideout of the Elves."

43

Tevin Jenkins

As the sun goes down, Tevin returns to his apartment. He sneaks up the fire escape and climbs through a cracked window. He tiptoes on the squeaky, wooden floor and nearly slips over the dust and plaster from the large holes Sparkle left in the walls.

As he rushes into his bedroom, he digs through all the torn newspaper articles, dirty jeans, and t-shirts, fumbling past his mud-stained socks and balled-up boxer shorts until he finds the leather jacket that Richard gave him. He shakes it clean and puts it on.

There is no telling how the weather will be in the World of The Fairies. It changes so much that I better be prepared for all the elements. I'll stop by the store to get some food and drinks.

A cold sweat goes down his back. He flinches as he hears people talking outside his apartment. Grabbing his backpack, he fills it with a pair of wrinkled black jeans, a crumpled-up black sweater, and his holy water.

He creeps back out through the fire escape and spots his landlord's used red Corvette with gold-tinted rims parked by the alley's entryway. He tries not to make a noise while stepping down the metal, clanky steps.

I know Mr. Franklin is furious about how messed up my apartment is. I better not take any chances and let him see me.

As he reaches the ground, he sprints down the other side of the alley, trips over a garbage bag and falls face-first into a puddle of water.

Around the corner, he enters a small, congested liquor store. He coughs and gags from the skunk-scented weed from a blunt that one of the customers is smoking.

The stoner inhales a puff of the marijuana. "Hey, bro, do you want to buy some of this strong stuff?"

Tevin walks past him. "No, thank you, sir." As he approaches the glass counter, full of scratch-off lottery tickets and an orange lotter machine, Hal Richardson, the store owner, waves his long, thin hands at Tevin as he grabs two packages of frosted honey buns and a bag of flaming hot potato chips.

"Will it be the usual four slices of pizza, Tev?" Hal asks.

Tevin puts the junk food on the counter. "Yes, sir."

Hal twists his black mustache. "And the usual pint of James Dennis Whiskey?"

"Yes."

Hal leans down the twenty-square-foot wall of liquor and grabs a dusty, brown bottle of James Dennis Whiskey from the bottom shelf. He blows the dust off the plastic pint and wipes the rest of the dirt off it with his shirt.

"Um, Mr. Richardson, sir, have you been bulking up?" Tevin asks.

Hal places the pint on the counter and flexes his tall, thin arms. "I sure have, Tevy Tev. You know, Hattonville is full of drug addicts. This city may look nice, but it has its share of crime. I have to stay strong."

Tevin scratches his dry black afro and tries to add up the items he is purchasing.

A man in a wrinkled blue jean outfit with bloodshot eyes staggers in the store. He has an unpleasant smell, and his curly hair leaks from Jheri curl grease. The guy takes a revolver out of his pocket and fires a bullet toward the wall of alcohol. A bottle of White Russian blows up.

Everyone in the store ducks to the tile floor.

The deranged guy points the gun at Hal. "Give me some money now!"

Hal raises his hands in the air. "Okay, calm down."

Tevin's heart races.

I don't want Mr. Richardson to die. I can't die, either. I must go to the fairy world to save everyone.

The gunman screams, kicking the counter and busting the glass. He fires the weapon throughout the store, putting bullet holes in the walls and shattering expensive vodka bottles on the top shelf. "I want some money now!"

Hal pulls out his double-barrel shotgun and fires back, missing the assailant as the pellets hit a bag of barbeque potato chips, spilling them on the floor.

The gunman ducks down and fires back, shooting the owner in the shoulder, splattering his blood over the cash register. The maniac aims his gun at a trembling Tevin as he covers his head on the ground and shoots him in his back.

The wound on Tevin's back burns, and he lies on the cold floor. His blood pools on the ground around him.

As the robber jumps the counter to get to the cash register, Tevin coughs and heaves. *Almighty God, please don't let me die. I must save my parents and everyone. Serenity means everything to me, and I must protect her. I love her. Please help me. In Jesus' name, Amen.*

He closes his eyes, his body numb. His collapsing lungs fail, and his heart stops beating. He can no longer hear the robber struggling to open the register or the weed-smoking drug dealer screaming.

In an instant, Tevin's body starts beaming a shiny blue and gold light. Gold pixie dust shoots out of his skin, removing the bullet from his body and healing his gunshot wound. Blue pixie dust seeps out of his skin, and blue smoke surrounds him, causing an explosion, knocking the white tile out of the ceiling, and rupturing pop, beer, and liquor bottles. The popcorn and potato chip bags burst, sending food flying.

As the smoke clears, Tevin has transformed into the handsome, muscular Rock. He opens his eyes in wonder. *How did this happen? Sparkle is nowhere near me.*

44

Tevin Jenkins

Rock wanders around the dingy store, studying the bullet holes in the walls, and Hal grimaces on the bloody mat behind the cash register with a towel over his wounded shoulder.

The gunman jumps up and down, touching his greasy hair as he bugs out. "I must be on an acid trip, man. You just mutated into some freak with muscles! Even your outfit has changed, man."

Rock ignores him. He flexes his chiseled muscles while looking down and admiring his shiny, black Testoni dress shoes.

I'm back, but how?

"I am the man." Rock chuckles.

The gunman points his pistol at Rock. "I don't know what freaky stuff is happening, man, but I want your clothes. I can make a killing selling them."

Red pixie dust incubates throughout Rock's body, causing immense blood to pump through his veins, giving him new fighting energy.

Before the gunman can discharge his weapon, Rock snatches it with incredible speed and bends the criminal's arm, throwing him over the counter into the cake display, breaking it and knocking him unconscious.

Rock puts his hand on Hal's wounded shoulder and injects gold pixie dust into him until the wound dissolves and the bullet comes out, healing his hurt friend.

Hal seems more alert. "Who are you?"

Rock helps him to his feet. "I'm the guy who just saved your life."

Hal repeatedly blinks. "Wait a minute. You're the famous MMA fighter who was supposed to fight Benny the Destroyer. I thought you were dead along with everyone else in Fairyville."

"Nah, man, I'm good," Rock says.

Hal's store is in ruins. Blood and crumbs are everywhere, and a row of honey buns and cupcakes are on the floor next to the gunman's body, who landed on the now broken shelf. Rock quizzically nods at the drug dealer in the corner, rolling another blunt instead of leaving the store.

Rock puts a box of honey buns and a few water bottles into his white Louis Vuitton book bag.

Hal's thin face turns red. "Put that back. You can't take that without paying for it."

"I just saved your life. This is my payment."

"Have you seen a skinny, nerdy guy around here? His name is Tevin."

Rock stands motionless and hesitates to answer.

Hal didn't see me transform. The drug dealer over there probably did, but who would believe him? Hal allows drug deals here for money, so he would never keep a surveillance camera for the cops to see.

"No, I haven't," Rock says. "He must have run out of the store during the robbery."

"I see."

"Hey, Hal, let me get that pint of Whiskey—make that a fifth since I did save your life. Give me the four slices of pizza as well."

"You and Tevin ordered the same thing."

"Never mind."

Rock quickly exits the store.

Did I blow my cover? You know what? I don't care. I'm Rock, and everybody should know my name.

***

Rock struts down the dark, wet streets, feeling the cold rain against his skin, but his ego will not let him shiver. He hops over a big puddle on the sidewalk to keep his outfit clean and smiles, looking at a reflection of himself through the window of one of the massive skyscrapers on the block.

He turns down Hatton Lane, the dance club district, and hears people dancing and smoking cigarettes outside Club Trizzys. There are crowds of people holding umbrellas while standing in line around the gold, three-story, tinted-window building. Rock passes by and they turn their heads and stare at him as if he were a supermodel.

"Dang, you are handsome," a drunk lady says.

Rock gives her a picture-perfect grin. "I know I am."

The men and women in the crowd take pictures of him.

"That's Rock, the MMA fighter," a man says.

"You're gorgeous. Be my boyfriend," a woman says.

"That's right, keep dreaming." Rock pumps his muscles for the crowd.

Rock's body weakens as blue smoke appears around him, making a loud banging sound. His muscles get thinner, his dreadlocks get smaller and fade back into an afro, as he transforms back into Tevin.

As the blue vapor clears, Tevin wears a black leather jacket and jeans.

"Ugh. Who is that? He's ugly," a woman voices.

"What happened to Rock?" another guy asks.

Tevin observes the veins in his skinny hands and how gray and dirty his uncut fingernails are. His jaw drops.

What happened? I changed back.

"Where's the handsome guy?" a club-goer asks.

Tevin runs down the street.

I guess I can't remain Rock for that long without the help of Sparkle. I must figure out how I transformed like that. I may have a better chance against the fairies.

Tevin takes his cell phone out of his pocket and punches the directions to Chief Bailey's place into his GPS. He jogs down Kamari Street, near Winstonville Condo Village, trips over a pothole, and stumbles into an orange construction barrel, falling over it. A possum flees into some bushes outside the condominium neighborhood.

"Aargh!" he cries.

He gets back up, brushing the sticks and loose grass off his now muddy knees, and enters the complex.

The GPS says, "In four hundred feet, turn left onto Ryan Street."

A short while later, he reaches the Chief's three-floor olive green condo and knocks on the door.

Butterflies dance in his stomach, and he tries to swallow the lump in his throat.

A bald man with gray stubble in his beard answers the door. "May I help you, sir?"

"Hello. My name is Tevin Jenkins, and I am from Fairyville. I need your help sneaking back into the town."

"Pastor Anderson told me that you were coming. Come in, and I will help you."

45

Tevin Jenkins

Tevin stands in the doorway of Chief Bailey's living room.

The smoke detector goes off, and there's an aroma of burnt biscuits.

Chief Bailey hurries toward the smoky room. "Darn, I forgot to turn the oven off."

Tevin peeks at the red Persian rug, the green porcelain vase, and the French empire crystal chandelier hanging from the ceiling.

How can he afford all this?

Chief Bailey returns to the room with a prescription bottle of Lisinopril to treat his high blood pressure. He sits in a chair, straining to get the cap off his medication. "So, you are here to find a way back into town so that you can jump off Fairy Rock? Is that right, Tevin?"

"Yes, sir, I must try to save everyone I can."

Chief Bailey gives up opening the bottle and tosses it against the wall. He drops his head on the Astor table. "I can no longer live with the guilt of all the money that Mayor Brunson and I stole from Fairyville."

"What?"

"When the fairies attacked the city, me and Mayor Brunson escaped through a tunnel in her mansion that led us here, to Hattonville. We took over a million dollars, and I used some of it to buy this condo."

"W-w-where is Mayor Brunson?"

"I don't know. She took off after my wife discovered our affair, and my wife called the feds on us before she left me. They're on our trail, but I decided to stay. For the first time, I will make amends for what I have done. I should have been out there fighting the fairies with my men."

Tevin picks up the prescription bottle, twists the cap off, and gives it to Chief Bailey.

"Thank you, my friend. There is an unused tunnel in the sewer canal in Remington Park. It is a long, straight walk through that disgusting thing, but a maintenance hole cover is at the end. Push it up, and you will be inside the mayor's mansion."

***

Later that night, Tevin sits in the Chief's black Dodge Challenger, listening to the ticking Hemi engine.

As they drive down Duke Street, couples hold hands under the streetlights of the white brick sidewalks near the massive skyscrapers.

He envisions Serenity in the car, resting her head on his shoulder. He imagines whispering in her ear, "I love you, and I'm sorry for what I've done to everyone."

Tevin turns toward the back seat and pictures Richard, Susan, and his parents. He smiles as they listen to Serenity play a soothing, soft melody on her saxophone, and he tells everyone, "I love all of you."

Chief Bailey pops another blood pressure pill and takes a swig of water to swallow it down.

They reach the entrance of the sewer canal, and the Chief parks the car. He runs the wipers to get the mosquitos off the glass. He reaches for his flashlight and steps outside onto the tall, muddy grass along with Tevin. They push through the shoulder-length, high aquatic weeds and swat the irritating bugs off their faces.

Tevin turns his head in every direction, trying to figure out where the sounds of the crickets are coming from while Chief Bailey studies the rusty fence blocking the large sewer canal hole. "Tevin, come over here. Kick that gate in, travel down to the end, climb the ladder, and open the maintenance hole cover."

"Are you coming with me, Chief?"

"No, I'm too sick."

Tevin steps back from the gate, pinching his nose and coughing from the smell of raw sewage. He glances at the cement walls around the sewer canal and the cars driving above the beam bridge.

Fairy Rock

I'm scared to death. I don't want to go through that dark place alone, but I must do this.

Chief Bailey hands Tevin his flashlight and gives him his revolver. "Good luck, Buddy."

"Thank you, sir, and please take care of yourself."

Tevin zips up his leather jacket and adjusts his backpack on his shoulders. He jumps down into the sewer canal and kicks open the filthy gate, slowly creeping through the black hole. Dirty brown water splashes above his ankles.

An oversized rat screeches at him in the right corner of the murky walls. "Aargh!" he squeals.

Mice scurry away as Tevin sprints full speed through the dark.

He reaches the end of the tunnel and finds a steel ladder coated in grime. He climbs up it, pushes the maintenance hole cover out of the way, and arrives in a dark, cold room full of cobwebs.

While attempting to brush the spider silk from his soaked, dirty afro, he accidentally trips on a broken wooden chair and falls on the floor. *Ouch!* The back of his head is bleeding from cutting himself on a rusty nail.

As he rises to his feet, he reaches for his gun. *Where's the light switch?*

He slips on a pile of sawdust and stumbles backward into a bookshelf, knocking all the books off it. He accidentally flicks a button on the bookshelf, opening a door.

I made it to the mayor's mansion. I can't believe that I'm finally back in Fairyville.

46
Tevin Jenkins

Tevin tiptoes through the dark room toward the open door and enters Mayor Brunson's bedroom. He points the revolver in all directions and creeps around the spacious chamber, trying not to make a sound.

I hope Queen Vanessa did not leave any fairies here. What if she has a goblin or an ogre keeping guard in this town? Oh my gosh, a dragon could fly outside for all I know. What if the cops arrest me for trespassing?

The rays of the moonlight glisten in the unlighted room. As he paces forward, he bangs his shin on the brown Oxara nightstand and knocks over the expensive Tiffany wisteria lamp, shattering it onto the red, silk Isfahan rug. He steps on the broken lamp pieces and hides under the king-size bed, praying that no one enters the room. He hunches his shoulders and hopes his heart doesn't thump out of his chest.

The wind blows tree branches against the window, causing a screeching noise as the sticks scratch the pane.

Please don't let that be one of those fairies. Okay, Tevin, relax. I must get to Fairy Rock as quickly as possible!

Tevin flees the bedroom into the pitch-black hallway, pointing his gun in every direction. He holds onto the guard rails, leaving his nasty footprints on the fluffy white carpet while continuing his journey down the stairs and straight out the front door.

He jogs fifty yards through the high, uncut grass of the mansion's front yard and climbs the chain link fence onto Main Street. To his relief, the city is a complete ghost town with no one in sight. The streetlights are off, and massive rubble from the destroyed skyscrapers and businesses is all down the block.

Tevin drops to his knees and buries his head on the tar-paved streets. *I can't believe this. Look what those monsters did to Fairyville. It is all my fault. I will never forgive myself for making a deal with those stupid fairies. I'm the reason the town's destroyed! Who am I kidding? I can't save these people.*

As tears stream down his face, he points the gun at his head. *I'm a selfish loser, a failure. I don't deserve to live.* He closes his eyes and pulls the hammer down on the revolver. He gets ready to pull the trigger.

But the ground starts shaking rapidly, causing him to lose his balance. He falls backward and lands on his back, dropping the gun out of his hand.

Bricks fall from the rock pile, and he rolls out of the way as the rocks bury the gun. In an instant, the earthquake stops, and he lies in the rubble, covered in gray dust.

He wipes his face and sits down for a few minutes, processing what just happened.

I have never heard of Fairyville ever having an Earthquake. Was this an act of the Lord? This means… God kept me alive. I do have a purpose. God does love me.

"Almighty, Father, thank you for saving my life. I'm sorry for testing you, and I'll never point a gun at my head again. Suicide is not the way. I surrender my life to you. Please give me the strength to save everyone in Fairyville. In Jesus' name, Amen."

He gets back up, sticks his chest out, and runs full speed through the town with a stronger feeling of confidence, thinking about all the fantastic people who have helped him. He looks at the stones, the broken glass, and the dry bloodstains and smells the odor of misery in the streets, motivating him to sprint faster. "I'm coming, everyone. I'm coming."

Soon, he arrives at The Fairyville Woods, sweaty and out of breath. Yellow police tape covers all the entrances. He ducks under it and trudges through the tall ragweeds, passing the oak trees. He claps his hands at a raccoon, scaring it away into the evergreen shrubs.

He pulls forward through the pasture, stepping on the damp dandelions as he climbs the grassy hill toward the mountains.

Come on! I know I can make it up. It won't be long until I reach Fairy Rock. I can't believe how dirty I am, and I stink. But nothing will stop me from helping my people, family, friends, and sweet Serenity.

***

At Fairy Rock, he climbs on the colossal, muddy boulder and observes the city. *The view up here is so different from how I left it. It used to be beautiful, but now there are no lights in the buildings or cars driving. Looking at this town with no kids flying their kites is hard. I can see Fairyville Amusement, and no one rides the roller coasters. My gosh, Mitch's MMA gym looks so empty and dead.*

A wolf is howling nearby, but Tevin pays it no mind. The bluish halfmoon light and all the stars aligning with it keep his attention, for this may be his last image of Fairyville. "Almighty God, please keep all the people trapped in the fairy world alive and protect them. You are my shepherd and my savior. Please give me the strength to make this leap one last time. In Jesus' name, Amen."

Tevin jumps off Fairy Rock and enters The World of The Fairies.

47

Tevin Jenkins

Tevin is in a field full of high grass in the West Forest of The World of The Fairies. The fog is as thick as he remembers, but the grass is taller and nearly above his neck. The howls of dark wolves and the grunts of the ogres are nearby. The gloomy atmosphere impairs his vision. He hurries through the forest and bumps his head on the bark of a Sycamore tree.

"Aargh!" he hollers.

He climbs the tree, concealing himself in the leaves, as he contemplates his next move. *I'm surprised the fairies didn't greet me when I entered the fairy world. I'm so scared because I haven't seen anyone, and I forgot my anxiety medication. I must be a brave hero and save everyone.*

The lonely orange star in the black sky shines bright as it had in the past.

The howls of dark wolves and the growls of ogres fill the air again. He grabs his cup of holy water from his bookbag and removes the plastic top.

The rugged, thudding footsteps of the ogres rattle the trees and knock the black and gray apples out of them. The dark wolves are barking, getting closer to him.

Oh, no, they must have found me. I hope this canister full of holy water works. Father in Heaven, please keep me alive. I want to save the people of Fairyville. Please let me see Serenity again. I love her, and I miss her so much. In Jesus' name, Amen.

The dark wolves surround Tevin's tree. Twenty giant ogres leap out of the mist. The gray-skinned monsters pull the tree up by its roots, bending it sideways. One of the ogres rapidly climbs aboard.

Tevin clinches his arms and legs around a thick branch on the tree, barely able to hold onto the holy water as the leaves and apples continue to fall. As it gets close enough, he splashes holy water in the monster's face. Its forehead bursts into flame, and black smoke pours from its jaws. It runs away toward the river, shrieking in pain and rage.

"It works," Tevin says.

The ogres push and pound on the tree again, tipping it over. As it's falling, Tevin pours the blessed water over his afro and black leather coat, soaking it as he grips the branch tightly. The oak tree lands in a black mud patch, leaving a crack in the ground as dirt flings up high.

Tevin injures his elbow as he jumps clear of the tree.

The grizzly bear-sized dark wolves shake the mud out of their thick black fur and violently bark at Tevin. The filthy dark wolves and ogres charge at him, and he curls into a fetal position.

But at the last minute, they stop as they sniff the holy water on him and step back.

Tevin opens his eyes.

I'm not dead. They must be afraid of the water on me. I better get out of here. I will have to run through them before the holy water evaporates.

He sprints through the pack of ogres and dark wolves and they jump out of his way, then scurries through the gray fog and runs face-first into the tall black tumbleweeds and thorn bushes.

The thorns cut his face and tear his leather jacket. "Aargh!"

The rain begins to fall heavily from the sky, flooding the ground.

Oh no. The rain will wash the holy water off me.

The dark wolves bark, and their beaming eyes burn through the fog. The ogres grunt and chase him. He trips on a stone, stumbles, and falls into a pink swamp.

He swims quickly to the top, then spits the warm, mildewy water out of his mouth. The ogres dive in and restrain him, and once they get ahold of him, they grip his wrists and ankles and they him up. Tevin shouts for help and tries to squirm his way free as they drag him out of the swamp and through the foggy wetland.

The elder fairy, Selena, appears in front of him. She wears a long purple Victorian dress.

"Please let me go," Tevin begs.

Take this prisoner to Queen Vanessa's castle. She wants to deal with him personally."

Tevin pulls and tugs to break free from the ogre's grip, but with no success. His voice becomes hoarse, and nausea is in his stomach as he wants to vomit from fear.

The ogres drag him, kicking and screaming, to Queen Vanessa's castle.

***

The ogres and Selena drag Tevin through Queen Vanessa's newly expanded courtyard and drop him on the short purple lawn.

He lies in the wet grass and whines as he rubs the bruises on his wrist. Selena hovers over him and blows purple pixie dust in his face. *No, not this stuff again.* It itches as it goes down his nose and throat. He becomes drowsy, and his mind goes blank.

The elder fairy instructs him to keep his head down as he passes hundreds of prisoners wearing purple tuxedos with glowing purple chains around their ankles and wrists.

Mammoth-sized ogres, wearing purple Armani suits, growl and swing their spiked horsewhips, forcing them to work harder. The prisoners pull thorn bushes out of the wet ground with bloody bare hands and plant grass seeds on the freshly grown, purple lawn across the five-mile campus.

Selena guides him to the front door of the queen's thirty-story purple castle.

"Queen Vanessa made the prisoners remodel this whole establishment," Selena says.

Tevin blinks at her, and she appears disgusted at his severely torn, muddy leather jacket and jeans.

"You are not in proper attire. Queen Vanessa now requires everyone to dress in purple suits. She desires everything in this castle to be purple. It is her favorite color."

She blows her transformation pixie dust around him. The particles stick to him and explode into magical threads that wrap around his body, transforming his clothing into a purple tuxedo.

Tevin remains in a trance, marveling that Selena's pixie dust is stronger than Sparkle's, as she also changes her dress into a new evening gown.

A fifty-foot-tall, triangle-shaped door opens, shining purple light, and Tevin covers his face and turns away from the brightness.

"Get on your knees," Selena says.

He crawls inside the entrance on the living room's soft carpet, listening to a group of Fairyville citizens dressed in tuxedos play violins, the viola, the cello, and the piano for Queen Vanessa's orchestra.

"They are rehearsing Mozart's symphony, *Old Lambach*," Selena says.

Bernard, the great little fairy composer, waves his baton back and forth. He's clearly nervous, and mutters under his breath, "We better get this right. Our lives depend on it."

They continue down the mile-long hallway toward Queen Vanessa's quarters, passing hundreds of crystal chandeliers, which make a clinging noise above them.

Many Fairyville citizens use ladders to apply purple paint to giant gold statues of Queen Vanessa near the long staircase.

He coughs at the smell of wet fur from a dark wolf chained to a wall, barking at a prisoner, who is attempting to bathe it. The poor man trembles as he pleads with the Armani suit-wearing fairies guarding him for help.

"You will clean the animal, boy," one of the fairies says.

"This thing will kill me," the man replies.

The dark wolf barks loudly at him, dripping its putrid drool on his face. The man screams and almost kicks the soap bucket over on one of the queen's Persian rugs.

They continue to travel down the hallway, passing by a painting of Queen Vanessa in a Renaissance dress and another portrait of the queen dressed as an Egyptian Pharaoh.

After a quarter of a mile, Tevin stops to rest.

A shadowy black creature flies across the room.

Was that a ghost?

"Keep moving, boy," Selena directs.

The pixie dust wears off as Tevin continues to crawl down the hallway. It gets darker and darker. Fiendish spirits fly sideways through the walls to scare him. Tevin yells and runs away, but Selena quickly grabs him by the collar and drags him back towards Queen Vanessa's door.

Soon, they come to a mega-sized door larger than anything in the castle. In the center is a face with a big nose, lips, and eyes. The spooky purple eyeballs light up, staring at them. Swiftly, the mouth opens, revealing razor-sharp fangs.

"Who dares disturb Queen Vanessa?" the door asks.

The elder fairy raises her hands in the air. "Linus, it's me, Selena. Let us in. Queen Vanessa is expecting us."

Linus opens its mouth wider, exposing a ray of purple aura that fills the long hallway.

Selena and Tevin enter Queen Vanessa's room.

48

Tevin Jenkins

Tevin and Selena are in Queen Vanessa's chambers. The room is pitch-black and hot. Purple energy gas surrounds the room, and purple steam emerges from the walls and the purple marble floor.

Tevin analyzes a colossal painting spread across the ceiling. In it, Selena and the pirates are on the deck of a ship. In the center of the canvas is another face with a big nose, purple eyes, a mouth, and sharp, purple fangs. The eyes light up, and the mouth hisses and gags as it opens wide, letting out hundreds of shadowy ghosts.

"Winton, calm yourself," Selena snaps.

Tevin screams, running for the exit, but Linus will not open the door.

The ghosts fly across the room as they hide in the walls.

Tevin bangs on the door again. "Let me out of here!"

Purple pixie dust goes up his nose, putting him in a calming trance again.

"Calm yourself before the queen," Selena says.

A tiny fairy sits in the back of the room on a miniature purple throne near the king-size bed with purple satin sheets. She snaps her fingers, and the room lights up.

Selena chants, "All praise Queen Vanessa."

The fairy queen ignores her and appears to be talking to herself. "I have everything I ever wanted—a beautiful castle, servants, power, and wealth. Yet, I am not happy. I always wanted to be a mother to an obedient child. Things are not the same since Sparkle is no longer my daughter. I miss her dearly."

Behind the queen stands a twenty-foot-tall shadowy spirit with dark red eyes.

"W-who is that?" Tevin asks.

"It's Spencer Unitas, The King of the Demon Ghosts," Selena replies.

Spencer floats around the queen.

"Your majesty," Spencer says, "I sense that you miss Sparkle. Are you going soft?"

"There is nothing wrong with missing your child," Queen Vanessa remarks.

Spencer roars and flies rapidly up and down the vast room. The mighty demon ghost king vents, vibrating the chamber and causing purple dust to fall from the ceiling.

"Do you remember when you first came to this world?" Spencer says. "You were hungry and begging to survive. At the time, I told you I couldn't help you leave this world, but I could do something better. You let me and my demon minions possess you, and in return, I made you very powerful and gave you this world."

"Some believe dragon meat and a particular star are the secrets to the fairies' power. No one knows how many demons we fairies allowed to possess our bodies to gain this great strength. I even held this secret from my daughter, who'd been born with demon energy," Queen Vanessa cries.

Spencer's voice becomes raspy. "I am a demon. The angels forced me down to this evil world centuries before you came here, Vanessa. I feed off, making my subjects evil. It's my rush."

"Spencer, why did my little girl rebel?" Queen Vanessa asks.

"Sparkle was always loyal to you until she met Tevin Jenkins. He got into her head and changed her," Spencer says.

Purple and red lightning flashes in the room, destroying the walls and leaving rubble everywhere.

Queen Vanessa's mouth widens, and several ghosts fly into it. She swallows them and her eyes roll back in her head. "It's Tevin Jenkin's fault," she mumbles, glaring furiously.

She twitches as her head and neck spin around in circles. Her jaw muscles twist and turn, leaving her face disfigured. A purple and red aura beams out of her body. Hair falls out of her head, and bloody, ivory horns inch out of the sides of her skull, making a popping noise.

The queen's skin is purple, and her eyes are dark red as she grows twelve feet tall.

Selena ducks down. "The queen is now a demon," she says solemnly.

Queen Vanessa sheds skin, and her bones pop as two bloody, white wings slowly form from her back. Tevin wails as tiny brown worms crawl out the queen's nostrils and down her warped, deformed jaw.

"Get me out of here," Tevin whimpers.

Selena chaotically blows purple pixie dust in the infected fairy queen's face, but it does nothing to her.

Queen Vanessa just swallows more ghosts. As she does, her arms and thigh muscles expand, and she grows fourteen feet taller. Her purple Renaissance dress tears into pieces as nothing but a purple girdle covers her half-naked body.

As the demonic aura beams out of her, the excruciating heat in the unholy room becomes hotter, and ghost blood leaks out of the walls onto what's left of the crushed, purple marble floor.

Selena uses more magical pixie dust to open a small yellow portal. "My queen is possessed entirely by evil. There is nothing I can do for her. I'm leaving now."

She flies through the portal, and it disappears, leaving Tevin alone in shock.

"Wait!" Tevin shouts. He makes a run for it toward the sealed entrance again. "Help me!"

Drool drips out of Queen Vanessa's dark purple lips. "Give me more power," she screams.

Spencer stretches his ghostly head, rubbing it against the queen's ear. "Tevin Jenkins is the one who told Sparkle to disobey you, and he's in this room."

The power of Spencer's words causes the queen to create a strong wind, ripping the roof off the room.

She lets out high-pitched, screeching noises. "Tevin Jenkins! Tevin Jenkins!"

Tevin continues to sweat through his soaked purple tuxedo. He squints through the flashing red light from the ghosts.

I must get out of here. Rock, please come out and save me.

His hands begin to itch and yellow pixie dust sprays out of them and quickly forms into a portal.

He jumps inside, and it disappears.

***

He comes out of the portal outside the castle and runs away through the mist.

How did that happen again? I still don't have Sparkle with me. She must have left enough pixie dust inside me to use it still when I'm in extreme distress.

He runs for hours through the high Ravenna grass, and he sits to rest. Tired yet restless, his head hurts as his knees bounce up and down. He gets up to pace.

How am I going to save everyone? How am I going to stop the fairies? Where are my family and friends? Where is Serenity? I need help.

His hands become sticky as green pixie dust comes out and forms into squares. Images of people in green cloaks walking through a rainy forest in the fairy world appear. Pink pixie dust emerges out of his other hand and forms into a straight line and moves east.

Wait, does the pixie dust want me to follow it?

Tevin follows the pink pixie dust down a nature trail of black sycamore trees and shrubs, hoping to find his family and friends. After several hours, he enters the Central Forest. Fifty yards away, a group of travelers is walking on a beach by the yellow mountainside.

As he pushes his way toward them, the group draws their swords and pulls out their bows. They look at him, immediately lower their weapons, and take the hoods off their heads.

It's his parents, Richard, Susan, Serenity, a few elves, and Sarah. Tevin falls to his hands and knees, tears pouring down his face.

"Tevin!" Mrs. Jenkins cries.

The group runs and circles him. They appear in shock. His parents sob as they hug him.

"We love you so much," Mrs. Jenkins says.

"I-I love you too," Tevin replies.

49
Tevin Jenkins

After a brief rest, the group leaves the area and travels through the rough terrain of the Central Forest. They walk through the marsh and follow the Pink River through the valley to their new temporary hideout.

"We should find Timothy, Lisa, and Leon as soon as we are close to the base," Elroy whispers quietly. They all nod.

Tevin has his arms around his mother and father as Serenity approaches him, and he blushes as she is as beautiful as ever.

"Tevin, I'm glad you are okay," Serenity says.

"Thank you," Tevin says.

"Have you seen my mother, or someone named Rock on the journey here? Rock is my boyfriend," Serenity asks.

Tevin's head drops. Dark twigs and decaying grass are below his feet.

She still doesn't know that I'm Rock. Will she be mad at me if I tell her? I must tell her.

"I am Rock," Tevin mumbles.

"What? Speak louder. I can't hear you," Serenity says.

"I am Rock," Tevin repeats.

Serenity drops her sword, and a look of disbelief spreads across her face. "What?"

50
Tevin Jenkins

Tevin is speechless as Serenity grabs him by the collar of his shirt and slaps him. He stumbles into the muddy, yellow pebbles behind him.

"You fooled me. How dare you?!" Serenity says.

Tevin's lips quiver. *Oh, no. Serenity's mad at me. I didn't mean for this to happen.*

"Who helped you, Tevin? Who helped you do this to me?" she screams.

"I-it was Sparkle," he whimpers.

Serenity punches him in his chest.

Susan and Sarah pull on Serenity's arm, attempting to separate them.

"Why did you do this, Tevin?" Serenity demands.

Tevin sobs. "I love you, Serenity. I believed the myth and jumped off Fairy Rock because I wanted the fairies to turn me into someone you would like so I could be your boyfriend."

Serenity pauses. "We are all stuck in this evil world because you decided to work with those wicked fairies. You could have just asked me out."

"I thought that you would say no," Tevin mumbles.

Susan and Richard pick Serenity up, keeping her away from him.

Tevin cries on Mrs. Jenkins's shoulder. "Mom, Serenity hates me."

Mrs. Jenkins hugs him. "Serenity is hurt right now. Give her some time, son."

As the mist gets heavier, Elroy gathers the group. "There are fairies in the area. We must keep moving."

They press on through the valley until they reach the South Forest where they approach the bottom of a yellow mountain near a yellow beach by the Pink River. Together they push a boulder out of the way and climb down a vine to the bottom of their lair, where Mr. and Mrs. Johnson wait silently near a fire, keeping Leon warm.

Mr. Johnson and his wife embrace their son. "Praise the Lord! You all made it back safe."

***

They wait for several hours, sitting in silence, on the leaves by the fire, resting their bodies.

Over the crackle of the fire, Tevin hears Mr. and Mrs. Johnson whispering about him. "I oughta kill this Jenkins kid! He's the reason we're all here. I used to have a life of luxury. I drove a fancy Cadillac and lived in a big house. Now, I'm living in a tiny hole in The World of The Fairies, hiding from monsters. I even had to eat bugs!"

Mrs. Johnson snuggles up against her husband. "You're right! I used to bake chocolate chip cookies for Tevin and Richard. Now I want to bake him. Everyone we know is a prisoner or dead! I haven't had a proper manicure in years. I miss my summer cottage. The heck with this, Tevin Jenkins."

Tevin slinks back into the shadows, guilt pouring over him. *Oh, no. Richard's parents are mad.* He rolls over silently and glances at Susan, wrapping herself in her green robe as she finishes rolling a blunt. He strains to hear what she's saying to Richard. "Elroy's magic makes some good weed. Dang, everyone looks so mad at Tevin. I'm not that mad at him. I mean, I know he didn't realize the fairies were evil. Yeah, I am a prisoner in this fairy world. I hope my family is okay, even though we never really got along. I don't want Tevin to die, but I do want to punch him in his mouth for getting us stuck here."

Richard puts his arm around Susan. "I know Tevin like the back of my hand. He didn't mean for this to happen. As far as being in the World of The Fairies, I blamed him for it, but I forgave him. I have my parents, you, and these cool new fighting skills. I could be on Earth, taking college courses. I know that I'll get back to that life. For now, I'm worried. When the people of Fairyville find out what he did, people will hunt him down. We've got to make sure that no one harms him."

Sarah writes in her notepad as she speaks with Serenity. "I have never seen you that mad before. This Tevin guy seems mental. But I can tell he is a nice guy by how his parents hold him. He just needs some confidence in himself. I won't kill him because I think God wants me to write this story despite all the negative stuff going on here. I think it's my destiny to do so," Sarah whispers.

Serenity leans against the muddy yellow walls, fiddling with her saxophone and pressing the keys on it as she says, "How can Tevin do this to me? Despite all this, I still love Rock. Does that mean I love Tevin, too? I feel bad for hitting him. I know he cares for me, and somewhere inside Tevin, there is Rock. What do I do?"

Tevin listens to his father quietly chatting with his mother. "Where did I go wrong with my son? I know that the doctors diagnosed him with what they think is schizophrenia. He has delusions that Serenity is like a goddess. Maybe if I had got him more into sports than the books, he would be tougher. I love my boy and will protect him with my life," he whispers.

Mrs. Jenkins rubs Tevin's back, comforting him, and offering up a prayer to the Almighty.

Tevin puts on the green robe Elroy gave him. *King Jesus, I'm sorry for making everyone mad at me and for what happened to everyone in Fairyville. Again, please free them all and get them home. Please help everyone, especially Serenity, to forgive me. I love her so much. In Jesus' name, Amen.*

51
Tevin Jenkins

The group remains in the dimly lit hideout, warming themselves by the fire while Tevin positions himself near the exit, ready to climb the vine. In the rear of the room, Mr. Johnson rambles to his wife. He is on his sixth cup of rum, and he pulls his bow out.

"Look at that Jenkins boy still breathing. He deserves to die for what he's done. That is my son's best friend, but I don't care. I'm going to kill that boy."

Mrs. Johnson sips her liquor slowly. She drunkenly wobbles as she steps on the crunching yellow dirt below her.

Tevin's head hurts as his gut-wrenching anxiety peaks. He can sense the tension in the room, but he's not sure how to break it. Finally, he takes a deep breath and quietly leans closer to Mrs. Johnson. "Hi."

Mrs. Johnson reaches for her knife. "Do you have the nerve to speak to me after what you have done? I want to slit your throat." She softens slightly and pushes the blade back in the sheath. "But I can't. I did help raise you."

Tevin hangs his head down and backs away from her.

Mrs. Jenkins nudges her husband and motions with her head in Tevin's direction. "Harold, check out how Lisa is staring at Tevin with her hand on her knife, and look at how Timothy is putting an arrow on his bow. They're going to kill him."

"Relax, sweetheart. We have known the Johnsons for years. They won't hurt Tevin. They're just drunk," Mr. Jenkins replies quietly.

Mr. Johnson points his weapon at Tevin.

"Bleeping crap, he is trying to kill him!" Mr. Jenkins says. Rising quickly, he shouts, "Tevin, get out of the way!" The sudden sound makes Mr. Johnson flinch and gives Tevin time to dive into the dirt. Recovering quickly, Mr. Johnson fires the magic arrow, missing and hitting the muddy yellow wall, setting it on fire.

"I'm sorry, Mr. Johnson," Tevin whimpers as he crawls across the floor, looking for cover.

Mrs. Johnson charges at him, swinging her blade as he ducks out of the way.

Richard grabs her and tries to stop her while Mr. Jenkins wrestles the bow out of Mr. Johnson's hands. They both slam into the wall as Mr. Johnson shouts over the noise of the struggle. "Give that back, Harold! With all the destruction that your son has caused, why are we protecting him?!"

Mrs. Jenkins jumps in front of her son to shield him from the onslaught. "He's my child, and I love him. I will always love him."

"Hey!" Susan shouts aggressively, and in that moment, everyone stops to listen to her. She crosses her arms. "Tevin," she says sternly, "you're my friend and all, but you deserve some punishment for this." She walks across the room to stand in front of him. "Why did you come back here?"

Tevin clears his throat and takes a deep breath. *Speak with confidence. I know that I can do this.* "You all have every right to be mad at me. I'm very sorry for all of this. I came back to save you all. I will do everything possible to get you guys back to Fairyville."

Mr. Johnson spits at him. "You can't save anyone, you coward. You don't even have the gall to talk to a girl."

"Calm down, Dad. Tevin is a good person. He helped us all out at some point in our lives. He didn't mean for any of this to happen. Forgive him, guys," Richard says.

Tevin drops his head. *They hate me, and Serenity is crying because of me. They don't want me here.*

For a few minutes, there's a standoff, no one sure who will make the next move, to forgiveness or vengeance. When he hears a groan from the corner of the room, the elder fairy, Leon, begins to stir as he awakens from his coma.

"You're awake," Serenity says with joy.

The mood shifts, and they move over to take care of Leon, putting their anger aside for the moment. But seconds later, thudding footsteps above the lair pound yellow dirt down from the ceiling. The hideout erupts, quaking as more dust falls, landing on the group and putting the fire out, making the room dark. Leon sits up and points to the roof feebly. "The other fairies are here," he says.

A red aura glows around the noble fairy, vibrating the room. The group covers their faces from the bright light of his power. His tiny arms and legs stretch as his muscles expand, and he grows seven feet tall.

Tevin stands there in disbelief, taken completely back by the sudden transformation. "We are in danger!" Mr. Jenkins says.

The group quickly grab their weapons and rush outside.

Queen Vanessa, Baker, Selena, Bernard, and six other giant, mutated fairies stand just outside their doors in a hollow area they've trampled clear. They are twice the size of Leon, with purple wings and skin, legs wider than tree trunks, and ivory horns on the sides of their heads. Hundreds of shadowy demon ghosts float nearby. The fairies increase their purple auras, turning the black sky and clouds purple as hundreds of purple lightning bolts flash, striking the black trees and sending them crashing to the ground, spreading debris across the sand.

"Oh, no," Mrs. Johnson moans.

The terror rushes through them as they draw their weapons and take their stand for what could be the final and ultimate battle of their lives.

Susan, ever mindful, looks around the bleak scene heedlessly. "Richard," she howls," what are we going to do?! I don't see the Elves anywhere."

52
Tevin Jenkins

Tevin stands, stunned, as everything around him seems to move in slow motion. It's terrible. Looking past Susan, beyond her, he sees the hills burning. His heart thumps in his chest as he scans to the north, south, east, and west, searching for an escape from the fairies. There's no way out. In front of them, hundreds of demon ghosts fly in every direction. Fire surrounds them, and the smoke shrouds the battlefield in a thick cloud.

Tevin comes to the realization that this is his fault. His friends are in danger because of him. He looks at their faces, contorted with panic and fear. With nowhere to run, he grasps that if they want to live, they must hold their ground.

Richard shakes him and snaps him back into real time. "It's time to make a stand. We'll finish these fairies off right here and save everyone from this evil place."

Mrs. Jenkins prays. "Lord, Jesus, the enemy is here. Please put your heavenly blessing on us and protect us. In Jesus' name, Amen."

Tevin puts his dukes up. *This is it. I can't be scared anymore. I must fix this and send everyone home.*

He strains all his muscles as hard as he can. "Come out, Rock. Come out, Rock. Let's transform one last time."

Nothing happens.

No, this can't be happening. What's wrong? Why isn't Rock coming out? I must not have any more pixie dust in me.

Queen Vanessa lets out a hoarse roar of triumph. She opens her mouth, and demon ghosts approach her. She inhales, sucks them inside her, and swallows them. Black and purple demonic energy gleams out of her, forming a purple cocoon around her as she sits down by the shore of the pink river. Selena, Baker, Benard, and the other fairies get in front of her cocoon, guarding her. Hundreds of demon ghosts spin around them, booing and hissing.

"What is she doing?" Tevin asks, trembling.

"I don't care," Richard says angrily. "I just want to end this!" He shoots a magical flaming arrow at one of the ghosts, and it goes through it, hitting a yellow stone on the mountain and melting it. He groans and reaches for another arrow, firing one after another, each firing true, but passing through the enemies, causing no damage.

Susan swings her sword at them, missing with every swing. "What are these things?"

Richard steps back. "If this keeps up, we're doomed!"

Baker, Benard, and the other seven fairies armed with their large, razor-sharp axes march through the fog toward the group while Selena stands near Queen Vanessa's cocoon. "Destroy them all!" she calls to them. "We must protect the queen until she transforms into her final form."

Stepping out of the smoke, Leon walks through his companions, each step defiantly bringing him closer to the coming fairies. He grunts, raising his power, creating a violent wind that uplifts yellow sand from the beach and thousands of stones in the air. The mighty wind forms into a tornado and blows many trees sideways, ripping them out of the ground. Raising his hands, he guides the tornado attack away from the group and unleashes it at the fairies.

Selena, Baker, and Benard fly out of the way, but the other fairies get caught in the tornado and spin in circles rapidly. The tornado sends them plowing into the Pink River, where they lie motionless.

Then, in a quick motion, he snaps his fingers, and the tornado evaporates, leaving tree limbs, leaves, and yellow stones littering the beach. He dashes at Queen Vanessa's undamaged cocoon. But just as he gets within striking distance, he clutches his chest and falls into the sand as his body shrinks back to a tiny fairy. He reaches one arm toward them and falls back. "My heart!" he calls out weakly before lying motionless.

"Leon!" Serenity screams. Ignoring the dangers all around her, she races across the littered battlefield, towards the cocoon – towards Leon.

Tevin throws all caution to the wind and follows her, ready to die if need be but unwilling in the midst of battle to be apart from her. *I can't let anything happen to her.*

53
Tevin Jenkins

Serenity drops to her knees as she reaches Leon's limp body. Scooping him up tenderly, she places him in a pocket of her cloak.

Tevin is two steps behind her, but he's drawn the attention of the demon ghosts who swarm by him, moving so fast he can't see their faces. They fly through the sage brushes and the cracks of the angular stones on the yellow mountain and out of the Pink River.

In a flood of overwhelming fear, he falls to the ground as they bear down on him. He's not sure what to do. *Is there anything left to do but die?* He closes his eyes and waits for the end.

But Serenity is on her feet, swinging her sword as she screams, fighting her way through the ghosts to get to Tevin.

Baker, Bernard, and Selena hoover over the others in the group. More demon ghosts fly down the yellow mountainside and enter Baker. The jumbo-sized fairy's neck twists in circles as his head faces the group. His beard grows to his feet and shines a dark red and purple light. A pair of eyes, a nose, and a mouth appear on the beard. The beard grows arms and legs. Baker rips the beard monster off his face.

Tevin's friends and family are about fifty yards from him and Serenity. His mother and father point their bows at the creature as it turns and charges at them.

Tevin's jaws lock. He tries to call for his mother but can't make a sound. *I'm so scared. I can no longer be Rock without Sparkle's help. I'm so weak that there is nothing I can do to help.*

Mr. and Mrs. Jenkins's arrows cut through the air and bury themselves in the monster, setting it on fire, but it keeps charging at them, a burning fury that can't be stopped.

Susan and Sarah step into the fray, swinging their glowing blades and chopping it into pieces of purple fluff, which blows around them, carried by the wind. When it lands on them, the hair flashes a purplish red light again, draining the women's energy and causing them to faint.

Richard uses his magical glove to pull the wicked hair off his girlfriend, but Baker sees what he's doing and teleports to Richard, slashing at him with his ax.

As Tevin sees Richard fall on his back and pass out in a ditch in the sand, he finds the courage to move. *Mom, Dad, Richard, I'm coming.* He surges forward, fighting his way in a fury, through hundreds of demon ghosts floating on the terrain. The long, dark shadows of the evil spirits distort his vision as he feels his way forward. He trips on a rock and falls into the gravel.

A soft hand pulls him up. "It's me," Serenity says.

The demon ghosts leave Tevin and Serenity alone and fly to the fairy Benard as he opens his mouth. The ghosts push and pull on each other, fighting for position. He chews on a demon ghost. His wings flutter faster and faster. His purple and red aura rises and reaches its limits, making thunder erupt. Reddish-purple lightning strikes the top of the yellow mountain, sending an enormous boulder down.

He waves his wand, and the sound of an enchanted violin appears out of nowhere. Swarms of bats and crows come into view from the purple clouds, with a reddish-purple aura around them. His new pets swoosh down and attack Mr. Jenkins, Mrs. Jenkins, Mr. Johnson, and Mrs. Johnson. The birds bite and peck at their flesh, and they scream.

"Mom, Dad, no!" Tevin shouts.

Serenity takes Leon out of her robe's pocket. "Leon had another heart attack, Tevin. I found him nearby. It's up to us to save everyone."

54

Tevin Jenkins

The thunderstorm continues to flood the ground, and the water in the Pink River overflows onto the shore. Black magic particles appear in the water as more sadistic demon ghosts become visible.

Tevin and Serenity are waist deep in the water as the evil spirits confront them. They show their fangs.

Serenity grabs hold of him. The loudness of her cry rings in his ears, and the moisture of her tears stick to his cheeks. A chilling sensation goes down his arms, legs, and spine. His heart feels like it's about to stop.

I don't care if I die. I will protect Serenity. He swings his fist in a windmill motion. "Leave Serenity alone. Your fight is with me."

The evil ghosts boo and surround them, stretching their phantom black bodies. As they get closer, Tevin quickly pushes Serenity into the water and gets in front of her. The demon ghost put their creepy, thin hands around his body, lifting him into the sky. Their ghostly fingers itch as they crawl down his back.

"Let me go!" He struggles in a frenzy to free himself.

"Tevin!" Serenity cries.

The demon ghosts blow out thousands of black magic particles. The sadistic particles fizzle into a large oval-shaped dark black hole, and they drag him into it.

The black hole closes and disappears.

He's alone. In silence, his body flips around in space. He sees no light and hears no sound as his body spins in the freezing atmosphere of darkness.

He tries to stop his teeth from chattering, and he wiggles his hands and feet, trying to get some warmth to his numb fingers and toes.

He screams into the nothing that surrounds him, "Hello? Is anyone here?"

"Hello? Is anyone here?" his voice echoes back.

"I can't see anything. Help me!" he screams.

"I can't see anything. Help me!" the echo replies.

The silence crushes him, and he begins to panic. Even the chaos of the battlefield was better than this endless blackness and eternal solitude. *Where am I? Am I dead? Where are my mom and dad? What happened to Serenity and the others?*

And then, out of the utter nothingness that extends to the edges of everywhere, he realizes he can just begin to make out an immense set of dark red eyes blinking at him.

Tevin flinches. "Please don't kill me," he begs.

"Please don't kill me," his voice echoes back.

Then comes another voice, a voice without an echo. One that seems to belong to this place. A voice that seems to come from inside his own head somehow, taunting him with its very presence. "I'm not going to kill you, Tevin Jenkins. Let me introduce myself. I am Spencer Unitas, The King of the Demon Ghosts."

"What are you going to do with me?" Tevin asks.

"What are you going to do with me?" the echo repeats.

Spencer expands his face, stretching it across the black hole, filling the endless void with his presence. He blinks his gigantic eyes and grins, showing plasma covering his fangs. "Tevin Jenkins, I bet you're wondering how you're breathing in this black hole. It's because my magic allows you to breathe, for I am the real ruler of this evil world."

Tevin coughs and he swears the Demon Ghost King's breath smells like blood.

Spencer blinks again and vomits shiny, white powder out of his mouth. The powder shakes and spins into circles. It explodes, leaving an incense of charcoal as it forms a sculpture. And that sculpture takes the shape of hundreds of the citizens of Fairyville. He cackles at Tevin. "Originally, I was going to let Queen Vanessa torture you to death, but I decided to thank you and give you a chance. Since you selfishly jumped off Fairy Rock, I was able to devour all these souls."

Tevin tightly closes his eyes and sobs. *Why is he tormenting me? I didn't mean for everyone to die. I just wanted to be with Serenity.*

The Demon Ghost King chomps on the pictures of the people until they all poof into white smoke and disappear. He opens his mouth and gags out more magical powder. The powder churns around, creating a snapping sound, and inches into a pair of arms, legs, and a bosom as it forms a clone of Serenity, wearing a blue Renaissance dress.

Tevin opens his eyes as he sniffles. "Serenity, is that you?"

"Serenity, is that you?" his voice echoes back.

"Moho ha, ha, ha," Spencer laughs. "Tevin, let's make a deal. You let me devour your soul and own you, and I'll let you have the real Serenity without you transforming into Rock. I will also reincarnate everyone in Fairyville and give them their lives back."

Spencer sprinkles his magical powder on him, stopping him from spinning and Tevin senses suddenly that he belongs to this place somehow. He knows without speaking that his own voice will no longer echo here; that Spencer has enchanted him, at least for a time.

Tevin stares at Serenity's beautiful face, circular-shaped afro, and fit physique. He blushes. *This is my chance to save everyone and fix things. Plus, I can be with Serenity.*

Tevin shakes his head until the thoughts go away. He thinks about a time two years ago when he attended a service at Pastor Anderson's church. That day, Pastor Anderson talked about Jesus Christ and how great and forgiving he was.

"There will be times your faith will be tested," Pastor Anderson said that day. "Accept Jesus Christ as your Savior, and God will be all you need to get through anything."

Tevin trembles at the astronomically large, demented Spencer.

"What will be your answer, boy?" Spencer demands.

Tevin turns away from The Demon Ghost King as he continues to sniffle. *My desire got me here, but I'm a child of God now and know what I must do.* "Spencer, the answer is no."

The Demon Ghost King's jaw drops. "Did you just tell me no?" His face vibrates as he yells, making the black hole quake. He flies his dim body up and down, booing.

"Aargh!" Tevin screams.

A red aura glows around Spencer, creating a stretching sound as his body slowly expands, making him twice as big as before. "No one has ever told me no. Tevin Jenkins, do you know that even your protector, Leon, has made deals with me in the past? That is why his aura is red and he is so powerful."

The Demon Ghost King spits more supernatural powder, sloshing it until it forms a square and sizzles, developing images of Mr. and Mrs. Jenkins, Richard, and Susan standing in black and white tuxedos next to Serenity. They all simultaneously say, "Tevin, please save us from this world. Do what Spencer tells you." Each of them catches on fire. Their flesh burns as blood and boils form over their skin as they moan, "Help us, Tevin."

Tevin waves his arms, attempting to float toward his family and friends. "Please stop hurting them."

Spencer blows the images away into white smoke. "If you don't let me have your soul, this will happen to your loved ones."

The Demon Ghost King hiccups and gags, vomiting another horde of white powder. The magical substance fizzles as it quickly mutates into a vision of an enormous castle that reaches the baby blue sky. The whimsical powder spins in circles and explodes, making a popping noise. A picture of palm trees with green leaves and a clear blue water lake form around the castle, showing Serenity, Richard, Susan, and the Jenkinses in green tuxedos, drinking green cocktails as they sit in beach chairs.

Tevin pulls his nappy afro. "Oh my gosh." *If I give in to Spencer, Serenity will be my wife, and everyone important to me will live in luxury. No, this doesn't seem right. Pastor Anderson and my mother are strong Christians, and they taught me that there is only one God, and I pray to God in Jesus' name. I know that he won't let them burn.*

"Spencer, the answer is no."

"What?!" Spencer hollers. He shrinks in size into a twelve-foot-tall phantom. He flies up and down, whining as he weakens. "Why don't you bow to me, Tevin Jenkins? How do you think the fairies became so strong? I gave them the pixie dixie dust, which gave them any aura color they wanted and any power their imaginations could think of."

Spencer expands his lungs and blows white powder into the image, bringing it to life. Suddenly, Richard, Susan, and Mr. and Mrs. Jenkins slowly turn their heads, and their neck muscles pop. Their faces are now pale, and worms are crawling out of their eyes. Their stiff bodies crackle as they turn into zombies. They say simultaneously, "It's all your fault, Tevin."

Tevin murmurs. "No... Mom, Dad, Richard, Susan... I'm sorry."

Spencer flies to Tevin, sticking his thin, pointy red tongue out as he gets in his face. "Listen to them, Tevin Jenkins."

"It's all your fault! It's all your fault! It's all your fault!" the zombies yell.

Tevin blurts out, "No!"

"I'll give you another chance. Surrender your soul to me, and I'll bring everyone back to life," Spencer says.

Tevin wipes the tears out of his eyes and thinks about the book of Job in the Bible. *Job had everything taken from him, but he never lost faith in God. Only God can fix this. I must keep my faith.* "Spencer, I said no, and I mean it!"

The Demon Ghost King's body creates a screeching sound as it shrinks six feet and starts to fade. "Die, Tevin Jenkins," Spencer whispers. The black hole gets smaller, forcing Tevin to gasp for air as he slowly loses oxygen.

But as he loses consciousness and surrenders to the nothingness, a yellow light forms a straight line and gets more expansive, opening a magical portal.

Elroy becomes visible and grabs Tevin, pulling him into the portal and out of the black hole.

55

Serenity Cooper

The downpour continues, and the water from the flood rises above Serenity's elbows. She puts the ailing Leon in the front pocket of her robe and draws her sword again.

Where are her friends?! She lost Tevin, and while she chased after him, she lost sight of the others. Now, with the rain, she can't see anything. She can't hear anything. A deep dread flows through her veins, chilling her from within. Everything's quiet except for the pitter-pattering noise of the torrential rain splashing on her. She's soaked, and her wet, bushy hair glues to her face.

"Serenity," a voice whispers.

She raises her elbows high and nearly bursts a vein in her hand from squeezing on the handle of her sword. "Tevin, is that you?"

Her blade glows its shiny red light, showing the tall, elder fairy, Selena, next to her with what seems to be a plethora of demon ghosts in the background.

"You cannot hurt us with your weapon," Selena calls out, taunting her. The fairy kneels in the pink water and smiles as the rain drips down her wrinkled, purple face. "I love the power they give me and want more of it."

Selena opens her mouth, and the demon ghosts race to get inside it. She gulps down as many of them as she can. Her aura expands. The elder fairy's skin tears and starts to shed. Her arms and legs fall off her, and she goes underwater.

Selena's skin turns into purple scales. Her body stretches fifty feet long as it transitions into a huge serpent and slithers through the water.

Serenity quickly tries to move out of the way and falls underwater. She gets back up, spits out the salty pink water, and draws her sword again.

She flashes her blade in every direction and in the faint light, she sees the bodies of her friends floating in the river.

She gasps. Dead. All of them! She heaves! Their vacant eyes look skyward, a couple face down, all lifeless, forever silent. Mr. and Mrs. Johnson still hold hands, undivided even in death.

She hears the demon ghost hissing as they taunt her.

The giant serpent lurks at the top of the wet, muddy yellow rocks in the middle of the mountain near the oversized Baker, whose armor is bloody.

He picks up the remains of the bearded monster and uses gold pixie dust to heal the furry creature as it builds back together. It jumps onto his stubbly purple face, reattaching itself to him.

Serenity slows her breathing as she now feels empty. Her emotions are numb. She no longer cries or trembles from the fear of death. *Everyone is dead but me. I've been a prisoner in the World of The Fairies for over three years. My life is over. My dreams of being a jazz musician are all gone. Dad, thank you for introducing me to jazz. I forgive you for divorcing my mother. Mom, I love you and hope to reunite with you in the next life. Finally, Tevin, please be alive. I hope you make it home. It seems like death is the only way out of this place for me. I'm ready to be with God. See you soon, everyone.*

The aura of the third enemy, Benard, radiates. He waves his musical batons, and hundreds of glowing crows and bats emanate out of the purple sky's atmosphere, assailing toward her.

She points her powerful weapon at them. "I may be alone! I may be finished." She growls at them and steps forward. "It is likely that I will die here, like my friends. But, before I die, I promise I will kill one of you fairies."

In an instant, the rain stops and the fog clears. The sky turns black and Benard loses control of the bats and crows as they scatter away. Green, red, orange, violet, and blue fireworks fill the sky, stopping everyone in their tracks. A magical yellow portal opens, and Sparkle pops out of it in her giant form. She's seven feet tall, wears a rainbow-colored Renaissance dress, and carries Pastor Anderson on her back.

The young fairy lands in the water next to Serenity.

"Hello, Serenity! It's been a long time!"

Selena crawls toward the young fairy. "Sparkle, you are a traitor. How dare you show your face in this world?"

Sparkle unleashes her rainbow-colored aura around herself. Her magnificent power changes the sky's atmosphere to the colors of a rainbow. It's the most beautiful light Serenity has seen in years.

Sparkle waves her hand and a long line of magic, rainbow-colored sand from the forest materializes into the shape of a teacup that is big enough to fit Serenity in it. It moves and scoops Serenity out of the water, bringing her closer to Sparkle and Pastor Anderson.

"Serenity, you did a great job staying alive here for so long," Sparkle says. "I'm going to get you and the survivors home soon. You and Pastor Anderson can wait in this cup while I finish this."

56

Serenity Cooper

Serenity floats inside the giant magic teacup with Pastor Anderson. She rubs the cup's rainbow walls and pulls herself up to the top of it. She sees the anxiety written over her fairy friend Sparkle's face.

"I cannot believe this is happening," Sparkle says. "Pastor Anderson taught me about evil spirits while helping me heal. Selena, Benard, and Baker helped raise me, and look at them now. The three of them have made deals with the demon ghosts."

Baker is by Queen Vanessa's cocoon, consuming another demon ghost. Each one seems to increase his powers. The veins in his forehead burst, and the blood leaks down to the bearded monster attached to him. Its eyes open, and plasma drips on its hair follicles. It twists, turns, and yells as its arms and legs punch and kick, trying to break free from Baker's chin.

Benard swallows another. The skin on his head splits open, making a nipping noise as spikey black hairs inch out. He waves his necromantic baton, creating the sound of a violin playing a high note. A rippling wave of music attracts hundreds more bats and crows with a glowing black light around them to come to his evil aid.

Selena hisses as hordes of bumps form on her scales. Her pores burst open, spurting dark magic powder and turning her snakeskin black. She howls in fury, "Sparkle, you will die a horrible death for betraying your Queen!"

Sparkle extends her arms in defiance. Red, orange, yellow, green, blue, indigo, and violet light emerge from her, creating a rainbow aura. The power of her magic fills the dark sky with rainbows.

The ground shakes, breaking the remains of the yellow mountain and crushing them into millions of pieces. Rainbow-colored energy funnels out of the rocks and goes straight up into space.

Sparkle snaps her fingers, making rainbow-colored dirt rise from the surface, forming it into a ball the size of a meteor, bursting with static electricity.

The crows and bats squeak as the dirtball's electric power melts and disintegrates them into ashes.

Serenity ducks down. *Will this work?* She peeks her head over the cup's rim to watch the battle.

With roars of anger, Selena, Baker, and Benard release a high-pitched screech, summoning more demon ghosts. Thousands creep out of the clouds and flutter toward the possessed fairies.

Sparkle frowns.

Pastor Anderson takes out a small brown cross from his stole. "The three of them have gone to the dark side. We cannot let this type of evil harm others."

Serenity grabs the handle of her sword. *They're coming in our direction.*

Selena opens her mouth and spits out globs of venom, almost hitting them with it.

Baker and his bearded monster fly toward him.

"You leave me no choice," Sparkle says. She throws the enormous ball of magical dirt at the demonic fairies, causing an explosion as rocks, water, and tree branches erupt in the sky, leaving the ground covered in rainbowed-colored fire. The mountains, trees, and bushes of Central Forest burn into dust. In a flash, Selena, Baker, and Bernard join the dead, and nothing is left standing in the area but the floating teacup and Queen Vanessa's cocoon.

Serenity sweats from the heat of the flames. She coughs from the black smoke.

Queen Vanessa's cocoon splits. The gigantic brown cartilage breaks open as green slime oozes out of it. As it continues to crack, it gleams a purple light.

"My mother is coming out of that thing. Stay here, and I'll protect you!" Sparkle shouts.

Pastor Anderson holds his cross out. "Your mother is a full-fledged demon now, and I will help you defeat her."

"I'm joining the fight, too," Serenity says.

57

Serenity Cooper

Serenity crouches down in the floating teacup with Pastor Anderson as the water from the Pink River floods the surface, rising above the trees. She opens her robe's pocket and touches the sleeping Leon's wrist. There's still a pulse. *Please pull through, Leon.*

She looks back over the top and is shocked to see the center of Queen Vanessa's cocoon expand as it reaches its final stage. Its silk fibers stretch across the river and grow taller, touching the clouds in the rainbow-colored sky filled with Sparkle's aura.

Serenity grasps her sword with both hands and gets into a long-point stance.

Pastor Anderson is next to her. He pulls on his cross as it briefly gets tangled with the beads around his neck. "Jesus, Jesus, Jesus. We must keep saying his name for protection from these demons."

"Do you have a weapon, Reverend?" Serenity asks.

"God is all I need for protection," he answers.

The cocoon's silk fibers break, and red, soupy liquids gush into the river. It opens wider and wider, shooting out black magic dust. Thousands of demon ghosts disperse out of it. They hiss and vomit mucus into the Pink River, polluting it as the poisonous substance boils the water, turning it into acid. They spit a circle of black magic that floats through the air and eats away at the rainbows, evaporating them as they disappear. A strange odor of incense spreads over the atmosphere.

Tears roll down Sparkle's face. "I won't let my mother come out of that thing. I must stop her." She raises her rainbow aura around herself. Rainbow-colored dirt forms another enchanted dirtball the size of a meteor.

Her magic causes mud to come out of the water, and as she lifts her arms, the wet dirt shapes into a round object, forming a protective lid over the teacup.

It's dark inside the cup. Serenity hears the electricity around the dirtball, enraging the demon ghosts as they snarl and chomp their teeth.

"Jesus, Jesus, Jesus," Pastor Anderson prays.

Serenity peeps out through a small gap in the lid. She gasps. The demon ghosts are surrounding Sparkle, and they stick their skinny, wet tongues at her.

"Jesus!" Sparkle cries out.

The demonic ghosts disperse at the sound of Jesus's name. Sparkle catches her breath and launches the dirtball toward the cocoon. When it hits, it causes a massive explosion.

Serenity and Pastor Anderson twirl in the teacup as the power of the dirt ball spins it around and around, tumbling across the water.

"Pastor, are you okay?" Serenity asks as the teacup comes to rest.

"I'm fine," he answers. "To God be the glory."

Serenity checks outside again. Sparkle's puffy hair is out of place, and her ripped dress has holes. Queen Vanessa's cocoon still nestles in place as Sparkle's dirtball caused no damage, and it knocks and thuds as a dragon's giant head smashes through it.

"Is that your mother?!" Serenity asks.

"Yes," Sparkle cries. "She's transformed!"

The dragon's enormous wings break the cocoon into pieces as the transformed queen, now 10,000 feet high, towers over them, its head lost in the clouds until she leans down and brings her head close, breathing fire out of her mouth and nose as she melts what's left of the cocoon. Hundreds of red spikes are on the scales of the colossal-sized monster.

"Mother, no!" Sparkle cries. She tucks in her lips as she seems to try not to let her sad emotions get the best of her.

Serenity's sword lights up. Energy from her weapon travels through her, energizing her spirit; her mind is clear of all thoughts of death. *I now fully understand the power of the Sword of Medicine. It heals not only my wounds but also my anxiety and fear. It keeps me ready for battle.*

Queen Vanessa seems to be getting familiar with her new dragon form. She rubs the ivory horns on her head and observes her mammoth-sized feet and the spikes and scales on her tail.

She laughs to herself, "My favorite color is purple." In an instant transformation, pixie dust comes out of her, changing her body color to purple.

She opens her mouth and sucks in hordes of demon ghosts. The muscles in her arms and legs swell up, making her physique more enormous than a mountain.

Sparkle shakes her head. "There is no way that I can beat her. We have to get out here."

Serenity and Pastor Anderson remove the lid and jump into the young fairy's arms. She carries them as they flee from Queen Vanessa.

Other dragons and the demon ghosts chase after them, and Queen Vanessa lurches towards them, each step covering hundreds of feet.

"Get us out of here, Sparkle!" Serenity says.

The vibrations of Queen Vanessa's aura cause the planet to wobble. She roars and the sound makes the mountains shake. "Sparkle, you are a traitor, and I will punish you for disobeying me." The wind from her dragon wings gusts dust and water away. She zooms toward her daughter, blowing purple flames at her. The young fairy dodges and screams as the sky catches fire.

Sparkle flies them into another area of the forest, but Queen Vanessa is close behind, shooting fire at the trees and bushes, setting them ablaze.

"Mother's burning everything! She's out of control," Sparkle says.

Serenity turns her face as she hears the prisoners' screams and ogres below, wailing as they slowly burn to ashes.

"Jesus, Jesus, Jesus, Jesus," Pastor Anderson proclaims.

They fly toward a high, black mountain at the end of the planet and land on it. The sky and ground below are in purple flames. They're soaking in sweat as they watch The World of the Fairies burn in fire and brimstone.

"The queen turned this world into eternal damnation," Pastor Anderson says.

"I can teleport us back to Earth," Sparkle says.

"You can send Serenity. I cannot let this type of evil live any longer. With the help of Jesus Christ, I'll stay and defeat her," Pastor Anderson declares.

"Pastor, I'm staying to help," Serenity says.

A bright yellow light appears next to them, opening a magic portal. Elroy, Melinda, Bartholomew, Reginald, Jason, and Tevin appear. The portal closes.

Serenity laughs in delight. It's a miracle! Tevin is still alive. She stops in her tracks. It's Tevin, but he's changed. There's a difference in him. He is standing tall with his chest sticking out.

"I came back for you," Tevin says as he puts his arms around her, pulling her close.

58

Tevin Jenkins

Tevin is on the mountain's cliff with Serenity, Sparkle, Pastor Anderson, and the elves. Their clothes are wet and doused in rainbow-colored sand. The sweltering heat has taken a toll.

"I thought you were dead! I'm so glad you're alive," Serenity cries as she clings to Tevin.

He strokes her hair. "I had to come back for you. I couldn't live without knowing you were safe. I love you, and, so help me God, I will protect you with my life."

Sparkle shrinks back down to the size of an ordinary fairy. Tevin picks her up in his palms. "I'm tired," she whispers softly.

Abruptly, Spencer, the Demon Ghost King's dark red eyes, spread across the smoky atmosphere. Tevin stares in disbelief. *What's he doing in this place?*

"I'm going to enjoy watching your demise," Spencer taunts him.

Hundreds of dragons fly with Queen Vanessa, blowing fire as they land near the mountain cliff, the heat of their flames raising the temperature to over 150 degrees. The power of her aura pulls the gray-colored oak trees out of their roots, sending them crashing to the ground as leaves and dirt plunge into the bushes. The surface cracks, splitting open, and orange molten lava rises from the planet, melting the forest into ashes. The smell of burning meat from dead animal flesh fills the area.

The giant dragon, Queen Vanessa, trudges through the pool of hot liquid growing above her waist. She appears unbothered by the heat as her scales are full of demonic sorcery.

Elroy, Melinda, Reginald, Bartholomew, and Jason point their bows and arrows at Queen Vanessa's enormous dragon-shaped head, which is almost bigger than the cliff of the mountain.

"Fire!" Elroy shouts as the elves shoot their flaming arrows at the queen. They fly through but evaporate as they touch her scales.

The lava rises, nearly reaching the top of the mountain, and it begins to boil rapidly as orange heads form with a purple aura around them. Orange arms and hands slowly creep out of the molten liquid, grabbing onto the mountain's rocks. As their bodies fully develop, each naked lava creature grows a neck, chest, waist, legs, and feet. They boil with lava bubbles and steam. As they climb the mountain, they melt everything they touch.

A sprinkle of plasma hits Tevin's shoulder, and he looks up into the sky. It starts heavily raining drops of blood. He screams, but his nerves are calmed as Serenity puts her hood over her head and touches Tevin with her healing sword. He gasps in surprise and grins. *This is almost better than the pixie dust.*

Reginald wiggles his pointy ears as blood drips down his face and through his newly grown white beard. "We should not have helped the humans. Spencer is going to let Queen Vanessa kill us."

Melinda buttons her drenching wet robe. "Show some dignity before you die, Reggie. We should've never dealt with those things in the past for survival. It's better to die free than be servants to the demons."

Bartholomew puts his arm around him. "Yes, Reginald, we all decided to come back to save them. It's the right thing to do."

"Remember, we all were human before," Elroy says.

Pastor Anderson grabs Tevin and Serenity's hands. "Everyone holds hands."

"She's about to kill us," Reginald says.

"Do what he says," Elroy says. "I have a hunch about this."

The group stands in a circle, clutching each other's hands.

Tevin puts the sleeping Sparkle in his pocket and listens to the reverend.

"I know that you are all scared, but there is a name more powerful than any sword or arrow. There is a name stronger than any fairy or dragon. There is a name that leaves demons running in fear. That name is Jesus Christ. If you want to live, say his name," Pastor Anderson preaches.

The demon ghosts race down from the sky toward them, booing as they lick their fangs.

The evil spirits get within inches of the group, and they hiss, spitting their slimy saliva onto them.

The ten-foot-tall lava creatures reach the top of the mountain. Their molten, hot feet melt the black, rocky floor as they march toward the group.

Pastor Anderson jumps up and down. "Jesus, Jesus, Jesus! Say his name!"

"Jesus, Jesus, Jesus!" the group chants.

Pastor Anderson bounces up and down, dancing and stomping as he catches the holy ghost. "Hallelujah! Hallelujah! Praise Jesus Christ, our savior of the world!"

The holy preacher drops to his knees as he speaks in tongues. "Sha la, la, la, la! Sha la, la, la, la! Jesus! Jesus! Jesus! Jesus!"

The demon ghosts tremble in their tracks and fly in the other direction. The lava creatures pause and rock their faceless bodies back and forth in confusion.

"It's working," Tevin says.

The blood stops raining down, and the dragons flee behind Queen Vanessa. Sunlight appears in the sky, shining through The World of The Fairies. A strong wind begins to blow, extinguishing the purple flames.

Gold light fills the sky, and a cosmic portal stretches open. The peaceful sounds of a harp play as thousands of soldiers resembling humans dressed in silky gold gowns with wings covered in brown feathers fly out of it, and they draw their swords.

Tevin senses a peaceful awakening in his heart and spirit. *I've never experienced this emotion. I feel safe and strong.*

"Are those angels?" Tevin asks.

"Yes. God is answering our prayers," Pastor Anderson says.

59
Tevin Jenkins

Tevin and the others in the group fall silent as thousands of eight-foot-tall heavenly beings float in the air, hovering over the river of molten lava below them. They wear brown gowns and have the well-sculpted, chiseled physiques of gladiators. The scorching hot wind blows through their woolen afros as they line in formation. Their skin remains cool and unaffected by the sweltering heat.

The leader of the angels appears in front of the crowd, holding a gold harp. "My brothers and sisters, we are here to do God's work," she says. "We must rid this world of this evil and rescue the frail humans who stand and fight these demonic entities in the name of Jesus."

"Yes, Denise," the other angels respond in unison.

Denise rubs her long fingers against the instrument's nylon strings, making an A-flat and A-sharp sound, creating beautiful music. The magnificent holy tunes turn the dark sky powdery blue and the clouds fluffy white. The lone orange star shines sunlight for the first time in The World of the Fairies.

The demon ghosts flee from the light. The lava creatures sway back and forth as their brainless bodies stand on top of the river of lava in bewilderment. As the sacred music becomes louder, a supersonic wave comes at them, and the sinister lava monsters slowly evaporate into ashes. The lava beneath them simmers, and the molten liquid calms and changes into clear blue water.

Fairy Rock

Queen Vanessa turns her dragon body and covers her ears as the Christian beats get louder. She places her spikey fingernails against the sides of her purple-scaly head and bounces up and down in the river. The sinister queen clutches her pointy ears and grunts, pulling on them tightly to block the music. Her eyes spring wide open as she rips her ears off. She screeches in anger and frustration, watching all she fought for vanish into nothing.

Denise pauses her harp playing. "She can no longer hear our music. Stop her." The angels raise the brown aura around them and sheath their swords.

Hordes of dragons fly toward them, but in a flash, thousands of angels teleport in front of the beasts, hacking away at their monstrous limbs and sending chunks of dragon flesh raining down to the ground. At the same moment, hundreds more angels appear in front of Queen Vanessa and aggressively chop away at her.

Tevin and the others in the group curl in a ball as scales and slime fall on them. Bits of a dragon's heart land in Serenity's afro. The angels relentlessly mutilate and slice into Queen Vanessa and the other dragons.

As the carnage grows and the sound of swinging swords thunders through the air, Denise says, "It looks like our work here is almost over. Now, let's get the humans back to Earth."

The water trembles, and black magic comes from its bottom, turning the river black. The river stream moves in circles, faster and faster, as a whirlpool takes shape. Queen Vanessa erupts from the water, transformed back into a tiny fairy. "Did you think I was going to die that easily?" Her hair and skin remain purple as she models her old Renaissance dress, but her ears are gone, with only bloody stumps to show where they'd been.

The angels cast their weapons again.

Queen Vanessa blows blue pixie dust into the river. It foams as giant purple arms spring out of the water and grab onto each angel, pulling them into it. Denise tries to fly, but the arms yank her into the spinning river.

Tevin gets up and nearly slips on the bloody black rocks of the mountain under him.

He checks his pocket, and he can feel Sparkle starting to stir. He stands up, boldly. "Guys, I think me and Sparkle can stop her. Sparkle, if you have any strength left for the sake of humanity and the angels, please turn me into Rock one last time."

"Yes," Sparkle murmurs.

She flies toward Leon as Serenity holds him. She kisses him on the forehead. "I miss you, Father." She gusts gold pixie dust into him, and he slowly opens his eyes as he wakes up.

He smiles, and his lips quiver. "I can't believe it! It's my lovely daughter. I missed you so much, dear."

She blushes and hugs him tightly. "Father, I love you so much."

"Be careful," Pastor Anderson says.

"I will."

Serenity runs over to Tevin. She hugs and squeezes him tightly as if she doesn't want to let go. She briefly rests her head on his shoulder and kisses him on the cheek. "I love you," she says.

"I love you too."

He slightly turns his head, keeping himself from blushing as the love of his life finally kisses him. Him. Tevin. Not Rock. For the first time, he feels that he is enough. That he has what he needs to rise up. The shy kid in him has left, and he's ready to fight.

"Bring us home," Serenity says.

Sparkle blasts blue pixie into Tevin, causing him to vibrate, and a small explosion of blue smoke appears around him. His muscles expand, dreadlocks grow down his head, and glowing blue threads spring from his nasty robe, mystically changing it to a blue suede suit.

Tevin has transformed into Rock.

60

Tevin Jenkins

The river of purple arms yank the last of the angels into the whirlpool of necromancy water. Denise punches and kicks the evil limbs, but they refuse to release their grip on her. Hundreds of the arms put their wet hands on her face.

Queen Vanessa grins, shining her new purple teeth. "I have finally regained control of The World of the Fairies. Did you think that you could come to my home and defeat me? Who can stop me now?"

Rock stands on top of the mountain. He straightens the tie on his suit. He uses a rubber band to tie his wet dreadlocks into a ponytail. *I love my hair. When I start smacking that fairy queen, none of her blood better get in it, or I will be mad. Why does Pastor Anderson look so confused right now? I get it. I must be the most fantastic person to him. He needs to do something to cover those liver spots, though.*

Pastor Anderson looks at him and closes his eyes. "Do not be afraid, my son."

Rock chuckles. "I'm not afraid of Queen Cranky." He puts his gold-rimmed stunner shades on his smooth, moisturized face and says to Sparkle, "It's been a minute, fairy. Long time, no see."

"It's good to see you, Rock," Sparkle replies.

"Why don't you make me one of those nice weapons so I can get to work."

Sparkle casts silver pixie dust around him. She winks, and a long silver sword appears in his hands. The skin on his back crackles, and rainbow-colored wings inch out of his shoulder blades, ripping through his shirt, growing taller than him.

Serenity blows a kiss at him. "Good luck, baby."

"Do me a favor, sweetheart. Play some music for me," Rock says.

Sparkle sprinkles blue pixie dust in Serenity's direction and snaps her fingers. A saxophone instantly appears and lands in her hands. Serenity puts her lips on the mouthpiece. She breathes into the instrument and plays a soft melody.

Rock flaps his gorgeous, multicolored wings and releases a rainbow-colored aura. He soars off the mountain's cliff and toward the river below.

Demonic arms spring out of the water to drag him under, but Rock refuses to go down. He slices and slashes, lacerating the fingers and wrists of the arms as the black magic dust gets on his clothing.

Queen Vanessa stretches into her giant fairy form. She sticks her arms into the river and pulls out a long purple metal staff, pointing it at him. "Rock, I will punish you for turning my daughter against me."

The boils on the clouds burst, raining daddy long-legged spiders out of them.

Serenity stops playing her saxophone. "Oh my gosh!" she screams as the spiders get near her.

"Queen Cranky, you killed my parents and my friends. I'm going to finish you off right here and right now," Rock says.

Queen Vanessa's staff gets thicker.

"Rock," Sparkle says. "I'm giving you all my red pixie dust." In a frenzy, she gushes red pixie dust into Rock. His arms, legs, and chest bulge out of his fancy suit as he gains fifty pounds of muscle. "You should be able to fight at your maximum ability now," she says triumphantly.

The two enemies fly head-on at each other. *Cling!* goes the sound of Queen Vanessa's staff colliding with Rock's sword. The energy of their two auras battle for control of the planet as half the sky is purple, and the other half represents the colors of a rainbow.

Clack! goes the sound of their weapons crashing into each other again. Queen Vanessa's staff snaps in half, and Rock's sword shatters.

Rock hits the evil queen in her face with a left hook and an uppercut, breaking her jaw as slime bursts out. She grabs him by the dreadlocks and drags him by the hair as she flies at Serenity and the others.

As she hovers before them, Queen Vanessa hangs Rock by his dreads. He looks at Serenity as she cries for him, wondering if this will be the last time he sees her. His eyes fill with flashing lights, and his legs kick in the air, desperately trying to break free.

Queen Vanessa shakes him. "This is the woman who you jumped off Fairy Rock to marry. You will never have her, but you can look at her again before you die."

Sparkle flies out of Rock's pocket and blows black pixie dust into the queen's face, forcing her to cough it out of her lungs.

As she sputters and chokes, she releases Rock, and he falls, down, down, down, crashing down in a pile of creepy spiders. He lies immobile as the eight-legged creatures crawl all over him. The excruciating pain of the eerie insects biting and sucking the pixie dust out of him is unbearable. Screaming in agony, he transforms back into Tevin.

Queen Vanessa snatches Sparkle and starts squeezing her as she groans in desperation. "This is what you get for being disobedient to your mother. You will die with Tevin and the others."

Sparkle's face turns blue, and she begs with whimpers and moans. "Mother, please!"

The demented fairy queen laughs at her daughter's ribs cracking.

Hearing her desperate cries, Denise and several other angels break free from the river and teleport themselves before the queen.

"Charge her!" Denise says.

The queen waves her hand, and on her orders, spiders hanging from the cliff wall shoot out thick webs to bind the angels.

Spencer, The Demon Ghost King, appears on the mountain, hovering over them. He laughs with pride as he sees what he's helped to accomplish. "You've done it, Vanessa. You became the all-powerful one of this world, and you destroyed everyone who defied you."

Sparkle continues to plead. "Mother, please stop this and let everyone go home. I'm sorry for being disobedient."

"Crush her," Spencer orders.

Queen Vanessa squeezes and suffocates Sparkle again. The young fairy lets out a high-pitched whimper. "Mother!" she cries out. "You're killing your only child!"

The queen stops, sets her to the ground gently and roars in anger at the sky, shaking the very edges of the universe.

The Demon Ghost King grits his teeth. "Don't go soft on me now. I gave you the power to take over this world. Kill her and make some new loyal babies. I promise you it will feel better."

"No, Spencer. I won't do it. I can't kill her. She is my only child."

Tevin sees Serenity's sword beside him. *Heavenly Father, please give me strength. In Jesus' name, Amen.*

As the Queen howls at the sky, drowning out all other noise, he fights through the spiders and takes her sword. Her roars mask the sounds of his approach, so undetected, he sneaks up behind Queen Vanessa. *Closer. Be careful! Almost there!*

Suddenly, the queen looks behind her, but she's too late. Tevin plunges the sword deep into her back, pushing with all his might as he drives the blade deeper and deeper through the queen's heart and out of her chest.

She freezes in place, stunned into silence. Purple fluids spread from her heart and down her dress. She coughs, and blood comes from her mouth in spurts. Blue, red, orange, purple, silver, black, turquoise, yellow, and pink pixie dust seep from the hole in her chest. The colorful dust seems to have no more power as it decomposes to brown dirt. The queen releases her grip on Sparkle, and Tevin catches the young fairy.

The weary queen struggles to move her decrepit lips. She staggers, then catches herself, but just barely. She falls to one knee and reaches out to Tevin. She's beyond help. She shivers like she's cold.

"Thank you, Tevin Jenkins, for releasing me from this pain." Her voice is weaker now. She has so much to say, but no more time. She looks at Sparkle. "It's getting darker. Sparkle! Sparkle, dear!"

She coughs. "Sparkle, I will always love you, and I'm sorry for what I've done," she whispers, her voice almost lost in the wind.

She wants to say more, but the sound won't come. After so long, and so much violence, the queen herself falls into the floor of spiders and dies.

61

Tevin Jenkins

The clouds stop raining. The purple in the atmosphere evaporates. The sky returns to its baby blue color. The lone orange star shines again throughout The World of the Fairies.

The demonic spiders crawling on the ground freeze in place, turning into ashes; the wind blows them away.

At the mountain's edge, Tevin stands over Queen Vanessa's corpse. He pulls Serenity's sword out of the queen's back, and she shrinks down to a bug-sized fairy. He kneels beside Sparkle, and she turns to look up at him weakly.

"Tevin, my ribs are broken, and I'm out of pixie dust."

"Don't worry. You are going to be okay. I'll pray for you," Tevin replies.

Sparkle whimpers. "Tevin… Tevin… Is my mother dead?"

Tears roll down his cheeks, and he strokes her hair. "Please forgive me."

Sparkle frowns. "Tevin, I'm not mad at you. You had to do it."

Dark red eyes and a big, black, shadowy spirit appear across the mountain's wall. Neither Tevin nor Sparkle flinch this time. Spencer doesn't scare them anymore.

"Congratulations, Tevin Jenkins. You are now a murderer. I knew you had it in you." Spencer laughs.

Tevin shakes his head. "I'm not a killer. I had to stop her." He shakes his fist. "You've been defeated!"

The Demon Ghost King wags his long red tongue, showing his yellow teeth, and breathes his bloody breath in Tevin's face. "I'm going to ask you one last time. Let me devour your soul and own you. I will make you the new king of this fairy world, and you can have Serenity as your wife," Spencer says.

Tevin closes his eyes and takes a deep breath. *I must calm down. I know The Demon Ghost King is a big fat liar and a manipulator. I resisted him once, and I can do it again.* "Away, Spencer, in the name of Jesus!" Tevin declares.

Abruptly, the soft sound of the harp begins to play.

"No!" Spencer shouts.

The mellow, low-pitch noise of the sacred music causes Spencer to tear apart. His body turns gray, becomes blurry, and splits in different directions. His face stretches, and his head swells to the size of a hot air balloon. He exhales black magic powder out of his mouth, spilling around the sky, and a black magic portal forms, sucking him away into nothingness.

The music stops playing, and Tevin pauses as Sparkle rests on his shoulder. He looks down the mountain. The black magic river has dried up, and the remains of skulls and bones of humans, ogres, dark wolves, and dragons lie on the muddy ground.

He turns to his friends, their hair, skin, and clothes drenched in dried-up blood, then squats down, puts his hands over his face, and lays down. He pounds his face on the rock surface of the mountain and wails, "It's finally over. I'm so sorry I got everyone killed. My parents, Richard, and everyone's gone. They're gone."

A brown light flickers, and thousands of angels with harps fill the sky. Denise stands proudly before him. "Don't be afraid! The Demon Ghost King may have escaped from us again, but all the angels of heaven will continue to search until we find him."

"I've helped to destroy everything by looking for help from Queen Vanessa. All of this is my fault!" Tevin looks around in sorrow; there's only death and destruction everywhere. "Will God forgive me?"

"God has already forgiven you. God gave you the strength to stop Vanessa at the end. God loves you, Tevin," Denise replies softly.

Tevin wipes the tears out of his eyes. "I just wanted to date Serenity. Sparkle transformed me into Rock, this amazing, super guy she loves. I realized God made me Tevin Jenkins, and I'm proud to be Tevin Jenkins. If someone doesn't love me for me, then it's just not meant to be."

Denise smiles. "Congratulations. You've learned your lesson."

Tevin gently rests Sparkle on the rocky, warm black mountain surface and stands back up, putting his hands on his head as he paces back and forth. "Was this whole experience just a test?"

Fairy Rock

"Every moment of life is a test, Tevin," Denise says. "You jumped off Fairy Rock with low self-esteem, searching for answers from an ungodly queen. Through this experience, you became more confident, found Jesus, and found yourself. Luckily, you have angels on your side. God is proud of you. Every human who died in this fairy world will return to life. You are going home, Tevin Jenkins."

Denise and the angels gently pluck the long strings of their harps, and a soft, metallic sound goes throughout The World of the Fairies.

As the music fills the air, it seems to move inside him too. He takes one last glimpse of the blue sky and the fluffy white clouds. The black, orange, pink, red, green, gray, yellow, and rainbow-colored trees have miraculously regrown as the river refills with clear water. A brown aura surrounds him, Sparkle, Serenity, Pastor Anderson, and the Elves.

Tevin gazes at Sparkle, who looks at him with shining, tear-filled eyes. "Goodbye, Tevin Jenkins," she says quietly.

"Goodbye," Tevin says. He tries to reach for her, but as he does, his hands and fingers start to fade as white light flashes before his eyes, and he disappears.

62

Tevin Jenkins

A heart monitor beeps, and Tevin opens his eyes to bright light and chatter in the room. A tight bandage covers the stinging knot on his forehead. Everything's a little fuzzy, and he tries to make out what he's seeing. He looks for Sparkle, but as his eyes come into focus, he can see his parents standing next to his hospital bed, dressed in their police uniforms.

He turns and tries to focus. "Mom? Dad?"

"My baby has woken up," Mrs. Jenkins cries.

"I'm so glad you're okay, son," Mr. Jenkins says.

"You guys are alive?"

Mr. and Mrs. Jenkins look at each other.

"Tevin, what in the world are you talking about?" Mr. Jenkins asks.

"You both died in The World of the Fairies," Tevin replies.

"Baby, the police found you at the bottom of Fairy Rock. You must have hit your head on something. Did you try to harm yourself?" Mrs. Jenkins asks.

Tevin touches the bandages on his head again. "I did jump off Fairy Rock. The last thing I remember is you all dying, and I killed Queen Vanessa. Then Spencer, the Demon Ghost King, got away from the Angels. Where is Serenity? Where is Sparkle? Where am I?"

In a mild frenzy, he quickly surveys the room. He looks at the ceiling, then down at the leather chairs near the window, giving an excellent view of the full moon outside. "Where am I?"

"You are in the hospital," Mr. Jenkins says. "The police found you in the Fairyville Woods, and the ambulance brought you here."

"I'm in Fairyville?"

Before they can respond, there's a brisk tap on the door and Richard and Susan burst through, carrying balloons.

Tevin stares at Richard. They're alive! Richard's chubby again. Susan looks the same as I remember her. How?

"Hey, buddy. Are you okay?" Richard asks.

Tevin buries his hands in his face as he wails, "I'm so sorry that I jumped off Fairy Rock, and I got everyone in the town killed."

"What are you talking about?" Richard asks.

Mrs. Jenkins leans in and looks at him, worried. "You didn't get anyone killed, baby. Everyone is alive and healthy."

"But I saw it all! Queen Vanessa and the other fairies killed everybody except Serenity and me," Tevin cries.

"Richard, you shouldn't have given this kid any weed. He's tripping," Susan says, rolling her eyes and crossing her arms.

Tevin tries to sit up, but his mother gently pushes him back down. "Where's Serenity?" he pleads. "Is she alive? Did she make it back to Fairyville?"

"Serenity is alive, and she never left Fairyville, buddy. You just had a nightmare, that's all," Richard says.

A tall, hefty doctor enters the room, holding a clipboard. He has curly hair and a smoothly combed beard. He approaches Tevin and starts writing. "Hello, Tevin. My name is Dr. Milton. How are you feeling?"

Mrs. Jenkins interrupts. "Is he going to be okay?" she asks. "He's talking crazy! He believes he went somewhere called The World of the Fairies."

"Well, that makes sense, if you think about it. We see this all the time! He took a nasty fall off the boulder and bumped his head. He has a mild concussion, but he should fully recover with a bit of bed rest."

Dr. Milton rubs his silky beard. "I think it's best if I send him home as soon as possible. We all know that they give you police officers crappy insurance. I don't want you to have to pay a huge medical bill. We'll get you discharged. Just make sure he rests."

***

Outside the thirty-two-story hospital, Tevin is wearing a new pair of jean shorts and a blue T-shirt his parents brought him. He rubs lotion on his bony legs and elbows.

Mr. and Mrs. Jenkins help him out of his wheelchair and into the backseat of their red minivan.

Richard takes his cell phone and hands it to Tevin. "It's my parents. They want to talk to you."

"Don't they hate me?" Tevin asks.

"No."

"Tevin, we are so glad you are okay, buddy," Mr. Johnson says.

"You are one of our favorites," Mrs. Johnson adds.

"Thank you."

Richard takes the phone back, and he and Susan hug him simultaneously.

"Thank you for coming to check on me, guys, but there is something different about you two," Tevin says.

"What?" Richard asks.

"You're both sober. You guys were drunk or stoned almost the whole time in the fairy world."

Richard and Susan both look at the ground, and Susan fidgets with her fingers. "Yeah, me and Richard decided to stop the pot and booze and focus on going to college next year."

"Am I still dreaming?"

"Come on, buddy, we are not that bad of stoners." Richard chuckles.

Mrs. Jenkins interrupts, "Thanks for coming to see Tevin." She pushes the button, closing the electric sliding door on the minivan's driver's side.

Tevin smells the pollen from the warm summer night air. He looks out of the window at the full moon. *It must have been a dream, and I am so happy I am home in Fairyville. Everyone is safe.*

As Mr. Jenkins drives down Main Street, Tevin takes in the vast buildings, the shopping plazas, and the crowds walking down the red brick sidewalks. Couples embrace each other as they survey the mannequins' model pink and red designer dresses in the store windows. He claps his hands at a group of senior citizens eating a chocolate sundae. He rolls down the backseat window and screams. "You are all alive! Praise Jesus!"

A crowd of onlookers stare at him as he shakes his arms in a circular motion.

"I love everyone in Fairyville!" he yells.

Mr. Jenkins stops at a red light, and a green Corvette pulls up next to them on the two-lane street. The fancy car's driver blasts a song from Brian Blaze, Fairyville's greatest techno music star.

Tevin leaps out of the minivan and dances on the white lines of the crowded intersection, shaking his hips as if he were playing with a Hula Hoop.

"Play the beat louder!" he screams at the top of his lungs.

Mrs. Jenkins sticks her head out of the front window of the minivan. "Get back in the van!"

An audience circles him, taking pictures with their phones, and hordes of cars behind them honk their horns.

"Who is that guy? He's cool."

"Isn't that the kid that got beat up in the mall?" a man in the audience says.

"Who cares! He can dance, and he's handsome," a blushing woman in the crowd says.

"I know I am," Tevin calls back. He wiggles his knees as he rocks the crowd.

Looking back at the car, he can see that his father is getting into his groove. "What did that bump on the head do to my boy?" Mr. Jenkins grins. "He looks so happy and full of life. I'm so proud of him. That's how you rock the bleeping crowd, boy. Gone with yo' cool self."

"Harold, stop instigating," Mrs. Jenkins says.

Tevin closes his eyes to soak up the music, and his mind suddenly flashes to Serenity. He shakes his head and takes off down Main Street, shouting back at his parents: "Mom and Dad, I'll see you guys later!"

***

Twenty minutes later, he arrives at Mitch's MMA Gym. Bursting through the double doors, he passes the new marble front desk counter and some of the big, sweaty, muscular fighters as they stretch to spar on the red mats under the supervision of Denver, Ron, and Rhyme.

Tevin gawks in amazement at a skinny fighter throwing a fast seven-punch combination on the heavy bag.

The large flat-screen TV screen near the ceiling is on. Benny the Destroyer is giving a press conference for his upcoming fight. The MMA champion chews on a raw steak right on national television.

"That nasty man hasn't changed a bit," Tevin says.

A long line of fighters is waiting for refreshments at the juice stand. Serenity, flustered and busy, races back-and-forth behind the counter making protein shakes for her customers.

Tevin pats his hair to ensure it's straight, and he laughs as he enjoys his new swag.

Cutting the line, he goes straight to the juice stand's front counter. He licks his lips at Serenity's beautiful face, gorgeous brown eyes, perfectly picked afro, and hourglass figure. *She is more radiant than I remember. I can't stop looking at her. Wait, lusting is a sin. I must stop thinking these dirty thoughts.*

"Hi, Serenity. It's me, Tevin."

Serenity stops the blender and looks at him as if she saw a ghost.

"Get in the back of the line, you skinny little punk," one of the fighters says.

Tevin pauses as his face goes blank, and he blinks. *Dang, I did just cut in front of everyone? This is something that Rock would have done, and everything in my behavior is something Rock would have done. I don't feel scared. What has gotten into me?*

A familiar voice yells, "Hey! Get away from my girlfriend!" Tevin turns around, and it's Daniel, who's walking quickly towards him, balling his fists. "I just beat the brakes off you for being around my girl the other day. I see you ain't learned your lesson yet!"

Tevin stands firm. "That won't happen again, I promise you that."

Daniel rips off his sweat-soaked white T-shirt, showing the tarantula tattoos on his broad chest.

Serenity leans over the counter. "Daniel, how many times do I have to tell you? It's over between us," she says.

Hearing the shouting, Mitch comes out of his office and toward the juice stand. "What's with all the commotion?"

"This little punk keeps trying to push up on my girl!" Daniel yells.

"I'm not your girl anymore," Serenity says.

Daniel grabs Serenity by her forearm, pulling her toward him, and almost as a reflex, Tevin cocks his fist back, swings with all his might, and punches Daniel in the jaw. Daniel falls onto the mats and lies there.

"Ooh!" go the fighters in the juice line.

Mitch rubs his chin. "You have a nice righthand, kid. Have you ever thought about fighting?"

Tevin shakes his head quickly. "No, I haven't." He stops for a moment to breathe. "I'm sorry about the scene I caused." He pauses again, then turns to look Mitch in the eye. "Do you know anyone named Rock?"

"Never heard of him," Mitch says quickly. He tries to put his arm around Tevin, but Tevin pulls back. Mitch frowns. "Look, kid, I'm a busy guy. So, do you want to join my gym or not?"

"No, thanks."

Mitch turns red and coughs. "Well, get out of here then."

Tevin turns to leave, unsure of where to go next. Everything feels so off now. As he pushes his way through the crowd and makes his way to the door, Serenity stands silently, looking at him walk away. She bites her lip.

***

Tevin arrives at Fairyville Woods. He pushes his way through the moist bushes, strolling through the tall ragweeds and Maple Trees. He ignores squelching noises from his wet, filthy shoes as he smacks his hands, scaring off a raccoon by a patch of rose bushes.

He trudges his way up Fairyville Mountain and gapes at the enormous muddy Fairy Rock again. He storms around the giant boulder, observing all the names carved into it. He uses a rope recently nailed into the humongous stone and climbs on Fairy Rock.

The yellow stars in the sky and the orange lights in the skyscrapers below refresh him. He smiles as he sees the cars driving through the city.

His sits for a moment, then feels someone climbing up. He leans over and smiles as he sees Serenity climb onto Fairy Rock to sit beside him. As she pulls herself up and slides next to him, she lays her head on his shoulder, and he takes in the perfume on her red sweater.

"I'm so glad that you are alive, Tevin."

"Thank you. The doctors said I took a nasty fall."

"I want to thank you for saving me."

"No problem. Daniel is a jerk."

She clutches hold of his arm. "It's weird, Tevin. I dreamed we were in this place called The World of the Fairies, fighting against fairies. Then, today, you asked Mitch if he knew someone named Rock. Right there, I knew it wasn't a dream."

"It wasn't? So, we were fighting Queen Vanessa and the fairies!"

"I know who Queen Vanessa is, and you killed her, Tevin. You saved us all."

"I guess we're the only two that remember then."

Tevin lays back and tries to process what she just said. Serenity lies down next to him with her head on his chest.

But in an instant, rainbow-colored pixie dust covers the area around Fairy Rock. Tevin and Serenity jump up. "Serenity, it's Sparkle's pixie dust!" Tevin shouts.

The oak tree below the mountain mysteriously has rainbow-colored leaves. "Tevin, look at that!" Serenity grins wildly.

Tevin studies the tree. Elroy, Melinda, Bartholomew, Reginald, and Jason are standing on a rainbow-colored branch waving at them. Sparkle and Leon blow kisses as they stick their little heads out of the leaves.

Tevin and Serenity wave back at them as their friends disappear and the tree leaves turn back to green.

Serenity puts her arms around Tevin and hugs him.

"I think they're gone now," Tevin says. "They just wanted to let us know they were with us."

Serenity puts her hand on his. "I think we'll always carry the memory of everything that happened."

Tevin kisses her on the top of the head. "I'm sorry I'm not Rock anymore."

Serenity grins and gives him a big hug. "That's okay. I want Tevin Jenkins as my boyfriend."

He blushes and tightly hugs her back. "I love that I'm your boyfriend. I love you, Serenity."

"I love you too, Tevin."

The End

About the Author

Jeffrey Roy Ford is a Fantasy Fiction writer and former substitute teacher. He has dedicated his life to creating stories that teach important life lessons. His latest novel, Fairy Rock, immerses readers in a mystical world where magic and reality intertwine through vibrant characters and captivating narratives. Jeffrey's goal is to inspire and educate, ensuring that each story is a journey of discovery and growth, leaving readers feeling enlightened and informed.

www.ingramcontent.com/pod-product-compliance
Lightning Source LLC
LaVergne TN
LVHW051037070526
838201LV00010B/231